ARK

ARK

A Novel

CHARLES McCARRY

A MYSTERIOUSPRESS.COM BOOK

NEW YORK

For Aamir

Scientists at Columbia University's Lamont-Doherty Earth Observatory have found that the Earth's inner core is rotating faster than the planet itself. The Earth's solid iron inner core . . . is surrounded by a much larger liquid outer core, and together the two form a giant electrical motor. . . . About a billion amps of current is flowing . . . across the boundary between the inner and outer cores. . . . 'The really surprising thing is how fast the core is moving,' said seismologist Paul Richards, who along with fellow seismologist Xiaodong Song made the discovery. . . . Over the past 100 years that extra speed has given the core a quarter turn on the planet as a whole. . . . [T]he motion is about 100,000 times faster than the drift of continents. . . . [Each] year, the inner core rotates about one longitudinal degree more than the Earth's mantle and crust. . . . Pressure at the inner core surface is millions of times higher than the atmospheric pressure at Earth's surface. . . . The mass of the inner core is about one hundred million million million tons—which is about 30 per cent greater than the mass of the moon.

—Excerpt from a Columbia University press release dated July 18, 1996.

The foregoing results were confirmed by subsequent research at Columbia University and the University of Illinois at Urbana-Champaign, as described in an article in the August 26, 2005, issue of *Science*.

ONE

1

ALTHOUGH HE WAS ONE OF the most famous men in the world, Henry Peel was a will-o'-the-wisp. Paparazzi could not plague him because they didn't know what he looked like. Hardly anyone did. The only known photograph of him was the one on his student ID at Caltech. He was fifteen years old when the picture was taken. The image was blurred. He never posed for a yearbook picture because, working alone during the summer between his junior and senior years, he solved the problem of the room temperature superconductor and shortly thereafter dropped out of college. Not long after that he patented a feasible design for a fusion reactor. His discoveries earned him a large fortune before he was twenty-five. As time went by, he perfected other inventions that had been regarded as unachievable and made more money—a lot more. *Forbes* magazine, estimating that he was richer than all the billionaires on its annual list of the filthy rich, called him a trillionaire. He was the only one in the world.

Henry Peel could not explain how he did what he did. Like Leonardo or Newton or Einstein, he worked by flashes of intuition and did the math afterward. Answers that had eluded the best scientific minds for decades or sometimes for centuries simply came to him—

an apple bounced off his head, and suddenly he knew everything about gravity.

One summer's day, someone purporting to be Henry Peel called me out of the blue and asked if we could get together. The caller had a pleasant tenor voice. He was polite but made no special effort to be ingratiating. I thought the call was a joke. I was busy. I said goodbye in a not-nice voice and started to hang up.

"Wait," the caller said.

He gave me the name of a mutual friend who could certify that he was who he said he was. I have to admit that I thought it was pretty cool that Henry Peel wanted to prove his identity to me. Melissa had been my college roommate and was still my best friend. I hadn't known that she knew Henry Peel, but when I called her, seconds later, she admitted that she did. In fact, she was his lawyer. She refused to answer any questions about him—what he looked like, whether he lived in New York, whether he was married or single. Was he a regular person or was he going to show up in an armored limousine inside a ring of bodyguards? Had I been invited out on a date, or was there some other reason for Henry's call?

"I'm not at liberty to answer those questions," Melissa said. "But trust me, the caller was Henry. I'm the one who gave him your phone number."

"What other information did you give him?"

"I told him no secrets."

"Can I be sure of that?" I asked.

A moment of silence. An exhalation. Melissa was telling herself to be patient, a losing proposition. She hung up.

Henry and I met two days later on a bench in Central Park at noon exactly. He turned out to be a lean, forty-something fellow with a few strands of gray in his close-cropped dark hair and brown eyes whose whites were so perfectly white that my first thought was, *This guy has never had a drink or a sick day in his life.* He wore a Yankees cap, a plain black T-shirt, blue jeans without a belt, Nikes, no socks. Slung over his shoulder by one strap was a daypack.

4

"Hi, I'm Henry," he said. Piercing blue stare, no smile. "I hope you like Chinese food."

I don't especially. He rummaged in the daypack and handed me a Styrofoam container of sweet and sour soup, a plastic spoon, and a paper napkin. The soup was excellent. The entrée, also delicious, was a vegetable dish I did not enjoy.

Henry made no conversation. Neither did I, though I studied him in stealthy, sidelong glances. He detected every single glance but did not react to any of them. When we finished eating, he gathered up the debris and threw it into a trash basket. Then he sat down again.

He said, "Let me ask you something. What, in your opinion, is the prime attribute of genius?"

As it happened, I had thought about this, in connection with Henry, on the way to this rendezvous, so I had an answer on the tip of my tongue.

I said, "The ability to see the obvious."

At last, a reaction, but so slight a reaction that I wondered if he had heard me. The hubbub of the city enveloped us—taxi horns, sirens, music, shouts, guffaws, shrieking brakes, breaking glass—all of it. Henry looked as though he heard nothing. His mind was working. This was almost a visible thing, as if inside his head, gears and balance wheel were spinning, springs were tightening, and a tiny Henry was walking around inside the mechanism, looking for a squeak, with a minuscule oilcan in his hand.

He said, "Let me ask you another question."

"Be my guest."

"Suppose an archeological expedition to Antarctica discovers a sphere, an artificial object, in a cave in the highest mountain on the continent. . . ."

"Mount Vinson?"

"Yes."

This geographical showing-off did not please him. He went on after the briefest of pauses.

"The archeologists pick up the sphere in their mittened hands and take it back to their laboratory in California," he continued. "They place it in an air-conditioned room, inside a transparent case at a temperature equal to the temperature in the cave in which it was found. The scientists touch it only with instruments. The sphere is made of a material that resembles Lucite, but is not Lucite. It is inert. It does nothing, teaches nothing, issues no warning. So what's the point of it? Clearly it comes from another world. Does it contain a message? If so, why doesn't it deliver it? Why would it have been left where we could find it, but in the last place on Earth we would look for it? Who left it?"

He paused. I waited for him to go on.

He said, "A genius is called in as a consultant. What does he do?"

"This object is untouched by human hands, right?"

Henry nodded.

I said, "The genius walks into the lab and picks up the sphere in his bare hands. For maybe thirty seconds, nothing happens. Then the sphere activates. It lights up. Data—pictures and what seem to be numbers—stream across the surface of the super-Lucite."

"Why?"

"Because the sphere is programmed to switch on when touched by something or someone who has opposable thumbs and a body temperature of 98.6 degrees Fahrenheit. In other words, *Homo sapiens* and nothing else that lives on this planet."

Henry's eyes widened. He didn't exactly smile, but his expression changed for the better.

"I like the way you think," he said. "I'll be in touch."

He lifted a hand in farewell and walked away. That seemed to be the end of it, whatever "it" had been.

Time passed. Henry did not call, he did not write. I called Melissa.

"Don't worry," she said. "You impressed him."

"How do you know?"

"He called to thank me for the introduction. He said you were amazing."

"Flattery."

"I doubt that. But Henry is hard to amaze."

Also, as cold as a stone. This didn't amaze me. Practically everyone I knew in my socioeconomic class had an emotional temperature just high enough to keep the blood from congealing, except when they went crazy with anger or jealousy or frustration or the self-doubt that had them all by the throat. Usually they were alone or in the presence of a therapist when such outbursts happened. It was the zeitgeist. Of course Henry didn't get in touch. Making that airy promise was just his way of saying so long.

After a while I stopped listening for the phone and went back to work on the book I was writing before Henry interrupted. Now and then I felt a twinge of pique. I was annoyed at myself. Without even knowing this guy, I had reported for duty, I had eaten Chinese food, which I loathe, on a park bench, and pretended to like it. I had let myself be interrogated like an applicant for an entry-level position. And I knew why: He was a trillionaire and he had awakened my inner gold digger. I was ashamed of myself. I was supposed to be hipper than that.

Shame never lasts. I went on with my life, getting up early, writing my five hundred words a day, going for a run when the sun shone, using my treadmill when it didn't, reading new books and enjoying old ones better, listening to music, watching sitcoms that featured smart-mouth women and cute, clueless men, going to the movies.

On a Friday in September, about three months after our meeting in the park, the phone rang. I had just finished writing, so I picked up.

A tenor voice said, "Hi, it's Henry."

Lifting the first syllable of his name into a higher key, I said, "Henry?"

He answered with a split second of silence, then he said, "I'd like to continue our conversation."

Oh, *that* Henry!

I said, "Same place?"

"No. I'm not in New York. I have an airplane parked at Newark Airport. I can send a car to take you there. The flight would last about four hours. You'd be back home Sunday night. Casual clothes. Bring a bathing suit if you like to swim."

"Where would I be going, exactly?"

"An island in the Caribbean, not far from Grenada."

"Does this island have a name?"

"No. It's a small island in the Grenadines."

"How small? One palm tree, like in the cartoons?"

Henry said, "Are you OK with this?"

"Not really," I said. "Who else will be there?"

"Just the two of us, but let me make myself clear. I'm talking about a business meeting, nothing else."

"Can you tell me something about the purpose of the meeting besides the conversation?"

"Conversation is the purpose of the meeting."

In other words, trust me, sweetheart. I could always leave a letter for the cops, in case I vanished. I love the Caribbean. It was January in New York. I said, "OK."

Henry's airplane turned out to be a Gulfstream. We took off almost as soon as I was seated and belted. Aloft, a smiling young steward offered me food and drink. I asked for a glass of water, drank it, and went to sleep.

When I woke up three hours later, it was dark. The night was moonless, so the stars seemed brighter than usual. As a child, I had learned from a stargazing father the names of the constellations and the galaxies that can be seen with the naked eye. They were clearer at forty thousand feet than they had been in our backyard on Long Island.

I can't say that anything else was.

The plane had been losing altitude. Now it banked, metal groaning. The pilot switched on the landing lights. The stars vanished. The plane touched down.

ARK

Henry stood beside a golf cart at the foot of the gangway. In Central Park he had kept his teeth beneath his lip, but now he smiled, fleetingly. He was dressed in the same nerdish style as before, except that he had gotten rid of the Yankees cap and wore shorts and sandals instead of jeans and sneakers. The steward heaved my bag and a large picnic cooler into the golf cart. I climbed into the passenger seat. Henry drove uphill, without headlights, over a bumpy track. Under this unpolluted sky, the starlight was enough to light the way. The plane took off, strobes flashing. Henry stopped the golf cart until the jet disappeared and all was silence and darkness again, then pressed the button on a remote control. A house sprang out of the pitch-black night, a large glass cube on a hilltop, filled with light.

Inside, the house was simple, not to say stark—minimalist furniture, sculptures and paintings, to nearly all of which an art history major like myself could put the name of a famous artist and a probable price at Sotheby's. We ate cold soup, lobster salad, and sherbet with blackberries. Henry served. He was as adept as a waiter in a three-star restaurant. As before, the food was delicious, the conversation minimal. Henry offered me wine. I refused it. I wanted no alcohol in my bloodstream in case I really had been brought here to think.

By the time we finished eating it was too late to talk, and despite my nap on the plane, I was too tired for conversation. When I mentioned this, Henry nodded his head as if to tell me he understood that I couldn't help it if I belonged to a species that slept half the time. He showed me to my room. Like the rest of the house, it was severe except for the Chagall on the wall and a bronze stalk of a woman by Giacometti that stood on a pedestal in the corner.

I woke up early. Outside the glass walls the world was bright blue. The house intrigued me—not the architecture but the mind of its owner. Why would Henry, the hidden man, choose to live in a transparent house? Downstairs, I found him seated under an umbrella at a table by the swimming pool, communing with a computer. On a table by the pool, breakfast had been laid out. I poured myself a cup of coffee and put some fruit on a plate. The sun was warm on my skin. I regretted having dressed so unseductively in shirt and slacks and sensible sandals. If ever there was a place to live in a bikini, this was it. From this vantage point it was possible to see the entire island. No other roof was visible, nor smoke nor movement. No noise, either, except for the palms, the surf, the gulls on the beach.

I stood up. The dishes in my hand rattled. Henry noticed my presence at last. He lifted his eyes from the computer screen and said, "Sleep well?"

"Like the dead," I said.

Henry said, "Good. Shall we get to work?"

He led me inside, to a room that obviously was his workspace: a desk, a computer, a large television screen, two identical space-age chairs facing each other. The only splash of color was a Finland rug lying between the chairs. He gestured me into one of the chairs and sat down in the other and gave me the same intense look I had noticed in Central Park. The eye contact lasted no more than a second or two.

He said, "You look as if you have a question."

"I do," I said. "Why am I here?"

"I want you to work with me."

"Doing what?"

"Helping me think."

"About what?"

"Something new I have in mind."

"Why do you think that I can help you, of all people, to think? I don't know a cosine from a hypotenuse."

"I've read some of your books. I liked them, liked the way your mind works. That thing you came up with about the sphere was impressive."

I said, "This new thing you mentioned. Is it a secret?"

"You could say that."

"Then maybe you've got the wrong person. I don't like secrets. I write books. My specialty is telling the world everything I know."

He took this calmly. "Are you saying you're not interested?" he asked.

"I'm not sure. You said you want me to be your confidant. But you hardly know me, or I you. It's like hearing a proposal of marriage on a blind date."

Henry said, "Let me explain what's involved. Then you can decide."

"Am I sworn to secrecy?"

"No."

For the next hour, Henry talked without pause, mostly about the cores of the earth. The inner core is made of iron and nickel. It is roughly the size of the moon, but heavier by a third. Its temperature is approximately fifty-five hundred degrees Celsius, or ten thousand degrees Fahrenheit, about the same as the surface of the sun. It is surrounded by the outer core, also composed of iron and nickel, but in a molten state. Spinning together, the two cores constitute a huge electric motor. This motor helps generate Earth's magnetic field.

The inner core is spinning faster than the planet itself. This was demonstrated in the late twentieth century by scientists at Columbia University, who compared the speeds at which seismic waves generated by two nearly identical earthquakes traveled through the inner core many years apart. Over the past hundred years, the inner core has gained a quarter-turn on the surface of the earth. That could mean that it has gained fifteen million complete turns, more or less, in the sixty million years since the extinction of the dinosaurs. This has created a tremendous amount of energy.

The question—Henry's question—was, where is all that energy? Some of it has been released in the form of heat to the rest of the planet. Some was transmitted in the form of electricity to Earth's magnetic field. No one knows how much, in either case. One possibility is that the energy, or most of it, is stored at the center of the planet. This energy is produced by a spinning object. Therefore it is kinetic energy, rotational energy, the kind of energy produced by a flywheel. What if the spinning cores, usually compared to an electric motor, more closely resemble a flywheel? Henry asked. How does a flywheel work? It spins, it creates energy through rotation, it stores the energy at the center of the wheel. At a certain point, it is logical to assume that the center will release this energy to the rim of the wheel.

"Think of Earth as a flywheel," Henry said. "Think of what such an event would mean, what it would do to the surface of the planet."

Recently there had been changes, a lot of them, in the magnetic field of the planet, first in Australasia, then in Southern Africa. In the South Atlantic Ocean, more or less overnight, the magnetism of an area the size of Brazil became much weaker. Something was going on in the core of the earth and it was manifesting itself on the surface of the planet. The North and South Poles might reverse. The North Pole used to be in what is now the Sahara Desert. In just the past one hundred years, it had moved almost a thousand miles out into the Arctic Ocean. It was still moving at a more rapid pace, in the direction of Siberia.

At this point, Henry stopped talking. He looked at the ceiling. The moment of quiet lengthened.

At last I said, "Henry?"

He said, "Give me a moment. I'm trying to find a way to say what comes next without convincing you that I'm a lunatic."

I said, "Go on."

Henry did as I asked. He believed that the energy stored in the core of the earth would sooner or later be released by the great flywheel of his imagination. When this happened, a colossal earthquake would take place. It would be entirely different from any other earthquake in history. The crust of the planet would be hurled forward not inches or feet as in an ordinary earthquake, but tens or hundreds of miles. Buildings would topple and, in many cases, be swallowed by the earth. The power grid and all communications would be wiped out instantaneously. Airports, highways, and railroads would be obliterated. Huge tidal waves would sink ships at sea and inundate most of the world's islands, large and small. Coastal regions of the continents would be flooded. Volcanoes old and new would erupt all over the world, including volcanoes on the seafloor. A miasma of ash and dust would rise into the atmosphere, blocking the light of the sun and bringing agriculture to a halt. Life would abruptly become nastier and more brutish than it had ever been before.

I was scared. If anyone else in the world had told me what Henry had just told me, I would have laughed. But this was Henry spouting this doomsday scenario. As far as I knew, or anyone knew, he had never been wrong about anything having to do with the behavior of nature.

I said, "You really believe this?"

"Yes."

"Henry, you're talking about the end of the world."

"No," he said. "I'm talking about an interruption of civilization."

"What's the difference?"

"The end of the world is irreversible. A civilization in ruins is nothing new. Man would put Humpty Dumpty together again."

I said, "How?"

"That's exactly what I want to talk to you about," Henry said.

2

HENRY SUGGESTED A SAIL TO a reef in his sloop. This took about an hour, so it was midafternoon by the time we arrived at the reef. The gleaming, gadgety boat was yar, to say the least. Henry was an expert sailor, and I knew enough about it to help with the sails and avoid being knocked on the head by the boom. The sloop, being Henry's boat, had no name. After dropping anchor we ate the very light, late lunch he produced from a picnic cooler. I chewed and swallowed to be polite. Apparently Henry couldn't have a conversation without offering a eucharist, but this meant that we had to wait half an hour before entering the water. We passed the time by talking about the Yankees. Not surprisingly, he was a walking encyclopedia of baseball statistics.

At last I went over the side into the blue-green water. Snorkeling had its usual otherworldly effect—the magnified images seen through the mask, the blood-temperature water, the creatures of the reef swimming around as if attending an evolutionary reunion, the sense of return to a lost existence, the escape from time. Would this reef in the Grenadines survive Henry's apocalypse? Of course it wouldn't. It would be obliterated like everything else. I commanded myself to stop thinking about that.

ARK

Quite soon I was doing less thinking than the fishes. The current carried me a long way. Much later, another part of my brain woke me to the realization that I was not a creature of the reef but a mammal that required air and fresh water. I turned over and pushed off my mask. The sun was sinking. I looked at my watch. It was almost five o'clock, and there was nothing in sight except water and the sun. No sloop, no Henry. I was alone in one of the most remote places in the world. I felt the stab of panic. Treading water, I made a 360-degree examination of the horizon—or thought I did. There were no points of reference. I knew that dozens of small islands lay all around me, but none was visible. I had no idea in which direction to swim. I was thirsty. My back stung and I realized that I had gotten a sunburn. After resisting the temptation for what seemed a long time, I looked at my watch again. Four minutes had passed. Panic revived. How would I attract the attention of a boat? Even if one came by at this time of day—a most unlikely prospect—the chances that it would see me lying flat on my back in the water were very slight. It would be dark in a couple of hours. What then? I kept looking at my watch. It was waterproof, so at least I'd know what time it was when everything stopped except the Rolex.

At 5:16 p.m., the tip of a sail appeared. In the moments that followed, the mainsail and jib of Henry's sloop rose out of the curve of the earth. I treaded water and waved. After a very long moment, Henry saw me and waved back. He swept by me, and then turned into the wind, and the boat luffed and came to a stop within ten feet of me. I swam two strokes and climbed aboard.

I wasn't feeling good about myself. I had committed a serious breach of etiquette, letting myself drift away on the current. Henry uttered no reproach.

As the sails filled with wind, I toweled off and flinched. Wordlessly, Henry rummaged in a bag and sprayed something from an aerosol can onto my back. We sailed home against the wind, which was brisk, Henry tacking the sloop expertly.

That evening we had another splendid dinner, this time with

a bottle of Bâtard-Montrachet, chilled to what I was sure must be precisely ten degrees Celsius. Henry drank about an ounce of this nectar. I consumed the rest. He asked how my sunburn was. I told him it was fine. He looked unconvinced.

"You shouldn't take this lightly," he said. "There's a thermometer in your bathroom and a bottle of aspirin. Take some aspirin. It relieves inflammation."

I thanked him for everything and pushed back my chair.

Henry said, "Wait. I'm wondering if you feel up to staying another day."

As a matter of reflex I started to reply that I had a book to write, things to do, appointments in the big city.

Before I could speak, he said, "It's important. We should finish our discussion."

I said, "OK, if I can fly back to New York tomorrow evening."

"Fine," Henry said.

Before going to bed I made the mistake of taking off my clothes in front of a mirror and looking over my shoulder at myself. How right Henry was. From nape to heels I was bright vermilion except for the white buttocks. I stuck the thermometer in my mouth. As Henry had predicted, I had a fever. I did not sleep well. In the morning I was sore, sick, feverish, dizzy, barely able to function. I had a medium case of the shakes. I crept to the kitchen and poured myself a cup of coffee. When I tried to lift the cup to my lips, I dropped it. Although it was only five thirty, Henry was up. He heard the clatter of his fine china on the marble floor and came to see what had happened. I was barefoot, surrounded by the shards of the broken cup. Henry told me not to move. I obeyed, and without protest let him clean up the mess. The aroma of the spilled coffee turned my stomach. Silent and scrupulously neutral, Henry advised me again to drink a lot of water. Dehydration was the enemy. I went back to my room and lay down on the bed. I was shivering worse than before. Quite soon, though, I fell asleep.

When I woke around noon, my stomach was more settled and

my embarrassment less disabling. I dosed myself with Solarcaine, took more aspirin, and got dressed.

I found Henry in the kitchen. He was standing at the counter, eating a lunch of crackers and cheese and a truly beautiful pear.

"Ah," he said. "You look better. How do you feel?"

"Not so bad."

Henry said, "Do you still want to fly back to New York tonight?"

"If that's possible."

"It's perfectly possible."

For Henry, everything was perfectly possible and instantaneously available. He was studying me, with something resembling a gleam in his eyes.

I said, "Then I'd like to go. I'm not much use to anybody at the moment."

Henry said, "Fine. You should see a doctor. I'll call the pilot. If you don't mind, I'll ride back with you."

I said, "Lovely."

In his light, pleasant voice, Henry began talking—lecturing, really—as soon as we were aloft.

"The Event," as he called the hyperquake to come, was a matter of planetary mechanics, part of Earth's design. It could be understood as the planet's way of renewing itself. Probably versions of the Event had happened before, maybe many times. There had been at least six mass extinctions in the past. Two hundred-fifty million years ago, ninety percent of species were destroyed by a cataclysmic event. Later, the dinosaurs and about half of all other species then extant were extinguished, over time, in another catastrophe.

"Elements of humanity will almost certainly survive this Event, though without help they may not survive for very long."

"What do you mean, 'without help'?"

"If humanity is going to survive the Event, it will have to be rescued."

I said, "Are we talking about rescuing all seven billion of us?"

"In a manner of speaking," Henry said.

"But that's impossible."

"Not really. In the first stages in their development, human beings and most other animals are so small as to be invisible to the naked eye. Embryos—millions of them, if necessary or desired—can be frozen for very long periods of time."

Not only would human beings be rescued. A skeleton ecosystem that could be transplanted when the ship reached its destination would also go along. Most of our fellow mammals would accompany us, of course. So would as much of the rest of the fauna and flora and bacteria as possible.

"And human knowledge, of course," he added.

"All of it?"

"Essentially, yes. Most of it is already computerized and the remainder soon will be. The whole of it can be contained in a package about the size of the Antarctic sphere."

It all made sense to him. It was not quite so clear to me. I had not felt my sunburn since the plane took off. Now I did, and squirmed. I asked no more questions. Henry's tale of the future seemed all too plausible, and I had stopped resisting the picture he painted.

In a way my mind had been prepared for something like this. I had seen this movie many times. So had everyone else. In films and books about the end of the world, there was always hope. Two people always survived, and they were always beautiful, and you knew that Adam and Eve were going to discover the secret all over again.

Not this time, said common sense.

Next morning at five sharp, Henry phoned. He said he was sending me something and asked me to name a convenient hour for delivery.

"It's fairly bulky, so give yourself time to clear off a tabletop for it," he said.

I said, "Actually, Henry, I don't want anything bulky. I have no room for anything. This is a one-bedroom flat."

My sunburn hurt. My throat was dry. My voice was a squeak.

Rising from sleep I had imagined myself swimming through a cloud of reef fishes. Did they nibble at my peeling skin or had I made that up after I woke up?

"It's essential equipment," Henry said. "The guys who deliver it will hook it up for you."

He hung up. I slammed down the phone. This was an annoying man. It was still dark. It was raining. I was too annoyed to go back to sleep and too agitated to work. A shower would be agony. I made coffee and toasted an English muffin and smeared it with apricot jam. I put on a thin, silk Chinese bathrobe I had bought from a catalog but had never worn. It lay lightly on my raw skin, but was intolerable just the same. I took off the bathrobe and sat down at the computer.

Usually it's a mistake to attempt to write while both naked and angry. Nevertheless I typed a few words. An hour passed before I wrote a sentence good enough to keep. Another sentence followed and soon others joined up. Doors opened in the brain. Time went away. I forgot the sunburn.

Then, at ten o'clock precisely, the door buzzer sounded.

"We've got your ten o'clock delivery down here," a male voice said from downstairs. I buzzed him in.

Henry's gift turned out to be a very sleek computer with an over-size screen. The delivery people set it up and turned it on for me. They were gone, taking the packing with them, in ten minutes or less. Seconds later, the computer sounded two musical notes, the monitor lighted up, and Henry's face appeared on the screen.

He said, "Can you see me and hear me?"

"Everything seems to be working."

He said, "Good. This computer is secure. It can't be hacked. Please use it exclusively to talk to me. I ask you never use it to talk to anyone else."

He sounded like he really intended to keep in touch. We gazed at each other's images for a long moment. His face was expressionless. I hoped that mine was, too.

At last Henry said, "So what's your answer? Will you work with me on this?"

A sensible person would have replied, *I'll think about it*—or better yet, *No*.

I said, "Before I answer, I'd like to ask you a question."

"Go ahead."

"Have you run a background check on me?"

"Yes."

"What's the worst thing you found out about me?"

"No significant sins were discovered," Henry said.

"No crimes, either?"

He paused before he spoke—sizing me up, I thought, wondering if he should give me an honest answer.

Finally he said, "Only the crime that was committed against you when you were fifteen."

"What do you know about that?"

"That you were raped. That you were injured. That the rapist was not brought to justice."

"Do you know his name?"

"No. The court records are sealed."

"What else?" I asked.

"That you spent fourteen months in a psychiatric hospital. That during that time you bore a child that was surrendered for adoption."

"None of that bothers you?"

"The crime angers me," Henry said. "But what happened to you against your will when you were hardly more than a child has no bearing on the subject under discussion."

I said, "It bothers *me*, Henry. It bothers me a lot. I had an excellent psychiatrist, and he tried to teach me how to live with this, and mostly I do as he suggested, but I never go out at night without thinking that the rapist might be waiting for me, and I never go home to a dark apartment without wondering if he's inside, hiding."

"Are you afraid of men?"

"I'm afraid of one man who was a boy when he did what he did. The others I judge for what they are, not what they might be."

I saw something in his eyes.

I said, "Really."

He nodded, moved a hand. Another long pause.

Henry said, "I can offer you protection."

I said, "There's no such thing."

He didn't argue. He waited patiently for me to say whatever I was going to say next.

I said, "The answer to the job offer is yes for the time being, provided we never return to this subject."

"Agreed," Henry said. "Melissa will deposit a retainer to your account for the first six months."

I said, "You do remember that I'm writing a book?"

"What hours are you undisturbable?"

"Six a.m. till noon."

"That's fine. Please don't get sick because I can't spare you. You shouldn't have much in the way of expenses, but whatever they are, you can bill them at the end of every month. Get a bigger place if you need one and charge it as an expense."

"I like it where I am."

Henry's image shrugged. He said, "I'll be in touch."

That was the entire negotiation. Later in the day, using my old computer, I went to my bank's website. My checking account showed a deposit of five hundred thousand dollars.

My balance was now $500,967.57.

3

SOON AFTER THIS—so soon as to take me by surprise—Henry called at the stroke of noon.

He said, "I want you to come to a meeting. A car will pick you up at two o'clock. You'll be gone for about a week."

"Same place?"

"No," Henry said. "Colder climate."

There were three other passengers aboard the airplane with me, tall men about Henry's age who were very clubby with one another. Not with me. They took me for exactly what I was, someone they didn't know, and ignored me. They dressed like Henry, in jeans and T-shirts and sneakers—but then, so did I. The steward, the same young Asian I had met on the flight to the Grenadines, brought drinks and dinner. Afterward the men went to the back of the plane and played video games. I read for a while before turning out the light.

When I woke, not remembering when I had fallen asleep, it was daylight. The men were sound asleep, stocking feet protruding from the blankets. The pheromones were quite strong. Only one of them snored. My watch said five after one. I had no idea where we were or what our destination might be. We had been in the air for about nine hours. The safety video had told us that the cruising speed of this aircraft, a Gulfstream, was six hundred miles per hour, with a range of seventy-five hundred miles. Ergo, we wouldn't run out of fuel for another two thousand miles.

The steward, this time wearing a name tag that identified him as Daeng, touched the back of my hand.

I said, "Where are we?"

"Almost there," he whispered, with a brilliant smile. "Better hurry before they all wake up."

When I emerged from the lavatory, the men were drinking coffee, eyes dull with sleep, hair standing on end, dark-chinned, not one bit friendlier than before. We broke through the clouds. A khaki desert, seemingly endless, came into view. In the middle distance, a dozen missiles, looking like great big rifle bullets arranged in a circle, materialized. They must be pointed at the United States—where else?

Beyond them lay a runway. The Gulfstream landed without so much as a squeak of tires and we disembarked—me first as the men, suddenly chivalrous, stood back and let me pass as if we had landed deep in the twentieth century. Outside, it looked and felt more like the tenth century. The wind moaned and stirred up dust.

There were no formalities—not a soul to be seen, no soldiers or police asking for passports. At the other end of the runway I saw a squat concrete building but could not make out the flag that flew above it. A large van was parked on the tarmac. Daeng loaded our luggage into it and we all piled in—the boys in the backseat, me in the front. Daeng got behind the wheel and drove smoothly along an absolutely straight macadam road that seemed to go nowhere.

We drove eastward—*whizzed* would be the better word, because Daeng had set the cruise control at one hundred miles per hour. No doubt parched desert creatures crawled and slithered in the sand beside the road, but the van seemed to be the only moving object in this drab and empty landscape. The radio, tuned to a satellite station, played twangy Chinese music loud enough to make conversation impossible—not that any was likely.

After an hour or so we arrived at a large round structure that was meant to resemble a yurt. Several smaller yurts surrounded it to make a compound. The yurts were made of some shiny space-age material I could not identify. A bank of solar panels and a row of wind turbines, propellers spinning, completed the tableau. Several fearsome-looking chow chow dogs roamed the grounds unleashed. Daeng handed each of us a chain necklace from which a blank plastic card dangled.

"Please wear these at all times for your own safety," Daeng said.

We got out of the van. Three of the chows left the pack, each choosing one of the men. A fourth, a lion-colored animal, attached itself to me. The rest—there were maybe a dozen dogs in all—kept their distance.

Daeng and the dog escorted me to my yurt. After he had shown me the amenities—the yurt was a little America—Daeng pointed at the plastic tag hanging from my neck.

"It's for the dogs," he said.

"They check people's ID?"

"They smell it," Daeng said. "Each tag has a different scent, to differentiate individual humans. The chows attack if they don't smell it, so don't forget to wear it. Don't be alarmed when they walk along with you. They're trained to do that. Don't try to be friendly with them. They don't like it."

I said, "Where are we?"

He flashed his perfect smile.

"Hsi-tau—Little Gobi Desert, the Chinese part," he said. "Henry will be expecting you in the big yurt in half an hour."

I left early, accompanied by my guardian chow, hoping to be the first to arrive, but the men were already seated around a table, engaged in a lively conversation with Henry. One of them was an American. The other two, though perfectly fluent in English, were not native speakers. This surprised me a little. Aboard the airplane they had certainly acted like Americans and dressed and sounded like them, too. But then, who in the world didn't, nowadays?

Henry explained to me that that these men were engineers who specialized in spacecraft design, then came straight to the point without explaining my presence to them.

"We are here to answer a question," Henry said. "What is the largest spacecraft that's possible to build and launch into orbit with present technology?"

"That depends on where you want to build it," said the genuine American in the group.

"Then where is the best place?"

"Low Earth orbit. You don't have to contend with gravity."

"Ha!" said another, who sounded like a Russian. "You will contend with a lot of gravity when you start lifting the parts of your spaceship two hundred miles straight up from the surface of the earth."

"One moment, please," said the third, plainly a German. "We're starting from the wrong direction. First decide what is the optimum size for the job, then design to that size."

In short, nobody answered the question, simple though it might be. Henry said, "Think in terms of a ship that could keep a crew alive and sane for a thousand years or more and deliver them at their destination in a condition to walk, speak, think, and remember what their mission was. And carry it out."

"You're kidding," the American said.

"On the contrary," Henry said.

"Forty generations in space?" said the German. "This is science fiction. With such a small gene pool, living in isolation from culture in an environment without gravity, they'll be grotesque monsters in far less time than a thousand years."

Henry said, "The genetic destiny of the crew is a separate question. The problem we are here to discuss is the design and construction of a space vehicle that can remain in space for a very long time and sustain a crew of several hundred human beings in such a way that they will remain human to the end of the voyage."

The engineers exchanged glances.

The Russian said, "Tell us, Henry. Is this an intellectual exercise, or do you actually plan to build this spacecraft?"

"It's not an intellectual exercise," Henry replied.

"What's the timeline? When does construction begin?"

"As soon as we have a blueprint."

"That would take decades and hundreds of engineers. It's a huge undertaking."

"We don't have decades," Henry said.

The American—these fellows were scrupulous about taking turns—said, "The crew would be self-sustaining—produce their own food and everything else?"

"Yes."

"Replace themselves in the usual way?"

"Yes."

"What if they multiply at the same rate as earthlings? World population in the year one thousand was maybe three hundred million. Now it's seven billion. Your ship would have to be the size of a planet to accommodate that."

"True," Henry said, "but irrelevant."

"Do we design this vehicle in such a way as to take population growth into account, or not?"

"You design rationally," Henry said. "What we want to know at the end of this meeting is, how big can the ship be? It's just physics, fellows."

The German said, "The International Space Station is the largest manmade object ever assembled in space. It took more than twenty flights by U.S. and Russian spacecraft to lift the components into orbit over a ten-year period. The space station has less than four hundred cubic meters of living space. That's about the volume of a small suburban house."

Henry said, "I'm not interested in being told what can't be done."

He pointed a finger at me. "What are your thoughts?"

All eyes turned to me and all asked the same silent questions. What could I know? Who was I, anyway? Henry hadn't bothered to introduce me. Why would anyone care what I thought?

"The space station," I said, "was made from modules that were launched into orbit, then fitted together. Why not do the same in this case, using larger components? Assuming that you have the means to launch an unlimited number of modules into orbit, the ship could be as large as you wanted to make it. It could even be disassembled when it reaches its destination and be maneuvered module by module onto the surface of another planet, or moon, and serve as living quarters for a colony."

The American said, "Why would you want to do that?"

Henry said, "Why not? Start there."

Without uttering another word, he left the yurt. In his wake, eyes were averted, silence reigned. Then the engineers went to work. I sat alone on my side of the table. The engineers huddled on their side, entering data in computers and scribbling notes—mostly crazy quilt equations—on legal pads. By noon, the tabletop was littered crumpled pages.

Meanwhile, I doodled. I drew modules and the rockets that would hurl them into orbit and string them together two hundred miles or more above the planet. I can draw and write. As I was not part of the discussion and had nothing else to do, I sketched colonies on our own moon and Jupiter's icy moon, Europa. By the end of the day I had put together a kind of graphic novel of the expedition. It was of no use to anyone who had a scientific mind.

Henry returned around five o'clock.

By that time I was ready to be a team player, to say generous things about my colleagues' ideas if they were better than mine, as my colleagues plainly were certain they would be.

The German acted as spokesman. He cleared his throat and to my great surprise, said, "Our new colleague has come up with an excellent concept." He smiled at me, bowed ever so slightly, and said, "Congratulations!" You could practically hear the exclamation point.

"The merit of this idea lies in its obviousness, its simplicity," the German continued. "Also its practicality. As the lady pointed out, we have already had some experience with assembling structures in space. We are impressed with the flexibility this approach provides in terms of design and materials. We believe the concept has other advantages, including the possibility that the crew could manufacture additional modules while the mission is in flight. We began with the attitude that the idea was unworkable. After only a few hours of consideration we cannot say for certain that it is, in fact, feasible, but the fundamentals are such that we are able to recommend further study."

Diagrams of the module as the engineers imagined it were projected onto a screen. Actually they had visualized several different modules—spherical, square, rectangular, tubular. In a computer image of the assembled ship, all these forms fitted together very nicely—beautifully, in fact, as they swam through space like a cartoon history of solid geometry.

"All this is provisional, intended merely to demonstrate possibilities," the German said. "However, Henry, our initial impression is that these possibilities are many. We are nevertheless somewhat daunted by the probable cost. We have made a rough estimate."

At this point the Russian took over. He based his estimates on the capacities of the space shuttle and its launch system. With some modifications, there should be no insuperable engineering difficulty in modifying the system to carry the modules into orbit. However, lifting the modules and their contents and the crew into orbit would involve an estimated fifteen hundred launches. The cost of a single space shuttle launch at current prices was about one and a half billion dollars. Total cost would be at least one trillion dollars.

Henry did not blink an eye. No doubt he had already calculated the costs. He asked the engineers to keep working.

"We'll be using a reusable launch system," he said. "Concentrate on the modules."

Eyebrows rose.

Henry said, "Think about new materials for the modules. Make all the modules the same size and shape. Otherwise we'll have to design and build several different launchers."

"Which shape?" asked the American.

"Spheres."

"What kind of materials?"

"Indestructible ones, not metals," Henry replied.

After five days, I went back to New York, back to my book. It would be inaccurate to say that the act of writing made me forget all about what Henry had told me. But the act of writing banished Henry and the end of civilization to brain compartments of their own. Or so I thought. Yet my characters got sadder and sadder as the story went on, as though they suspected something awful was afoot and I was keeping it from them. Maybe the watertight door between Henry's compartment and theirs was not so watertight as I thought.

4

AN OLD BOYFRIEND RANG ME up. He had tickets to an Off-Off Broadway play that evening. Did I want to see it with him and have supper afterward? I said yes. The caller was a presentable fellow. He never talked politics. He could be funny. I had always liked him.

The evening began happily enough, but during the play, the usual bitter poor-me meditation about the impossibility of love, I found myself floating above the characters on stage, looking down on them as if I were undergoing an out-of-body experience on their behalf. They were all going to perish, the audience was going to perish, I was going to perish, the species was going to perish. Nobody in the tiny theater but me had the slightest idea that life as we knew it was almost over. I made an unseemly sound. Heads turned.

My friend said, "Are you OK?"

I did not respond, but got hold of myself.

Afterward, at supper, large tears dribbled from my eyes without warning. My date put down his fork, reached across the table, and took my hand.

"Are you sure you're OK?" he asked.

"I'm fine," I said. "I guess the play made me sad."

"Why?" he said. "It was just the usual existentialist crap."

He took me home in a taxi. On my doorstep he asked if he should come upstairs. My memories of him were fond, and a sensible woman in my state of mind would have said yes. But for some reason I thought of Henry and felt like a wife attracted to another man but faithful to her vows, so I said no, not tonight.

In due course, after weeks had passed, Henry got back in touch. I examined his computer image in search of a deeper tan or a convalescent pallor or anything else that might explain his long absence. However, he looked just the same—the silent-movie eyes, the Zenlike calm, the suggestion of a fleeting smile that never quite showed up.

He invited me to lunch. His driver picked me up and took me to a house just around the corner from the Metropolitan Museum of Art. Like the glass house in the Grenadines, this place, an art nouveau mansion, was full of art. I knew most of the pictures, but only as photographs because the paintings had always been the property of the hideously rich. If Henry decided to sell just the pictures and sculptures on the ground floor in this house, he could probably have made enough after taxes to pay for a hundred shuttle launches with full payloads.

After lunch, Henry got down to business. He wanted to talk about secrecy.

"I thought you thought there was no need to go into that," I said.

"This is not about you keeping secrets. I mean secrecy itself."

Fascinating topic.

I said, "Henry, I understand that it would be a serious mistake to tell the world what you plan to do, if that's what we're talking about."

Henry said, "Quite soon we're going to start doing things that can't be hidden from the world—the launches, the assembly of the spacecraft in orbit, the recruitment and training of the crew, the collection of specimens. . . ."

I twitched. *Specimens?*

Henry noticed my reaction but did not elaborate. "And a lot more," he said. "How do we explain this?"

"Why not just tell the truth?" I asked. "Henry Peel is launching a spaceship. Nobody will be surprised."

"They'll want to know why I'm doing it."

I said, "You don't have to tell them. Everyone knows how secretive you can be. Maybe you just think it's time for private enterprise to break the government monopoly on space travel once and for all. Maybe you've had one of your amazing ideas, which you are not at liberty to describe."

"We can't mislead," Henry said.

"Who's misleading? Everything will be out in the open except the purpose of the enterprise."

"Exactly. So?"

"So who advertises purposes?"

A few days later, an earthquake registering 6.1 on the Richter scale occurred in rural Missouri. In the days that followed, tremors of similar magnitude occurred all over the world, including a number of places where earthquakes were unusual. A volcano in Ecuador and another in Alaska erupted. It snowed in summer on the South Island of New Zealand. Overnight, figuratively speaking, the North Pole moved a full degree of longitude in the direction of Siberia.

Without really knowing why, I worried about the compound of yurts in Hsi-tau. I felt even greater anxiety about the circle of big rockets we had overflown as the Gulfstream came in for a landing. Were these really nuclear missiles aimed at the USA, as I had assumed, or were they launch vehicles for components of Henry's spaceship? If this was a secret missile site, why hadn't the Chinese blown it up? If the rockets belonged to Henry, as seemed more probable every second I thought about it, I had less to teach him about hiding things in plain sight than I had given myself credit for.

My life had become a marathon of uncertainties.

Sometimes, crazily, I thought I was in love.

5

IN SOME WAYS, I MIGHT as well have been. I was getting practically no sleep. My routine was taking a beating. My habit was to finish work, lollygag for four hours, go for a run, take a shower, put on my pajamas, make a salad or order takeout and read a junk book while eating it, then watch a movie or a ballgame. In the pre-Henry era I had usually fallen asleep halfway through the movie or in the top of the fifth inning. Since going through the looking glass, I was more likely to watch the movie or the game until the end, then read until dawn—good book or bad, it didn't matter. The alternative was to lie on my back, thinking about the end of things, eyes wide open, watching a window full of yellowish city light pulsing as if synchronized to my breath.

Listen to me! I would tell myself. No matter how certain or how near the end might be, worrying, much less imagining a romance that would never happen, was a waste of whatever time was left to the world. But I didn't listen to my saner self—who does?—and I didn't sleep. The enemy I lived with was not fear. It was realization. This thing, this Event was going to happen. Henry said so. Even if I fell asleep for a while—and now and then I couldn't help but do so—I would wake with a start, realizing I would see it sooner or later—waves of solid ground filled with boulders sweeping in a towering tsunami across the continents, dust bursting like umber spindrift from the monster as it knocked down cities and mountains and sucked the water from lakes and seas and inhaled all this into itself, changing everything forever. It was always the destruction of inanimate objects—not the death of man but the erasure of his works—that made my heart ache and my lungs fail me. I could not explain this to myself.

Gradually, I got over my insomnia by running a little farther every day and adding an hour of yoga to my routine and just not thinking about extinction after the sun went down. Nevertheless, when I turned off the lights, psychosis crouched at the foot of the bed.

Henry came back and life got busier. We began running together—his idea, like nearly everything else I now did. But Henry ran six miles, or ten kilometers, every other day, always in the park. The distance around the Central Park Reservoir is 1.5 miles, or 2.4 kilometers, which meant four complete circuits—a lot. Usually we went our separate ways at the end of the run. But one day in March—patches of dirty snow underfoot, mist on the water, breath visible—we cooled off by walking to the Ramble. We found a bench and sat down.

A bird sang, and Henry pointed a finger at a small, black-headed bit of fluff that hung upside down from a naked twig.

"Black-capped chickadee," he said. "Wonder what he's doing here."

The bird fluttered away.

I began to shiver. I pulled a thick sweatshirt out of my daypack and put it on. This did little good. The sweatshirt had no hood. It captured less body heat than the amount that was escaping through my scalp.

I said, "Henry, let's go. I'm getting a chill."

He looked me over, nodded, and got out his cell phone. By the time we walked to the gate, the car and driver were waiting. I expected to be taken home, but instead we headed west. Traffic was light. The car, which smelled brand-new with the heater on, was toasty. Gradually I dried out and warmed up. Henry asked if I was feeling better. I replied that I was fine now. This was a lie. I just didn't want to be alone.

I asked him about the black-capped chickadee. Why had he been so interested in it? Had it been in the wrong place, far from its usual habitat, or what?

Henry said, "Why do you ask?"

"Well, magnetism has something to do with bird migrations, no? I just wondered if the patterns might be changing as a result of what's happening to the magnetic field."

"Interesting thought," Henry said, "but the bird wasn't in the wrong place. Its range includes Central Park, but just barely, so I was a little surprised to see it, that's all."

At West End Drive and Seventy-ninth Street, Henry asked the driver to pull over. The driver, showing no surprise, stopped the car and got out. Leaving the driver on the sidewalk, Henry drove onto the West Side Highway and we sped north on back roads along the Hudson River. He was a fast driver. Pretty soon we were in Westchester, then beyond it. It began to snow. Henry didn't slow down one iota as he rounded curves at eighty miles an hour. Somehow I kept from gasping and waving my arms.

Around noon Henry turned into a driveway that led to a house overlooking the Hudson. It was a showplace, pillared and porticoed. The view of the river alone was worth millions. Three other cars, all made in Germany of course, were parked in the driveway.

A fiftyish man who looked like the young Vittorio De Sica—hawk-nosed, tall and trim, with a head of curly, jet-black hair—opened the door. With a brilliant smile and a glad masculine cry he embraced Henry, then extended his hand to me.

"Amerigo Vespucci," he said, slowly and distinctly pronouncing the first name correctly: *Am-air-EE-go*.

The foyer was cavernous. The décor seemed to have been chosen by a decorator. A faux Flanders tapestry hung on the back wall.

Bland white nineteenth-century statuary stood in ranks, portraits of ancestors hung on the walls. From deeper in the house, voices floated. Amerigo led us toward them. A tall, dramatically slim woman with a Garbo face flew to Henry and kissed him three times on the cheeks before pulling him into the crowd. Others greeted him so enthusiastically I thought the party might at any moment burst into applause or "He's a Jolly Good Fellow." They were a stylish crowd. No woman in the room was wearing less than ten thousand dollars' worth of clothing and jewelry. I was still in my sweats and sneakers. Garbo noticed. Before leaving me alone in a corner, she gave me with her own hands a glass of champagne and a triangle of toast loaded with caviar. Also something that might have been a smile. She did not tell me her name or show the faintest interest in knowing mine.

Outside the windows, snow continued to fall—big fat flakes. By three o'clock it was ankle deep. The guests brushed off their Mercedeses and BMWs and drove away. Henry and Amerigo vanished. Garbo and I were left alone in the chilly foyer.

"I'm told you and Henry and my husband have things to talk about," she said. "So I'm going to disappear."

She did so without further ado, drifting up the double staircase and leaving behind a smile as if it were another point of toast and caviar. What was I supposed to do now? How would I find Henry and Amerigo? I was feeling worse by the minute, coughing, sneezing, burning with fever.

Amerigo appeared. He offered his arm.

"Henry awaits," he said, then marched me through lofty rooms to the library, where Henry was indeed waiting for us, goblet of springwater in hand.

Hanging on the wall behind the desk was a large oil portrait of a man in Cinquecento costume.

"Your seafaring ancestor?" I asked.

"My father certainly thought so," he said. "This was his place. Would you like something to drink?"

I shook my head. To make sure I meant it, he tempted me with coffee, tea, San Pellegrino water.

"Lemonade?" he said. "Hot lemonade?"

Again I declined.

Amerigo said, "Henry tells me you're his amanuensis in this new thing of his."

I had never before heard the word *amanuensis* spoken aloud. "Nothing as fancy as that," I said. "How do you fit in?"

"I am the mission pharmacist. I own a little drug company in Milan."

I started to speak, failed to get a word out, cleared my throat, coughed spasmodically. My earlier symptoms were getting worse. Amerigo instantly fetched a box of Kleenex and a glass of water.

"You don't get to go on the spaceship with that cold, young lady," he said, wagging a finger.

He then spoke at length about the many kinds of pills and serums his company, Vespucci S.p.A., made and sold.

"The Vespucci are still making discoveries," he said. "And going on great voyages. Our crew will be well protected."

"Maybe the better approach would be to select a crew that doesn't get sick," I croaked.

Henry pounced. "What do you mean by that?"

"Select people whose DNA suggests they have little or no chance of developing a fatal condition. Once in space, and effectively in permanent quarantine, you could breed a replacement population that was even healthier than the original crew. Smarter, too. As I understand it, embryos are easier to work with than adults—fewer cells, therefore simpler procedures."

Henry and Amerigo looked appalled.

Amerigo said to Henry, "She *knows*?"

Knew what?

By now I was coughing uncontrollably. I excused myself. In the lavatory mirror, I looked as awful as I felt—tangled hair, swollen nose, red eyes, chapped lips, chalky skin. No wonder Garbo had quarantined me from her other guests and fled up the stairway. I was still wearing the gizmo that measured my heart rate and blood pressure when I ran. I pressed the button. Blood pressure one sixty over ninety, heart rate ninety-two. Head stuffy, stomach sour, curiosity activated.

We talked some more—aimlessly, it seemed. The snow continued to accumulate. I felt worse by the minute. The last thing I wanted to do was sleep in this house. I asked Henry to take me home. We left immediately, tires crunching. It was dark, winter-dark. Snow swirled hypnotically in the headlights. Sunday-evening traffic was heavy, as weekenders streamed back to Manhattan. My stomach grew queasier. I figured out how the front passenger seat worked and tilted it back, meaning to sleep or at least feign sleep.

At this moment, Henry decided to abandon the taciturnity that had been the most noticeable thing about him since he returned from the Hsi-tau. He began talking about the Event and the thousands of things that remained to be done to prepare for it. The discourse went on for some time—the ship, the crew, the cargo, the itinerary, the many subcategories under each of these headings, and the uncountable details attaching to each subcategory. I pretended to listen. I never wanted to meet another Garbo or another Amerigo or another engineer.

While Henry went on about our epic to-do list, I fantasized about writing him a check for the money that remained in my checking account. Very little of the five hundred thousand dollars he had deposited had been spent. Only the week before I had received a royalty check that would keep me afloat for six months, so I could afford to return Henry's half million and call it quits and just perish with everybody else.

In the theater of my mind I wrote the check, smelled the ink, tasted the envelope flap.

6

I HID OUT LIKE A sick cat for a week. After that, the old boyfriend who had taken me to the depressing play and the trattoria phoned and asked me out again. We arranged to meet in a restaurant in Chelsea. I went down a couple of hours early so I could wander through the galleries by myself. In one place that displayed gargantuan paintings of galaxies, I noticed a man. He was around six feet tall, Roman nose, nice jawline, curly hair, body fat close to zero. Nothing he wore was new: a suede blazer over a black knit shirt, scarf, corduroy pants, scuffed loafers. We stood side by side, looking at the same picture.

He said, "What do you think?"

"I like it. But I don't have a place to hang it."

The canvas was about twenty feet long and maybe twelve feet high.

He said, "I've got the same problem."

He followed me to the next picture—same galaxy, bigger painting.

He said, "Would you like to grab a drink?"

I looked at my watch. I had ten minutes to get to the restaurant, which was about fifteen minutes away.

He said in a flatter voice, "You've got to go."

I nodded.

He smiled with just the right amount of regret. "Nice talking to you. I hope you find a bigger place."

"What?"

"I said I hope you find a bigger apartment," he said. "So you can buy the picture."

At the restaurant, another trattoria, the old boyfriend was seated at a table with another couple. The woman was a pretty, bosomy blonde, a lot younger than her husband. She wore a wedding ring and a large diamond engagement ring. She told me that my date and the husband had gone to Colgate together. They played varsity lacrosse and almost won the championship in their senior year. She was from Wisconsin. There was an empty chair at the table. Was another Colgate chum on his way?

The wife confided that she was a new wife. Her husband was wonderful in every way, but his three teenage kids came to stay with them every other weekend and on alternate Wednesday nights. They made it obvious—she described exactly how they did this— that they wished she had remained in Wisconsin, or better yet, been killed in a plane crash on her way to New York. Her eyes filled with tears. I said, "There, there." We retired to the ladies' room.

By the time we returned to the table, the extra chair was occupied. The newcomer was the man I had met in the art gallery half an hour before. My friend introduced him to the wife, whom he greeted with grave formality, gazing into her eyes as if forbidden by some code of chivalry to look at any other part of her wondrous person. He gave no sign that he recognized me.

His name was Adam.

"Adam is a big fan of your books," the old boyfriend said. "When he found out I knew you he gave me no peace until I said I'd introduce him."

"How sweet," I said. "So tell me, Adam, which is your favorite book?"

"All of them."

That's what they all said.

"Give me a straight answer or I won't let you sit down," I said.

Adam rattled off the titles of five of my six novels and then quoted the opening paragraph of my first book, which was set in Perugia, where I had spent my junior year abroad. The passage contained a phrase in Italian that referred to the huge white truffles of Umbria. He pronounced the Italian perfectly, and then translated it to show that he knew what it meant.

I said, "OK, Adam, you can sit down."

My date said, "After all that, you should maybe sit on his lap."

Not such a bad idea. The waiter delivered a large platter of anti-pasto.

Adam said, "I'll be mother."

"Why you?" asked the husband, who also seemed to know him.

"Because I was late," Adam said.

"Late? Is that what you call it? You practically stood us up."

Without looking at me, Adam said, "Yeah. Well, I was recovering from a terrible disappointment."

I said, "Did Adam play lacrosse for Colgate, too?"

"No," my date said. "He played for Syracuse. They kicked the crap out of us three years in a row. Adam did most of the damage."

Handling serving spoon and fork with one hand, Adam filled our plates and handed them around. Suddenly I had an appetite. I gobbled the antipasto and ordered gnocchi. It was after midnight when the party ended with half a dozen empty wine bottles on the table. Adam picked up the tab. The other two insisted on taking care of the tip. After they stood up and turned their backs, Adam counted the bills they had left on the table and added another twenty.

Hmmm, said the wine.

On the sidewalk, the old boyfriend wondered if I'd mind finding my own way home. He was staying with the newlyweds, and they lived in New Jersey. He'd find a cab for me.

Adam said, "I'll see her home, if that's OK."

"Same old Adam," said the husband.

My date just smiled nicely and waggled his fingers at me. Apparently Adam had won me in a long-ago lacrosse game.

Adam and I walked to his car, one of those convertibles with a metal roof that folds into the trunk. Despite the weather he put the top down. It wasn't snowing, but it was cold, and as the car moved, the windchill factor took effect. He asked where I lived. I told him. The air smelled washed. Adam smelled like coffee, having drunk two double espressos in the restaurant, and the aroma reminded me of Italy. I felt safe with him. I felt other things besides. I had drunk a lot of wine.

I asked him what he did for a living. He pretended not to hear me. We arrived at my building.

Adam said, "Shall I park the car or say goodnight?"

I didn't answer the question, but I didn't open the door, either.

He put the car in gear and found a parking space about half a block away. He backed into it expertly and turned to me. I must have looked like I was going to ask another question, because he put a gloved finger to my half-frozen lips and said, "I'm a lawyer."

"You don't smell like a lawyer."

"Neither do you," Adam said. "Let's go upstairs."

The next morning, while Adam slept, I wrote a scene that described in exquisite detail what had happened between the two of us the night before. Unbeknownst to me, Adam stood behind me as I typed and read over my shoulder.

He said, "I really hope you're going to do this every time we have sex."

I was naked. He put his fingertips on my shoulders and pressed lightly.

Later, while I regretfully took a shower—all those olfactory delights swirling down the drain to be replaced by the aroma of Olay soap—Adam prepared breakfast. It was nothing like one of Henry's gourmet repasts, but it was fine. This guy knew how to poach eggs in the microwave, make toast, pour orange juice.

Over coffee, Adam told me he had grown up in Saratoga Springs.

He had had a happy childhood. Like me, he was an only child. His father was a stockbroker who in his youth had played football at Syracuse. His mother, who had almost made the Olympics as an equestrian, owned a stable and taught kids to ride. He had spent four years on destroyers, and then gone to law school at Georgetown. After that he worked for the government in Washington for a while, and finally hung out his shingle in Manhattan—in SoHo, on Wooster Street, in fact, because he wanted to live a funky life. He had his own law firm, no partners yet. He made a living, he had a little money of his own. This recitation sounded like a wedding notice in the "Sunday Styles" section of the *Times*.

Adam said, "Your turn."

I said, "If you've read the author blurb on my books, you already know everything."

"You're right. My favorite thing is the photograph, that look in your eyes."

"Cut it out."

"Actually, I Googled you," he said. "You made Phi Beta Kappa. You've got an MFA and a PhD. You were an all-conference lacrosse player in college. Did you have a lacrosse scholarship?"

"Women's lacrosse? Are you kidding?"

Adam said, "One more thing. Our meeting in the gallery was no accident. I spotted you on the street and followed you."

This was kind of sexy to know, but also kind of not. I said, "Why, when you knew you were going to have dinner with me?"

"I didn't know you were you. Meeting you was supposed to be a surprise. It was a surprise. I was late at the restaurant because I was looking for you all over Chelsea."

This was good for my ego. On the other hand, it was eight thirty already, practically midday according to my usual schedule, and I hadn't yet written a word, except for the smut.

"Looking for me all over Chelsea?" I said. "What's the plan from now on? Are you going to go on stalking me?"

My tone was not as light as maybe it should have been.

Adam recoiled, then shook his head as if he had never imagined that I could say such a thing to him after what we had been to each other. He left without another word. The door closed behind him. What had I done? Was I out of my mind?

I sat down at the keyboard. Words flowed as from a mountain spring. At noon exactly, Henry's face popped up on the computer screen. I felt a little current of guilt. It didn't last long.

I said, "Hi, Henry. Nice timing."

Henry said, "Can you come for dinner tonight? There's someone I want you to meet."

"Another Amerigo?"

"I'll send the car around seven."

The other telephone rang. I let it ring. Adam was leaving a message on the answering machine. He wanted to know why I had turned into such a spiteful bitch so soon after we had gotten out of bed? Why? He was at a loss to understand.

To Henry I said, "Fine, seven o'clock," and hung up.

Adam's disembodied voice was telling me that if he had any sense he would never want to see me again. However, he was prepared to give me one more chance.

He said, "Let's get over this bump in the road. My place. Grab a cab, now."

He gave me an address on Broome Street. I didn't pick up.

Adam said, "Fine. I know you're there. The hell with you."

After he hung up, I went to the computer and Googled him. He didn't have much of an entry, but what there was checked out with the life story he had told me.

Evening shadows were falling. What would I wear to Henry's? I pulled on my tightest jeans and a pretty good top and my favorite necklace made of alternating polished and unpolished silver links, and a ruby ring I had inherited from an aunt, and sat down to watch the news while I waited for the intercom to buzz.

Henry's other guest was a very laid-back Chinese in a two-thousand-dollar suit. He looked like a younger and taller version of the late Zhou Enlai—same handsome face and obsidian eyes, same coiled manner. I was glad I had dressed up a little. He handed me his business card. I tried to make points by reading the side printed in Mandarin. His name thereon was Ng Fred. He was chairman and CEO of CyberSci, Inc., of Beijing.

He said, in Mandarin, "The *Ng* is pronounced *Wu*. It's a long story. The Cantonese ideograph is the same as the Mandarin character but has a different sound. But maybe you already know that."

In English, I said, "Is Fred really your first name?"

"My business name," he replied.

"So what should I call you?" I asked in Mandarin, showing off again.

"Fred is fine," he replied in native American English. "Your Mandarin is quite good. You have a Shanghai accent. Where did you pick it up?"

"In Shanghai. I taught there for a year after grad school."

"What subject?"

"Western art history, in a high school."

"So you taught in Mandarin?"

"Sort of, sometimes. I was supposed to talk English, a twofer. Lots of giggles from the kids when I broke into Chinese."

He gave me a real look of amusement. I liked this guy.

As Henry explained while we dined, the topic he wanted to discuss was defense systems for the spaceship. Fred's company, in which Henry held a lot of stock, was going to build the ship—in fact, had already built a factory not far from Henry's yurts in Hsitau. He and Henry were old friends—classmates—roommates, even. Fred's mother was an American Chinese who as a Movement chick had been such a fervent Maoist that she moved to China and married a Red Guard. She sent Fred to a New England prep school, but I had already heard that in his voice just as he had heard Shanghai in mine. Later he had gone to Caltech, where he met Henry.

"I used to copy his notes," Fred said.

Henry and Fred had been exchanging ideas about a defense system for the ship. The question of weaponizing a spacecraft was a difficult one, ethically speaking. Should humanity go unarmed into the cosmos or not? Theoretically mankind had no enemies except itself, in space or anywhere else. I said as much.

Henry said, "So what are you saying? That we should concentrate on countering a threat from Earth? That human beings would destroy the ship out of resentment or disappointment?"

I'm no great believer in the proposition that human beings will act rationally if given the opportunity to do so. Their natural state is irrationality, especially when they turn into a mob, which is essentially what they would become in the hypothetical circumstances we were talking about.

"The people who are being left behind might go crazy," I said. "That's always been the expectation in a worst-case scenario. But however crazy they went, I don't think they'd be stupid enough to shoot down the spaceship. That would mean shooting down their only hope of escape."

"Maybe not," Ng Fred said. "But a boarding party might be dispatched to capture the ship before it launched—or if it had already left, to pursue it, overtake it, and commandeer it."

Henry said, "Where would they get the ships for an expedition like that?"

"Do you really think the U.S. government is not going to build its own ship when it finds out about yours? Not to mention the government of every other technological state in the world."

"So how do we protect the ship?"

"You find a new way to protect it without destroying it or killing too many pirates."

Ng Fred said, "That rules out sabers and muskets."

I said, "Hornets, maybe."

I was kidding. Henry liked the idea.

"Not a bad thought," he said. "Hornets wouldn't kill, but they'd disable and confuse the attacking force without damaging anything on either ship. And afterward they'd return to the hive."

I said—I couldn't stop myself—"Wouldn't the hornets have to have little space suits?"

Henry said, "I'm not talking about real hornets. But we could design a robot hornet, a manufactured device, that would do the job. That's feasible, isn't it, Fred?"

"Provided the robots' stingers are long enough to penetrate space suits but thin enough not to make them leak, why not?"

"Can you do it?"

Fred said, "You design it, Henry, and we'll manufacture it."

I asked questions. Would the hornets' stings be lethal, or would they just hurt so much that the pirates would surrender? How would we keep the hornets from attacking our own crew as well as the pirates?

Henry told me to remember the chows of Hsi-tau and the ID tags. Something similar—chips implanted under the skin of the crew, maybe—could solve the problem. The hornets would sting only the enemy, never the good guys.

Just the same, I wondered. If there was life on other planets, was there an organism anywhere in the universe that could defend itself against Henry's hornets, especially as they would surely be improved by the crew of the mother ship? And what might the combination of human beings and indestructible hornets mean for the universe?

7

LATER, GETTING OUT OF THE car in front of my building, I half hoped that Adam would spring from the shadows and plead for another chance. However, I saw no sign of him or anyone else except the usual dog walkers and couples staggering home after dining out. It was almost one o'clock in the morning. Across the river, beyond a row of leafless trees washed by streetlight, New Jersey was a lattice of lighted windows. The city was unusually quiet. A full minute passed during which I did not hear a siren or feel a subway train beneath my soles. A couple of bicyclists in full racing gear whirred by, taking advantage of the light traffic. Somebody got out of a taxi across the street—nope, not Adam, just a woman with a briefcase. I liked this city in the same way that I liked my body—nothing was new, yet everything was always new. For the first time in ages, I felt the exhilaration of being where I was.

That changed when I reached the door of my apartment. I leaned against it, thinking to prolong my moment of euphoria while I got my keys out of my bag. The door swung open under my weight, and I staggered backward into the hall.

The door was unlocked. All four deadbolts, the chain, and the steel bar were open, every one of them. This was impossible. I never failed to lock the door. Locking it was an obsession. I distinctly remembered locking up before I left for dinner.

Were the intruders still inside? Where else would they be? I should have run for the elevator. Instead, don't ask me why, I dashed into the apartment, slamming and locking the door behind me and trapping myself inside with whatever killer or rapist might be waiting to pounce. There was no one there—no one under the bed, no one in the closets, no one behind the shower curtain. The thousand dollars in cash I kept in a Baggie in the icemaker were still there, but the inside of the freezer looked different, as if things had been moved around and then replaced. Same thing with my dresser drawers, with the bookcase, with my address book and diary. All were in slightly different places. *Someone had touched them.* Likewise the clothes in my closet. I examined the clean glasses in the cupboard for fingerprints but found none.

The apartment had been searched. I knew it. Nothing had been taken, but my space had been violated. Why? What were these people looking for? Beside the telephone I kept a scratch pad and a pencil. I held the pad level with my eye and looked across its surface. Yes, there definitely were indentations. I scribbled over them with the pencil and there it was, the proof. A number had been written on this pad and the page on which it was written had been torn off. The number was written in somebody else's hand, in large figures that slanted to the right. My own handwriting was small and perpendicular. I had worked for years to make it so.

I dialed the number on the pad. There was no answer, no answering machine. I dashed to the computer and tried to do a reverse lookup of the phone number. No luck.

Now what? What were my choices? If I dialed 911, the cops would treat me like a hysterical female. There was no point in calling a locksmith. If these people could pick these locks that had cost me a fortune, they could pick any locks ever made. Were the intruders lurking in the hall? On the roof? Where was I going to sleep from now on, where could I work? To whom could I turn? My father was dead. No lover protected me. I didn't want Henry to know what had happened. I was alone.

They had left the door unlocked. They wanted me to know they could come again whenever they liked.

8

THERE WAS ONLY ONE THING to do—leave. I stayed awake all night
reading For Rent classifieds on the Internet, then went to the bank
as soon as it opened and withdrew several thousand dollars in cash.
Before noon, I found a spacious, utterly sterile place on York Avenue
in a tower whose enormous windows overlooked the East River. It
came equipped with phony Bauhaus furniture and awful pictures
and rugs and a wonderful bathroom and state-of-the-art kitchen.
The building manager did not blink when I mentioned that I wished
to rent the place under an assumed name. The rent was astronomi-
cal. However, I was getting value in return. This was the last neighborhood in which anyone who knew me would think to look for
me, and the manager assured me that the building had a squad of
large, no-nonsense doormen and a security team of ex-cops that
prowled the corridors day and night, on the lookout for intruders.
Front and back doors had keypad locks, backed up by deadbolts and
what I was told was an undefeatable alarm system.

Before leaving my old apartment, I copied my manuscript onto
a flash drive. I left everything else behind—the bed unmade, dishes
in the dishwasher, clothes in the closet. I poured out the milk and
threw other perishables down the disposal—spoiled food in the

refrigerator would be a dead giveaway. I shredded my credit cards and checkbook. I felt a pang when bidding my books good-bye and a surge of anxiety about the new computer Henry had installed until I realized that the intruders had no doubt already drained it of any secrets it might contain.

I put on jeans and sneakers and a coat and hat and sunglasses, and went out. It was a short walk to a bookstore on Second Avenue. I ordered a dozen reference books, paid cash, and had them delivered. A few doors down the avenue I found an electronics store and bought one of those throwaway cell phones that drug dealers use. In a mail store I bought some stamps and envelopes and rented a mailbox. Henry was on my mind. I thought of walking to his house, only a few blocks away. I thought better of this, and instead wrote *Please call me at once* and scribbled the number of my new cell phone on a page of my notebook and mailed it.

Back in the new apartment, I disguised myself. I changed my hair—shorter, fluffier, darker. I wore my glasses all the time now instead of contacts. I walked more briskly, as if I had places to go and too little time to get there. I felt like a secret agent setting up a cover identity. When I ventured out to do some shopping, a man who needed a shave made eye contact with me. Was he stalking me? Was my every move being watched? Was this going to last forever? Was there no escape? Should I go to the airport and buy a ticket for Rio de Janeiro? Was I losing my senses? Did I have any further use for my senses? The apartment was inhuman in its sterility. The takeout I ordered for supper was blander than the takeout I was used to. The river I saw through those huge windows was the wrong river. The apartment, the neighborhood, were deathly quiet. Everyone was all dressed up. I had woken up in hell.

Henry didn't answer my note. He could be anywhere, doing anything. The media gave me many reasons to think about him: An ice shelf the size of Connecticut broke loose from Antarctica, carrying thousands of penguins and seals out to sea. The North Pole inched ever closer to Siberia. The magnetic field continued to fluctuate. Migrating birds appeared in countries where their species had never before been seen, and vanished from destinations where they had been arriving on schedule since the Stone Age. Still no one saw a pattern.

By the time Henry called, at the end of a week, I had accepted that he would never find me, that I would never hear from him again. I told him I had moved, as he had suggested. I told him why. I told him my new name.

"I'll be right there," he said. "What's the address?"

When he arrived, minutes later, he looked around, taking it all in, object by object—the furniture whose minimalism made it all the more showy, the gaudy faux Jackson Pollock carpets—*carpets!*—the imitation Warhol silkscreen of Marilyn Monroe as a sheet of postage stamps, the trompe l'oeil that looked like a framed sofa cushion until you saw that it was really a zebra. I won't go on.

"Wow," Henry said. "No wonder you changed your name."

Now he was being funny? I didn't reply.

He said, "It's not possible that you just forgot to lock the door?"

"Never in a million years."

He said, "OK, then somebody is trying to scare you."

"They've succeeded."

He looked around again. "Beyond their wildest dreams," he said. "Pack a bag. You can't live here and think at the same time, and I need your brain."

I didn't argue. Fifteen minutes later we were headed for the airport. For a change he told me where we were going. We stopped at my old place while I picked up clothes suitable for Hsi-tau, our destination. The driver collected the computer Henry had given me and lugged it down to the car. Everything was as shabby and jumbled as usual, but nothing was the same. The atmosphere had been disturbed. An invisible presence had moved in and it had no intention of ever leaving.

I could feel it.

TWO

1

WE ARRIVED IN HSI-TAU AT dusk. After dinner in the big yurt Henry amazed me by asking if I played chess. I did, sort of. I won the Camp Wingenund grand championship when I was twelve, and five years later made it to the semifinals of a high school tournament. In the here and now, I sometimes played a few games online, though I almost always lost because I overstated my skill level. That night, versus Henry, I played far beyond my abilities, and actually won one game out of three. If he let me have that victory (how else to explain it?), I didn't catch him at it.

Outside, after the chess, a grit-filled wind blew. The beam of my flashlight reflected from the swirling dust as from a snowstorm. The chow dog that had assigned itself to me walked me back to my yurt. Its presence made me feel absolutely safe. Not only was my protector on duty, but the rest of the pack roamed the howling darkness, ready to attack any intruder at a moment's notice. Inside my little yurt, America awaited—air-conditioning, satellite television and radio, a refrigerator full of wine, springwater and fruit and healthful snacks, clean sheets on a king-size bed, hot water. I showered and got into the bed and fell asleep. I was safe here on the far edge of China, with my attack dog curled up on the doorstep.

As the sun rose, the chow and I walked together to the big yurt. I was finishing my coffee when Henry appeared. He had a carefree air. He was smiling, relaxed, practically jovial. He wished me good morning and suggested an outing. He raised his eyebrows slightly when I didn't leap at the chance. I had come here to work with Henry, to learn new things, to behold new wonders, not to go sightseeing. Besides, Hsi-tau did not leap to mind when you heard the words tourist destination. I had already flown or driven over hundreds of miles of its tawny surface. Everything looked the same even when the wind blew, which was all the time.

"Sounds great," I said weakly, anticipating yet another gourmet picnic lunch and hoping against hope that the natives I kept expecting to see, but never did, had invited us to share Mongolian hot pot in an authentic yurt.

Reading my face—and for all I knew, my mind—Henry gave me a quizzical look. He led me to a Humvee that stood with engine idling outside the door of the yurt. Two chows—mine and Henry's—sat in the backseat with black tongues lolling. A couple of Kalashnikov assault rifles and two large holstered pistols were clipped to a rack behind our heads. A canvas bag, perhaps containing spare ammo or even hand grenades, and a pair of army-green, state-of-the-art binoculars dangled beside them.

At breakneck speed we raced down the arrow-straight road to nowhere for a few miles, then Henry turned off the pavement and we proceeded much, much more slowly across a trackless wilderness, Humvee lurching over the rough surface. The bag of grenades, if that's what it was, swung wildly, banging itself against the window posts, and I kept twisting my head to make sure it hadn't yet exploded.

"Do the guns bother you?" Henry asked.

"Only if they go off."

"They're not loaded."

"Then what's the point of bringing them along?"

"The Boy Scout motto," Henry said.

The country was more rugged here, and as we traveled the dunes got progressively larger. The Humvee's big knobby tires spun, gripped, spun some more, and gouged deep tracks in the sand. Despite the fact that we were equipped with a two-way radio and a couple of satellite phones interfered in no way with my fear that the Humvee might get stuck and we might die of thirst and exposure. Consider the consequences: If Henry died, so did humanity's last chance to take command of its fate, unless he could get the president of the United States on the phone before we perished and tell him what was coming.

The Humvee crested a hill. In the distance I saw some tents clustered in the shadow of a mesa. I got out the binoculars and focused on the campsite. People were scurrying around the tents or working on the wall of the mesa, which was pockmarked with excavations of various sizes. As we drew closer, I kept on sweeping the site with the binoculars. The lenses were powerful and self-focusing. Details emerged in great clarity. People were climbing down from the mesa. Most of them were local, but a few who were larger and clumsier than the others were Caucasian. One of them was a brawny fellow with a red handlebar mustache who wore a cowboy hat and, sure enough, when I panned down with the glasses, cowboy boots.

I stifled a gasp. I knew this man. And as soon as I got out of the Humvee, he recognized me. Apart from a look filled with hatred and loathing, which I returned, he gave no sign that he had ever seen me before. He was grotesquely huge, a slab of muscle and bone nearly seven feet high. In a windchill factor of about thirty degrees Fahrenheit, he wore shorts and a T-shirt with the sleeves cut off. His biceps were the size of a normal man's thighs. Even his teeth, when he grinned at Henry, were half again as large as standard human teeth.

In a booming bass voice he shouted, "Hot damn, Henry! I thought you'd never get here."

He enveloped Henry in a bear hug, lifting him off his feet and pounding him on the back. After giving him a final shake that dislodged his Yankees cap, Bear put him down. The cap, snatched by the wind, skittered away. The giant chased it as nimbly as a kid, recovered it, and screwed it back on Henry's head.

Henry introduced us. We stared at each other, neither of us offering a hand or a smile or uttering a sound. I wouldn't have touched this creature or spoken to it if someone had put a gun to my head. The giant's name, as I already knew, was Bear Mulligan. As a young man he had been an All-American left tackle who got his nickname in college from the ferocious way he tackled opponents. It was written in the newspapers that he didn't just bear-hug running backs, he ate 'em alive. Stadiums boomed with his name, shouted in unison by fifty thousand Texans in a state of bloodlust. Bear had a knack for fame. He grew up to be a paleontologist who was invariably described by the many reporters who traveled far to interview him as "legendary."

Henry, glancing first at Bear and then at me, immediately picked up on the revulsion between us.

"Come on, Henry," Bear cried. "I want to show you what your money has bought."

The two of them rushed away, Bear's tree-trunk arm around Henry's shoulders. I followed, uninvited and ignored. Pretty soon we reached the mesa and with Bear in the lead, clambered up a network of aluminum ladders that had been bolted to its face. In minutes we reached the top, which was perfectly flat, and there, in an enormous ditch, lay an enormous skeleton.

"Biggest dad-gum land animal ever seen by human eyes!" Bear shouted. "We're gonna name it for you, Henry."

"Oh, no, you're not," Henry said.

"It's a girl," Bear said. "Looks like a *Sauroposeidon*, but she ain't. She's bigger—about forty meters long. She stood about twenty meters high. Humongous long neck, like a giraffe, but a lot bigger. Weighed maybe forty-five tons. Older than *Sauroposeidon*, too."

"What era?"

"Late Jurassic, prob'ly, but don't hold me to that till we've worked on her a little more."

"Did you find her intact, as we see her here?" Henry asked.

"Intact, more or less," Bear replied. "We did a little retrofitting, mostly small bones that got scattered by the earthquake that done her in, but the big parts you see lie pretty much the same as they laid for all them millions of years. Found us some eggs, too. Huge— bigger 'n medicine balls. She must've been settin' on the nest when the world turned upside down on her."

The way Bear talked like an old cowhand grated. Whatever else he might have been—and we'll get to that presently—he was one of the most famous scholars in his field. He was also well-off. In the 1920s, his grandfather, an authentic redneck, had struck oil in Wink, Texas, and later on, all over the world. The family owned a private bank in New York, among other things. Bear had gone to a well-known New England school, the same one his father had attended, and after his football days, earned a doctorate at Harvard. I knew a lot about Bear. He didn't grow up talking like he had a mouthful of barbecue.

He showed us some fragments of fossilized dinosaur eggs.

"Imagine being the size of this here lady and all of a sudden finding yourself flyin' through the air doin' somersaults," he said. "Must have been pretty disorienting."

"I don't see any broken bones," Henry said. "The ground must have opened where she was standing. She probably was buried instantaneously, to have stayed together, like she's done for a hundred and fifty million years."

"Could be, old buddy. But we're talkin' about one hell of an earthquake."

Henry and I exchanged glances. Yes, he was talking about one hell of an earthquake.

Henry had brought treats for the workers—vacuum chests of hot Chinese and American food, coolers filled with beer, ice cream and apple pie for the Americans, Chinese sweets for the locals, huge boxes of Godiva chocolates for everybody. In the mess tent, speeches were made. Henry—meaning Henry's money—was cheered. By the end of lunch everybody was drunk except Henry, who didn't drink in any meaningful sense of the word, and myself, who hated beer and would not drink with Bear Mulligan, who was too large to be affected by alcohol. Afterward, we toured the bone collection. This included a nearly intact *Tarbosaurus*, a carnivore slightly smaller than *T. rex*, and many other creatures, all of which had been alive one moment and entombed the next on a day more than a hundred million years before.

Through it all, Bear had neither looked at me nor spoken a word to me—nor I to him, because the sight and sound of him made my skin crawl. The time to depart finally arrived. We walked over to the Humvee. Henry visited the latrine, leaving the two of us alone. Bear looked down on me with raw hatred in his eyes.

"Be warned, bitch," he said in the Chip-and-Buffie English he spoke when I knew him.

"Of what?"

"If you repeat one word of your rotten dirty lies about me to Henry," he said, "I'll hunt you down and tear your head off."

"Better do it now, then," I said.

"You're going to tell him, aren't you?"

"You've made it pretty obvious that you and I have a problem. If he asks what it is, I'm not going to lie to him."

Henry emerged from the latrine tent. Still glaring, Bear muttered, "Here he comes. One lie and you're dead. That's a promise."

He reached out for Henry and gave him a gentle hug. So tender was the look on Bear's face that for a moment I thought kisses might come next. Bear stood waving good-bye to Henry until we couldn't see him anymore.

Henry checked the Humvee's navigation screen and told me we had just time enough to get to the road to nowhere before dark.

I said, "Good," but dreaded the bumpy ride ahead. Already the Humvee was pitching and yawing. I wished I had worn a sports bra. The windows were closed because of the dust. The chows, carsick already, whimpered.

After a silence, Henry said, "What was *that* all about?"

I didn't pretend that I didn't understand the question. I replied, "Bear was surprised to see me, I think."

"You know him?"

"We knew each other in the past. It didn't end well."

"Why not?"

"He's the rapist."

Henry stopped the Humvee. "Go on," he said.

"His family bought the judge and Bear walked on a legal technicality. The cops were so busy trying to subdue him—he broke some bones—when he resisted arrest they forgot to read him his rights."

Henry took my hand. I was astonished. He had a nice hand, dry and sinewy.

"I had no idea," he said.

"How could you have?"

"It should have turned up when he was vetted for the grant."

"That was long before you knew me. Wouldn't you have given him the grant anyway? It would have been the broad-minded thing to do. He wasn't convicted of anything."

"Probably," Henry replied. "Are you afraid of him now?"

"Terrified. I know him. When you were in the latrine he warned me that he'd rip my head off if I told you who and what he is."

"He meant it?"

"Of course he meant it."

Henry was still holding my hand. His face was grim.

"You're going to tell Bear about this conversation?"

"No," Henry said. "But he'll know. The money will stop."

"Then what?"

"Then we contain him. You're safer than you think."

2

DARKNESS FELL BEFORE WE REACHED the yurts. We saw their lights, a white blotch in the anthracite sky, from a long way off. Their brightness puzzled, even startled Henry. He floored the gas pedal and the ungainly, rattling Humvee sped onward, headlights poking into the darkness.

When we arrived, we found a couple of military vehicles parked inside the compound. One of them was equipped with a machine gun, its long barrel pointed at the sky. Six impassive soldiers with assault rifles slung across their chests watched as we approached. Henry drove right by them. We were not challenged. Our dogs—the ones in the backseat—began to bark. There was no answer from the rest of the pack, and as the Humvee rolled on we saw that all the other chows lay scattered on the ground. They did not move. They looked stiff, as if frozen in place like Bear Mulligan's dinosaurs in the last nanosecond of life. I saw no signs of blood or mutilation. I had never before seen the slightest sign of anger in Henry, but he was furious now. He drove up to the big yurt, slammed on the brakes, and leapt out of the vehicle. I followed. Before I could stop them, so did the dogs. They broke discipline, abandoning us humans, rushing to the prostate animals, sniffing and whining.

Inside the yurt, a slender, erect Chinese with a Waterford glass in his hand was conversing amiably with Henry. He wore an immaculate uniform with many campaign ribbons and decorations. His blue-black hair was turning gray. Three younger men, also in the uniform of the People's Liberation Army, stood by, also holding glasses. I smelled Scotch whisky. Daeng appeared, smiling as though he knew nothing of the dead dogs lying just outside the door. He carried a tray of canapés and passed light-footedly among the officers as if serving at a cocktail party.

Henry beckoned me closer and introduced me to the older man. His name was General Yao. He was from the China Association for International Friendly Contacts, otherwise known as the counterespionage arm of the intelligence service of the People's Liberation Army.

Smiling, he said in flawless California English, "I must apologize for the dogs. Let me assure you they will soon wake up and be as good as new. Unfortunately they attacked us when we arrived. We were forced to subdue them with a humane gas. Had I realized they were going to sleep so long, I would have had them removed from sight. We didn't know exactly how much gas is required to render a dog unconscious. I am assured they will soon be all right."

"Thank you, General Yao. That's very comforting," I said.

The general's eyes became colder by a degree or two. Henry shot me a cautionary look. Clearly he and General Yao knew each other well. Just as clearly, the general found it difficult to be entirely frank in my presence. I drifted away and joined the young officers. For the fun of it, I gave no sign that I spoke their language. I understood fragments of the things they were saying about me in Mandarin. Two of them didn't like my blue eyes—"ghost eyes," one man called them. The third found them mysterious. They all liked my body even though they agreed that the breasts were a little too large to be truly beautiful.

General Yao joined us. If he harbored resentment of my earlier snippiness about the gassed chows, he showed no sign of it.

"The dogs have awakened," he said. "They're quite frisky. In humans, recovery time is related to body weight. No doubt the same is true of dogs. Or elephants. You are an animal lover, I gather."

"You could say that. After all, we're animals, too."

He smiled charmingly. He escorted me to the table and helped me into my chair. He poured mao-tai into my glass. He placed food on my plate in the Chinese manner, as if I were the honored guest and he the host. He asked polite questions about my family, my work, my education, my time in Shanghai. I got the impression that he knew the answers to his questions before I supplied them. He regretted that he had not read any of my books. I offered to send him one. No, no, he wished to buy one. He would order it from Amazon.com. Perhaps I would be so kind as to inscribe it the next time we met. He was charm itself.

"It is so interesting that the American people and the Chinese people became friends again on the very day that the great President Nixon came to China and the animosity between our two populations ceased to exist," he said. "Forty years of the most outrageous propaganda vanished like the smoke of a couple of cheap cigarettes."

His smile asked how anyone could possibly question this sunny view of Sino-American relations.

Over coffee, General Yao turned to Henry.

"Something rather curious is happening," he said. "The American government is suddenly very interested in you, Henry."

"Really?" Henry said. "How so?"

People from the American embassy, Yao said, had asked him and certain of his colleagues questions about Henry's activities in Hsitau and elsewhere in China.

"We are puzzled by this gossip," General Yao said. "It's unusual for the Americans to ask us about one of their own citizens, especially one as prominent as Henry Peel."

These Americans had heard that Henry was investing heavily in certain Chinese companies. They were especially curious about his dealings with Ng Fred and his company. They were curious about the mysterious ring of booster rockets. They knew from their satellite images that they were not military vehicles, but they were somewhat alarmed by their size. What was their purpose? The CIA had asked permission to visit the site to inspect the boosters. They told General Yao that the president of the United States himself was concerned about them. CIA briefers had shown him photographs taken from orbit. He had been intensely interested, even agitated. He thought the rockets might be a threat to America's national security. He had demanded more information. The situation was uncomfortable.

Henry said, "Have you granted permission for an inspection?"

"Our government has taken the request under advisement. It will move slowly, Henry, but it's difficult for us to say no to the CIA. As you know, it has done good and valuable things for China."

For instance? I was dying to hear, but Henry did not ask the question, no doubt because he, like his friend General Yao, already knew the answers.

"And there is another problem—two problems, actually," said General Yao. "The booster rockets do not belong to the Chinese government, nor are they in China. As you know, they are just across the frontier in Mongolia."

Henry said, "I don't mind their having a look from a suitable distance, in case that's part of the dilemma."

"It's not. They have already had a look from a suitable distance. Our concern is that the president might conclude that we are going to boost some sort of military hardware into space that will be targeted on the United States or its space station and satellites."

"But the rockets are harmless. The satellite photos should tell them that."

"One would think so. One would also think the CIA and the Pentagon know that the rockets are in Mongolia."

"I'm sure they do," Henry said. "So why are you humoring them?"

"Because humoring them seems to be what they're asking us to do," General Yao said. "It's all very puzzling."

"Why not just state the obvious? Why play this game?"

"The president of the United States is a nervous man. He might not believe the obvious. He leads a volatile democracy that might throw him out of office for letting China get ahead of America. He might be tempted to reassure the voters and assure his reelection by putting some kind of battle star in orbit, with all missiles pointed at us."

Henry said, "I'll talk to him."

"And tell him what? The truth?"

"As you say, that's probably the last thing he'd believe."

"Don't be so certain of that, Henry," General Yao said. "He's been briefed on the core of the earth problem."

"He has?"

"Of course. He was strongly affected. Maybe he has made the connection to you and this new project of yours. Or his experts have made it, which is the same thing."

"Who are his experts?"

"Who knows?" Yao said with a smile. "In China they would of course be astrologers, geomancers."

Henry did not ask how General Yao happened to know what the president of the United States had been briefed on and how he reacted. His demeanor suggested that he just took it for granted that Yao knew what he was talking about.

"It's only a matter of time before your government sees the future, or the possible lack of it, and decides to save itself," General Yao said in his reasonable manner. "After that will come the European Union, Russia, Japan, India. And private enterprise, which is already busy—meaning you, of course."

"Not China?"

"That's a different question. But my government is worried. We fear this situation is a recipe for space war."

"Which Henry Peel will have caused?" Henry said.

"Quite possibly. You mean well, Henry. You are greatly admired in this country. The whole world owes you its gratitude for your inventions and for what you're trying to do by virtuous stealth to preserve civilization. But if your work is mistaken by the American government for a Chinese plot to conquer space, which could only mean to a mind like the president's that China intends to conquer the United States, the speed with which things could get out of hand could take the world's breath away."

Henry gave General Yao a very long look. He said, "I hear what you're saying to me, General. May I ask why you're saying it?"

General Yao stopped smiling. The difference this made in his appearance was astonishing. The light in his smooth countenance went out as if a circuit breaker had popped. His eyes dulled, his complexion became a shade darker.

"I was not told why I should deliver this briefing, Henry," he said. "But I hope nevertheless that you are hearing what I am saying to you."

3

I FLEW OUT THE NEXT morning. Henry remained behind. As usual, there were no good-byes. In Newark, Melissa, whom I had not seen for weeks, was waiting for me outside customs. In her severe dark suit and perfect maquillage, she looked every bit the big-time Wall Street lawyer.

"Henry has a surprise for you," she said.

"What kind of a surprise?"

"If I told you that, it wouldn't be a surprise."

On the drive into the city, we talked about her children. They were teenagers now. The girl was beautiful and boy-crazy. Melissa suspected her son, who was a soccer star, of taking steroids. She suspected both kids of living dangerously behind her back. With their looks and allowances, how could things be otherwise? As a single mother, Melissa was a worrier and a spy. She had a tracking device that could pinpoint both kids' precise whereabouts by locating their cell phones. It wouldn't have surprised me if she implanted computer chips beneath their skin.

The car pulled up in front of an apartment building on Central Park West. The doorman watched appreciatively as Melissa's very long legs unfolded from the backseat.

"Hello, Edward," Melissa said. "Remember this lady."

In the elevator, Melissa provided a short biography of the doorman. Edward was a retired army sergeant, a former member of Delta Force who had gone on secret missions all over the world, shooting bad guys and rescuing good guys. All the other doormen were ex–Delta Force or Navy Seals or had even more impressive top-secret résumés.

The apartment was on the top floor. Melissa unlocked the door with a remote control like the ones that come with expensive cars. Four deadbolts snapped open, one after the other. Then the door swung open. The lights switched on by themselves. A large painting, unmistakably an original Edward Hopper, dominated the hall. Other pictures were displayed in the lofty living room, including what looked like a lost Seurat and a pre-Raphaelite portrait of a postcoital woman that could only have been painted by Dante Gabriel Rossetti himself. Every other room in the apartment was also loaded with pictures and sculpture—a Rauschenberg in the master bedroom, a wall of Old Master drawings in the second bedroom, Henry Moore bronzes and at least a thousand leather-bound books, including all of mine, in the study. The ceilings were at least fifteen feet high. The view of the park was terrific.

My clothes were in the closets, my books on the shelves, my computer in the study.

"What's all this?" I asked.

"It's one of Henry's places," Melissa replied.

I said, "And we're here for what reason?"

"Henry wants you to live here."

"Really? Why?"

"Maybe he couldn't bear the thought of you living in that drug dealer's pad on York Avenue."

"So he just up and moved me out?"

"Actually, I did, on his instructions. He didn't tell you?"

"Not a murmur."

Melissa wore the look of perpetual amused condescension that is affected by the very rich. It was Melissa who belonged in this Xanadu. She knew this.

She said, "I've taken care of the lease on York Avenue. Your own place is sealed and wired, so we'll know if the intruders call again. The rent will be paid by a bank. You should have no problems with the mobsters who own the York Avenue place, but if you do, call me immediately. I advise you to move your money to a different bank and get rid of your cell phone. Buy a cheapo and throw it away and get another one when you've used up the minutes. Do not install a regular phone. Change your email account. Use a different server. Encrypt everything. If you want to get laid, go to a hotel. But don't use a credit card."

I said, "How thoughtful you are. Are you telling me I'm in protective custody?"

"No," Melissa replied. "I'm telling you how to be careful."

She looked at her watch. "I have to go pick up the kids," she said.

She showed me how to operate the remote—one button to unlock the front door, another to open it, a third to turn off the alarm system, another to close the door—it was too heavy to close by hand—and lock it behind me and set the perimeter alarms and turn off the lights. She refrained from telling me not to lose the remote.

Melissa had one more item on her checklist. "By the way," she said, "this building doesn't allow pets that weigh more than ten pounds. So no chow chows." She kissed the air beside my ears, *mmmm, mmmm*, left and right.

"Ciao!"

She was gone in a paradiddle of five-inch heels.

Melissa or another of Henry's innumerable helpers had stocked the refrigerator and freezer with enough gourmet food for a month. I did not go outside for a week. I couldn't tear myself away from the pictures. And besides, I still had enemies, and one of them was Bear Mulligan.

However, nobody can live forever without fresh air, so eventually I did venture out. For old times' sake I took a run around the Reservoir. I stayed away from the Ramble and other hazardous parts of the park. Was I being stalked? A person might as well be stalked by *T. rex* as by Bear. I stopped once or twice to tie my shoes while glancing artfully behind me. I saw nothing except the usual aimless crowds. Bear would have towered over them, but he was not the only one who might be keeping an eye on me. The fact that my enemies knew how to blend into the mob could only mean that they were professionals. I wished that I did have the chows to protect me. How I would have prevented them from attacking everyone in the park who didn't wear a "Me-Friend" ID strung around their necks, I could not imagine.

Despite my anxieties, I was hungry. It was warm enough today to eat outdoors if you were wearing a sweater, so I walked over to the Boathouse and bribed my way onto the deck. While I waited for a waiter to notice me, I watched the ducks and swans on the Lake. Their balletic movements induced a sort of trance.

I snapped out of it in a hurry when Adam sat down at the table with me.

"Another fateful encounter," he said. "May I join you?"

I didn't say a word or make a gesture. That was all the encouragement he needed.

He said, "I'll take that as a yes."

He ordered grilled sole and a salad for both of us and a bottle of Meursault. He was as handsome as ever. He was charming. He was warm to the touch. He had a mind-reader's look in his eyes. I'm not used to drinking alcohol at lunch. After the third glass, I was quite seriously relaxed. Candy is dandy, liquor is quicker.

Hours later I woke up in a hotel room with the faint taste of sole and butter on my tongue. Adam was gone. He had picked up my clothes and folded them neatly before he left. On the floor, my running shoes stood primly side by side, socks draped over them. He left no note, but on the bathroom mirror he had soaped his phone number and, *ugh*, a heart pierced by an arrow.

Once again, Adam had stalked me. How did I know he was the only one? When I left the hotel I took a local train to South Ferry, then rode back uptown on an express, took a crosstown bus to the East Side, walked for a while, staring into store windows at the reflections of several hundred strangers, any one of whom could have been tailing me. Finally, I darted into the Waldorf by one door and left by another, then dashed across Park Avenue and leaped into a taxi that took me home.

Suspicion took charge of me. I *knew* Adam had followed me to the Boathouse. He had followed me once before, in Chelsea. Now he had done it again. Whom did he work for? How could he afford a bottle of Meursault?

For most of the night I lay awake, furiously lecturing myself: *You idiot! What have you done?*

At 5:00 a.m. on the dot, exactly an hour before I began writing, Henry called.

He said, "About what time will you finish work today?"

"If I start now, around eleven," I replied.

"I'll pick you up in front of your building at noon."

"When will we be coming back?"

"Tonight, late, I think. But maybe tomorrow."

Click. Henry never said hello or good-bye. He called, he hung up. He arrived, he left.

He was right on time in a sports car that was new to me. He was driving himself. As before, he turned north on the West Side Highway. My heart sank. Garbo again, Amerigo again.

Gleaming German cars again, when we arrived. Amerigo met us at the door. The house smelled of wax and air freshener and the bitter sap of recently cut stems of greenhouse flowers.

Awaiting us in the library were Ng Fred, the spacecraft engineers I had met on my first trip to Hsi-tau, and a tall horse-faced man I had never seen before. The men wrung Henry's hand and nodded absently to me. I saw no sign of Garbo and gave thanks. Chairs had been arranged in a circle. We all sat down and waited for Henry to tell us why we were here. The grandfather clock in the library—an odd place for it—struck two after a lengthy overture of chimes. Henry waited politely until the mechanism had done its thing, as if the clock might be a living being whose feelings he did not want to hurt.

He said, "We've come to the hard question."

He paused for a long moment, glancing from face to face.

"That question," Henry said, "is the Choice, capital *C*. Apart from the crew, who and what goes aboard the mother ship? More difficult still, who and what do not go aboard? How do we decide?"

Minutes passed. The grandfather clock ticked, a sound long lost to human ears. Henry waited patiently for someone to say something. No one wanted to go first. In his own mind, Henry may have been first among equals. To everybody else, he was a half-god, possessed of powers that mortal minds could barely comprehend. Finally the newcomer cleared his throat. His looks were unusual: long bones, balding crown with horseshoe fringe, big ears with lobes the size of egg yolks, pince-nez hanging from a black shoestring. He blinked a lot. He wore a wide-wale corduroy suit, rumpled and stained, and Birkenstock sandals with thick woolen gray socks. His manner suggested that whatever shyness the rest of us might have, he was no newcomer to the hall of the demigods.

Henry said, "Yes, Prof?"

In a faintly transatlantic accent, Prof said, "Let's begin with the ethical question, shall we? I believe that's why I'm here."

He gave Henry an inquisitive look—I *am* right about that, am I not, old chap?

Henry answered with one of his tiny smiles and said, "Why not?"

"Why not indeed? This enterprise will stand or fall on the question of ethics. More than any other factor, ethics has the power to imperil, even to destroy the enterprise before it ever gets"—he chuckled—"off the ground."

The Prof began his presentation. He knew his subject inside out. The material was dense. His delivery was practiced. It went on and on. I listened carefully. Much of what the Prof was telling us about the history of right behavior was interesting in its way, though by no means unfamiliar. After an hour or so, the others began to fidget. Henry called a break. Everyone rushed to the toilets, including me.

Henry ran me down in the hallway.

"How do you like the Prof?" he asked.

"Love him," I said.

"When we get back, interrupt him," Henry said.

I was the last to return to the library. The moment I appeared in the doorway, the Prof drew the breath that clearly was going to be exhaled a millisecond later as a cloud of words.

I said, "Excuse me. I have a thought."

Actually, I didn't. I had no idea what I was going to say, but I was under orders.

I received a sour look from the Prof, who said, "How very interesting. However, I haven't quite finished."

I held up a palm. "If you'll indulge me, sir, my thought is this— survival is the issue here. It is the moral imperative of moral imperatives. No smaller issue can be permitted to intrude."

The Prof's eyes widened. His lips twisted in contempt, disguised as amusement. He said, "You take my breath away."

Henry said, "Go on."

The Prof shook his head in deep puzzlement. Henry was giving this empty-headed floozy the floor?

I said, "The idea is to save the species. Nothing else matters."

"In other words, play God," said the Prof. "Do whatever you feel like doing and devil take the hindmost?"

"No, sir. Do what's possible in the circumstances."

"Nonsense," said the Prof.

I developed my nonsensical thoughts at some length while the Prof stood helplessly by because Henry let me talk, seemed even to want me to talk.

At last the Prof spoke. "Balderdash!" he said.

He turned on his heel without so much as a nod to Henry, let alone the rest of us, and strode out of the room, then out of the house. Apparently he did not brook contradiction.

"Shall we go on?" Henry asked.

We did so, until the sun went down. I took little part in the discussion, which turned practical and technical the moment the Prof departed—how many engineers did we need, how many physicians, teachers, pilots, navigators? Should the ethnic balance duplicate the numbers on Earth, or should selection ignore race and consider only usefulness? No one else referred to my behavior toward the Prof, but it bothered me. If past experience was any guide, it would probably continue to bother me for years.

Embarrassment had been my faithful companion for most of my life. Now it sat down beside me at dinner, when the German engineer, while pulling back my chair, congratulated me on my victory.

"Pompous ass," said the German, who had been educated in England and gotten his money's worth in terms of accent. "A bit of humiliation will do him good."

"I wasn't trying to humiliate anyone."

"You rang his bell anyway, old girl. Well done."

After dinner, Garbo materialized and murmured into my ear.

She said, "I'm told everyone is spending the night. And that brings me to a question."

"Which is?"

"You and Henry. One room or two?"

"Two."

Her eyes were bright, and in them you could read her thoughts. She wasn't fooled by this deception, not Garbo. What else could I be for if not to sleep with the trillionaire?

But as things turned out, I did spend part of the night with Henry. Before dawn—it was still dark of night—I heard someone tapping on my door. My visitor was Henry. He was fully clothed, Yankees cap and all.

"I'm going out for coffee," he said in a half whisper. "Want to join me?"

In the nearest town he found a Dunkin' Donuts with a bunch of pickup trucks parked outside. Inside, everyone was dressed pretty much the same way Henry was—that is to say, like people who lived from paycheck to paycheck. Most of the guys were beefy, and when he came back to the table with our breakfast, I understood why. Each donut represented an instantaneous weight gain of not less than twice its own bulk. Henry had bought us two apiece, along with two enormous cups of coffee.

"The ones with coconut are really good," he said.

I took a bite. How right Henry was. My mood lifted. After we finished the donuts, Henry went back to the counter and bought breakfast sandwiches made of fried egg, ham, and melted Velveeta, fishing ones and fives out of several different pockets and dropping a couple of dollar bills into the tip jar. We finished our sandwiches and had more coffee.

Henry said, "Are you all right? You looked like a ghost after supper last night."

"It was the lobster," I said. "Also, I had a conscience."

"You're all right now?"

"Yeah. I took the donut cure."

"Why the conscience?"

"I was rude to a guest, didn't you notice?"

"I noticed. He's old enough to take care of himself. Usually he does."

"You've known him for a while?" I asked.

"Years," Henry said. "Don't worry. He probably argued with you all the way home, shouting all the things he should've said if only he had thought of them. He'll say them the next time you meet."

"The Prof and I are going to meet again?"

"Why not? Sparks flew. That's a good sign."

At the next table a man with a loud voice was telling a dirty joke. Henry paused to listen to it, then grinned. One breath later he turned to me and said, "How serious were you yesterday?"

I had spent the night trying to forget what I said the day before. The last thing I wanted to do was reconstruct it.

However, I was on duty, so I said, "About what?"

"Forgetting about ethics."

I said, "Henry, I was babbling. I don't remember what I said."

"I do," Henry said.

He then quoted back every word that I had uttered during my monologue in Amerigo's library. I had heard of total recall. Henry actually possessed it. I felt that I had been eating donuts with an alien.

I said, "Tell me, Henry, did you have any help with remembering the balderdash?"

"Like what?"

"A tape recording? A chip implanted in your brain?"

He shook his head.

I said, "Can you recall everything I've ever said to you?"

"Most of it," Henry said.

"Also everything you've said to everyone else you've ever known?"

"Not everything is worth remembering. Or everyone."

He sipped his coffee and studied me. There was something he wanted to tell me, but he hesitated to take the chance. I felt this as if I had just read it on his forehead. Then, speaking in his usual soft voice, he told me. Or started to.

When he got to what he called "the enhanced embryos," and started to explain just how they would be enhanced and what the results would be, I said, "Stop. I don't want to hear this."

Henry said, "But I need you to hear it."

"No. You're making me very uncomfortable."

"I don't see why, but I'll stop now if you really want me to. You need time to think."

The last thing I wanted to do was to think about what Henry had just told me.

I said, "Frankly, Henry, at this point I don't know what I need."

Remorselessly, Henry said, "We'll talk again when you're ready."

Outside in the parking lot, he gave me the keys to his car, a BMW convertible, and suggested that I skip the rest of the meeting and drive back to the city alone. I could think of nothing better to do, so that's what I did. Henry didn't ask for a lift back to Amerigo's.

4

I DIDN'T SEE HENRY FOR days. I assumed he had gone somewhere. I didn't mind. I was falling in love with loneliness. This was a defensive measure, in case Henry never came back. To be alone again was like living with the ghost of an estranged husband. He was gone, but even when he was absent, there he was, right behind you, breathing on your neck like a ghost. Who knew if he was real? Who had the guts to turn around and surprise the ghost by actually looking at it? Two of my fictitious characters, lovers, had a quarrel from which there could be no escape. I deleted the passage. It didn't make me feel one whit better about my situation with Henry. I had failed him. I was paid to listen to him, and I had refused to listen to him. I assumed he would delete me from his life.

What would my post-Henry world be like? I still had the BMW he loaned me, parked in the basement garage. Once again I considered leaving Henry's money and everything else behind except my manuscript, and driving to, say, Utah. I could ship the car back to him, then live in a used trailer in the high desert, a good place to be when the Event happened. Absolute simplicity, that was the ticket—old clothes, a parka, boots, a warm hat, frozen food, Eight

O'Clock coffee, writing with a pencil on the back of junk mail, not even a cat for company.

In the end, I did not light out for the territories, but my habits changed. I turned off Henry's videophone and all my throwaway cell phones and stopped checking for email. I no longer answered the intercom when the doormen called. I began to sleep late and write far into the evening. One evening I was still writing—it was dark outside—when the doorbell rang. Oddly, I felt no fear. I opened the door without even asking through the intercom who was there. Whoever it was, whatever it meant, let it happen. What more could fate have in store for me?

The answer was Henry—a faintly smiling Henry. He cocked his head, checking me out, I guess, for signs of emotional distress.

He said, "Hi. Sorry for the surprise visit, but you don't answer the phone."

He made no move to cross the threshold on his own authority, so I invited him in. I sat down primly on the sofa, knees and ankle bones together, hands in lap. To my surprise, Henry sat down beside me.

He said, "I expressed myself badly in Dunkin' Donuts the other day."

I said nothing.

Henry said, "I'm here to try again."

One of our silences gathered. Then Henry spoke.

"To begin with, humanity is the first species with the capability to influence its own evolution," he said. "You won't be crazy about this analogy, but we are now able to perform most of the wonders attributed to the beings in Genesis. Quite soon we'll surpass them."

"By doing what?"

"When you think about what I started to tell you, think about it in terms of what you know as a twenty-first-century person instead of a character in the Old Testament. Consider the case of Sarah, wife of Abraham. Genesis tells us that God and a couple of his angels stopped by Abraham's tent one day and stayed for lunch—

freshly baked bread and a barbecued calf from Abraham's herd. God reminded Abraham of the many gifts he had bestowed on him. Abraham replied that he was grateful for the herds and flocks and land, but these things didn't really mean all that much because he had no children. God said he would rectify that. Abraham's wife, Sarah, would conceive a son by Abraham. Sarah, who was a very old woman and had long since ceased to menstruate, laughed at the idea. God reproved her for doubting that he could do all things, and said he'd be back in a year and she would, by golly, bear Abraham a son. God did return, and Sarah did bear Abraham's prophesied child. Abraham was a hundred years old and Sarah not so very much younger when Isaac was born—a miraculous event in his time. But in the late twentieth century, embryos implanted by mortal physicians in the wombs of women in their sixties were carried to term and delivered by caesarian section."

"You plan to do something similar?"

"If not exactly the same thing."

"How?"

"Technically, it's no great feat," Henry replied. "All you need is a computer program, detailed knowledge of the genome, and a certain amount of DNA. We have those three things."

"Including the computer program?"

He nodded. I didn't doubt that he himself had written the program.

"Where do you get the DNA?" I asked.

"Every human being is a walking DNA factory."

"So you plan to harvest it from living people?"

"Obviously."

For the first time ever, Henry's tone was unpleasant. So was mine. I said, "What kind of people?"

"We'll be working with embryos."

"Why embryos?"

"Because they're easier to modify, and because they are so small they can't even be detected by the naked eye. They weigh practically nothing. You can transport tens of thousands of them in the same amount of space that one adult human body would occupy."

"How do you keep them alive?"

"It's done every day in clinics all over the world. Properly frozen and stored at the right temperature in liquid nitrogen, they will, in theory, live forever."

"They live?"

"Of course they live."

He then told me many things about DNA that I already knew and even more that I had not known. It came down to this: It is possible to mold DNA into almost any form. Billions of species had evolved willy-nilly on Earth from the same DNA. What the coincidences of evolution could do, design could also do, and do it much more quickly.

I said, "Henry, cut the crap. Are you telling me that intelligent design is a fact?"

"If you leave the supernatural out of it, why shouldn't it be? Why does it have to be one thing or the other, God or natural selection? It's not outside the realm of possibility that a design team from outer space deposited our species on this planet forty or a hundred thousand years ago and let evolution take its course. The whole human race has been a design team at work on itself and everything else ever since it was turned loose on this planet. Agriculture, our invention, or maybe the instructions programmed into our DNA, gave us food that made us taller, stronger, smarter. Medicine gave us longer life. Technology gave us the power of gods. Sometimes, even usually, there was no obvious reason to alter the original, but we did it anyway. Look at the many specialized kinds of dogs and other livestock we've developed through selective breeding, which is just another term for planned evolution. Look at ourselves. Thanks to all of the above, plus managed marriage, present-day human beings are as different from earlier hominids as the inch-long ears of maize cultivated by the Anasazi Indians are from modern corn on the cob—same DNA, different outcome."

I said, "Henry, this is twentieth-century eugenics. You sound like a lunatic."

"I do? What we're thinking about doing next in the case of human evolution—the enhancement of embryos that has you so shook up—is nothing more than the next logical step in an ancient process. Humans have always bred systematically to improve themselves and their fellow animals. Keep an open mind. If I may quote, what about survival being the moral imperative of moral imperatives?"

Gotcha. I was trying to keep an open mind, but Henry wasn't making it easy for me. It was DNA, the yeast of the gods, we were talking about here. He was dismissing every ethical standard I had been educated to live by at great cost to my progressive parents. Nevertheless, as so often happened with Henry, I felt myself giving up my doubts.

Hours had passed, or so it seemed. I had no idea what time it was. Henry yawned, stretched, groaned a little. He wandered into the kitchen, not quite remembering the way, and returned with two bottles of springwater. I visited the bathroom. In the mirror I saw a bewildered woman with dark circles under her eyes. She looked as though she had never, ever smiled and meant it. I smiled at her. She smiled back, most insincerely. I washed my face and went back to the living room.

Henry said, "Please tell me exactly why you were so upset the other night."

Was it possible he really didn't know? I said, "All I could think about was man and chimpanzee. Is it not true that the DNA difference between man and chimpanzee is very small?"

"Less than five percent," Henry said.

"And you want to produce a new kind of human being who will be as superior to people like you and me as we are superior to chimpanzees? Furthermore, you want to send this creature into space instead of sending people as they now exist?"

"Yes."

"Then what is the point? I thought the idea was to rescue the human race, not mess around with it."

"Rescue is the purpose. But that doesn't mean we shouldn't enhance the species to give it a better chance of survival, which is what the enterprise is all about."

I said, "Henry, have you yourself figured out how to fabricate this Übermensch?"

His voice was calm, his eyes steady. He said, "Yes, I think so."

"You think so or you know so?"

"I see how it can be done. I haven't actually done it. It's illegal."

"Even in Mongolia?"

"No."

I said, "But the truth is, you really do plan to do it somewhere on the planet before the ship lifts off?"

"Very likely."

"And you have no qualms about it?"

"None."

"You've just answered the question you asked me at the start," I said. "How can you be without qualms? *That's* why I'm so upset."

Henry said, "Why should I have qualms?"

"Let me count the ways. First, you might create a race of monsters."

"In science fiction, that would probably be the outcome. In a real-life laboratory, properly managed, it will not. If the experiment fails, we will realize that and abandon it."

"Really? And what do you do with the product of the failed experiments?"

"Dispose of it."

"Like lab rats."

Henry said, "Stop it. Enough human embryos to populate Mars have already been disposed of on Earth without bothering anybody's conscience, including yours. The idea here is to preserve life, not prevent it."

"But the method, the purpose, the arrogance."

"Ah. What picture do you have in your mind about how this is going to be done?"

"The usual one—the terrified victim strapped to a table, the mad scientist injecting him with something and reaching for his scalpel."

"It won't be that way at all."

"Oh?" I said. "And how exactly will it be?"

"You know the answer. We'll be working with embryos, not conscious beings."

"So they're not human after all."

"Of course they're human. If left alone to develop they become the same as you and me."

"Oh, Henry," I said.

Henry gave me a look filled with genuine confusion. It was all crystal clear to him. Why could I not understand? *What* could I not understand? Why couldn't I understand his purposes? Why wouldn't *he* understand my misgivings?

Something primal was going on within me—but what? Why was I so outraged? Of course I knew the answer. The instinct of self-preservation was at work. Not so very long ago at Amerigo's house, I had argued that self-preservation trumped everything. These enhanced creatures of Henry's were not only going to replace us, they were going to *enslave* us. How could it be otherwise?

Feigning calm, I said, "The intention is to make our successor species *X* percent smarter and bigger than we are—right?"

"More or less," Henry replied.

"So if *X* equals five, the average IQ of a superhuman would be one hundred five instead of one hundred, and the entrance-level test score of genius, now one forty, would become one forty-seven, and the average American male would be six foot one instead of five foot ten. That's not a whole lot of difference. The average American has grown at least three inches in the last century with no help from anyone, and probably is just as much smarter on the average. So what's the point?"

"It doesn't work that way. The difference would be greater."

"How much greater?"

"As great as the difference between a human being and a chimpanzee," Henry said.

We parted in anger. And sadness, in my case. Did Henry know sadness—or anger, for that matter? Or anything whatsoever about the thoughts of the heart?

5

APPARENTLY NOT. NOTHING CHANGED. HENRY and I went on exactly as
before. He called, I responded to his summons, we met, I remained
a part of what I assumed was his inner circle. My own qualms lin-
gered, even strengthened. I could have resigned for my principles,
but that would have meant life without Henry, so I found a way to
live with my misgivings. In my fury I had told Henry he was crazy,
but at the same time I thought it was more likely that he was saner
than the rest of us in some way peculiar to Henry. He saw what
others could not see—was famous for it. Maybe genetic engineering was the way to go despite its vile reputation. Maybe Henry's
idea was repugnant to me because it contradicted my notion of who
Henry really was. Had he proposed the genetic alteration of human
embryos aimed at the production of a new version of *H. sapiens*
that resembled himself, instead of a race of supermen with rippling
muscles, I would have been all for it.

Genetic engineering and the Torah aside, there were other things
to think about. A few days after our quarrel about Nietzschean Man,
Henry brought me a present. It was a Lucite sphere that looked a lot
like the imaginary Antarctic artifact he had described on the day
we first met on that bench in Central Park. It came in two boxes,

borne by a couple of men. Naturally, Henry didn't tell me what was in the boxes.

"Would it be OK if they set it up in the study?" Henry asked.

It was Henry's apartment. I said, "Why not?"

"Stay here," Henry said. "It's a surprise."

I waited in the living room until the men had done their work and departed. Henry then led me into the study. A gleaming sphere about the size of a honeydew melon was balanced on a pedestal.

Henry said, "Go ahead—pick it up." I knew what was going to happen next, but he was in such a state of boyish glee that I did as I was told. After a second or two, the sphere vibrated like a cell phone, then lighted up. Data streamed across its surface—a photograph of Earth taken from orbit, followed by a graphic locating the planet in relation to other bodies in the solar system, the galaxy, the known universe. Then came a slide show about the formation of Earth, its geological ages and life forms past and present. This faded to videos from many angles of men and women and children of many ethnic types. Now a man and woman, both naked, engaged in what appeared to be unsimulated sex, followed by a slide show about sperm and ova and gestation and a video of a live birth and another sequence showing the woman from the sex scene suckling an infant. Then came the animals, trees, plants, grasses, mathematical equations with ingenious illustrations of their meaning and a virtual tour of man's knowledge. Zeroes and ones streamed across the surface. Music played, the camera zooming in on the instruments, followed by graphics illustrating how they worked.

Finally, the sphere went dark.

"It's just a demo," Henry said. There will be much more—all of human knowledge, just as we discussed."

I said, "Brilliantly done."

"Brilliantly conceived. Congratulations."

"For what?"

"Your answer that day in the park was what made all this possible."

"Come on. We were just fooling around."

"Nevertheless, this sphere was your idea, and what you imagined actually will happen."

"But it's you who made it happen."

"With a lot of help from Ng Fred. The basic idea was yours—on that point I will not yield. Human hands will pick up the sphere, it will detect a temperature of thirty-seven degrees Celsius, and it will activate just as it did in your imagination."

"That's a romantic prospect," I said. "You're going to leave the sphere behind on Earth when the mother ship leaves, to be found at some point in the future?"

"Several of them, so as to give coincidence a better chance," Henry replied.

"What about other planets, or a few spheres wandering the universe?"

"Too risky. Forget all that and give yourself credit."

"Thanks. How much time do you figure will have elapsed before the sphere is found by someone and does its thing?"

"Mere centuries, if we're lucky. Maybe sooner, or longer. Maybe never. It's a gamble."

"Won't the batteries be dead by that time somebody finds it?"

"I don't think so," Henry said.

I took that to mean that Henry had once again invented something that was new in the world—batteries that lasted forever or maybe weren't even batteries. But I didn't ask.

Instead I said, "Has it occurred to you that those who find it might worship it instead of studying it?"

"Maybe they will. But if they follow the instructions, what does it matter?"

THREE

1

EARLY ONE FOGGY MORNING, AS I ran around the Reservoir, I felt someone close behind me. I had been running in a daze. The realization that I was being followed startled me awake. I looked over my shoulder, but saw nothing but fog. However, my other four senses told me a thing or two about the person who was following me. He was a male. The footfall was heavy. So was the breathing. So was the smell. This guy was out of shape. I picked up the pace. The footsteps behind me quickened, then faded. Inside the fog, someone was gasping. This stalker, whoever he was, was not going to catch me. I stopped and turned around, running in place. Clearly the weirdo wasn't going to catch me. Pretty soon I discerned a staggering figure, then a more substantial silhouette, and then, Adam. The pace at which he was moving barely exceeded a walk. He stopped a step or two away, bent over with his hands on his knees, and fought for breath. Runners burst out of the fog bank and brushed by him on either side, showering contempt as they passed.

Adam said, "You don't make these meetings any easier, you know."

The words were spoken laboriously, one syllable at a time. He smiled his lovely wide smile, all those perfect teeth. He was red in the face, still struggling for breath.

I said, "You look like you've got about four minutes to live. Is there anything I can do for you?"

Not long afterward, quite predictably, we were both short of breath in a king-size bed in a hotel room. Quite soon he fell asleep, snoring. It seemed safe to leave him for a moment—after all, I could hear his snores through the bathroom door. When I returned, he woke up—or maybe just pretended to. I trusted no one. At the moment, trust didn't matter much. Adam was nothing if not good-looking. Sprawled on the sheet, uncovered, he resembled a recumbent David, but hairier. I got back into bed.

At a little after nine, Adam looked over my shoulder at the big red numerals of the bedside clock, snatched his cell phone off the night table to make sure the clock was right, and said, "Oh, boy! I've got to get to court."

He jumped out of bed and pulled on his sweats at cartoon-character speed, arms going one way, legs another. He kissed me, crushing my unclothed body against his damp sweatshirt.

"For God's sake, call me," he said hoarsely, and was out the door, untied shoelaces flying.

It was Sunday. The courts were closed. Who cared?

I took no precautions against surveillance on my way home, just headed for my building as if no one were watching, as if there were no such thing as a trap. I stopped at a coffee shop for a takeout latte. When I came back outside, I spotted a man who was leaning against a utility pole. He was reading the *Post*, holding the gaudy tabloid in such a way as to hide his face. I flagged a taxi and had the driver take me across the park, then down Fifth Avenue to the library, where I ran over to Sixth Avenue, took another cab to the nineties, caught a train to Columbus Circle, and finally took another cab back to the apartment.

As the weekend and then the first days of the next week passed, I thought about Adam. On Thursday, I realized I wanted to see him again—soon. Maybe he had just been half-asleep and confused about the day of the week. Sexually, he was a real find, and if he hadn't murdered me by now it seemed unlikely that he ever would. But how to manage a rendezvous? I didn't like hotels. He couldn't come to this apartment—couldn't even be trusted with the knowledge that it existed, let alone with my new address. I checked out the red stars on the calendar that denoted surprise encounters with Adam. Every one of them had happened on a Sunday. Should I go running in the park and hope for the best? Then I remembered: He already knew the address of my old apartment.

As soon as dark fell on the following Saturday, I went for a walk, then took the usual series of cabs and trains and buses to bewilder whoever might be watching me, and arrived at my old apartment. It was as squalid as ever, and it seemed undisturbed—not a finger mark in the dust that covered every surface. I got out my cell phone and dialed Adam's number. He answered on the second ring.

I said, "I want you to stop stalking me."

Adam said, "Too bad, kid, because I can't wait to catch up to you. But no more running."

I told him where I was and hung up. Half an hour later, the buzzer sounded, the decrepit elevator whined and clanged, and Adam came in through the unlocked door.

At five thirty on Sunday morning, minutes after Adam left, my cell phone vibrated. The caller ID said that Melissa was calling. I picked up. Even at this hour her voice was musical. There was absolutely no sleep in it, but ever so faintly, I heard exasperation.

"Then this is your wake-up call," Melissa said. "Invite me to breakfast."

"When?"

"Today, seven o'clock."

"What about the kids?"

"The nanny will feed them when they wake up, not that they'll eat anything. Are we on or not?"

"OK, seven o'clock. You bring the food."

"Seven it is," Melissa said. "Not where you are now. Where you're supposed to be."

How did she know where I was now? Before I could ask, the phone went dead. I locked up and walked back to Central Park West.

Melissa was exactly on time, bearing a Whole Foods shopping bag. She had no smile for me, and only a single air kiss instead of the usual Old World two. She spoke not a word. The determined look on her face was one I knew as of old. It meant I had done her an injury without even realizing it.

She unpacked the shopping bag. Absolutely everything she had bought was certified to be good for you—even the coffee. She shook a meager handful of organic granola into bowls, sprinkled organic raspberries on top, and poured organic skim milk over them. The organic coffee she left in its recycled cardboard containers.

Finally, I broke the silence. I said, "Let me guess, Melissa. I've failed to do something I ought to have done, or done something I ought not to have done."

Melissa said, "How did you guess?"

"Just tell me what the problem is."

"This is embarrassing for me," Melissa said. "I resent being put in this position—having to talk to you about this."

Melissa embarrassed? Melissa leading up to something instead of just laying down the law?

"Embarrassed about what?"

"Your behavior."

"Which part?"

"You've got to stop acting like you're in a spy movie."

These were pretty much the last words I expected to hear. I laughed.

Melissa said, "You may think it's funny, but believe me, it's not."

I said, "Melissa, I have no idea what you're talking about."

"You don't? Then let me be more specific. Nobody cares if you want to pick up men in Central Park and take them to hotels. That's your affair, your private life, your folly. Enjoy. But this business of jumping in and out of taxicabs and subways afterward like you're the star of *The French Connection* is driving everybody crazy. So

96

enough already. Stop it. Break the habit. You're making a fool of yourself."

"I am?" I said. "Who's everybody?"

"That's what I'm here to explain."

I was furious. Obviously someone had been spying on me and gossiping about it with Melissa and who knew who else? Did the spy dish with Henry?

"You've been watching me," I shrieked. "You've been on me every minute. You knew where I spent the night last night. You follow me everywhere. I knew it! I felt it. Call off your creeps."

"Believe me, they're a long way from being creeps," Melissa said. "But yes, you're under protection."

"Under *protection*? What's that supposed to mean?"

"You've spent a lot of time with Henry. Surely you realize he's a kidnapper's dream. Has it not seemed strange to you that you and he always seemed to be entirely alone?"

"If you're asking if I ever wondered where the bodyguards were," I replied, "the answer is yes, from the day we met in Central Park."

"That showed up in your body language on the video. You were looking around for the security."

"You took video of me?"

"Not me, security. It's routine. It helps them profile people, which helps them anticipate what the subject is going to do next."

"Lovely," I said. "What else? Fingerprints from my wineglass? A used Kleenex to check out my DNA?"

Melissa waited for me to subside. She wasn't going to waste her time swatting away my witticisms.

"Anyway," she said. "Security has been looking after you ever since that day in the park, and for a while before that. It's their job. They were impressed that you seemed to be aware of their presence on the first day, and that you've sensed them, even spotted them, on other occasions."

"I'm flattered," I said. "Just so my paranoia is complete, how many such occasions have there been?"

"They're *always* with you, dear. Sometimes right beside you, sometimes at a discreet distance. Even Henry doesn't know whether they're at his elbow or across the street."

"Well, I do. I may not see them, but I feel them."

"They know. That's why I'm talking to you."

I said, "What about right now? Are we being watched by hidden cameras? Is the apartment bugged? Should I look to see if there's a fake window-washer outside right now? Are you wired?"

"No, I'm not. About the rest, I have no idea. But as Henry told you when you moved out, your old place is wired, which is how I knew where you were."

"Are these admirable creeps hiding under the bed or in the woodwork and protecting me right this minute?"

"I don't know. But I wouldn't rule anything out. Henry has ordered them to keep you from harm. That's what they're doing."

I said, "What they're doing, Melissa, is stealing my privacy. What gives them the right? Is there one shred of my privacy left? Have they bugged my computer so they can read what I write at the moment I write it? Do they watch what I do in the shower, what I do with men? Can I *ever* assume I'm alone?"

Melissa said, "Nobody in this day and age should ever make that assumption."

"Not even you?"

"Not even me. The secret of a happy life, believe me, is to have no secrets. Then you have nothing to worry about. Most people don't realize that till they get to divorce court."

I said, "Thanks for the axiom. I mean, wow, that certainly puts the whole deal in perspective. What do the gumshoes do with all this vital information they gather? Give it to Henry?"

"They type it into a computer in encrypted form—no real names, everybody has an alias."

"But they know which code name matches which suspect."

"Of course they do. So what? Nobody else knows, not even Henry. Of what interest to anyone is your humdrum life or mine?"

"If I'm so boring, what's the point of all this surveillance?"

"You work for Henry. He shares his thoughts with you. There are people in the world who would love to get their hands on Henry. Some of them are merely greedy. But some of them, maybe the majority, are crazy. The purpose of the security is to protect Henry. In order to protect him, they have to protect everyone who's close to him. A threat to you is a threat to him, and vice versa. Nothing sinister is going on. The only possible interest anyone except a horny stud like your companion from last night can have in you is your connection to Henry."

"So the working hypothesis of these infallible and mostly invisible people who are protecting me is that I have no enemies, which is why I need protection?"

"Cut it out," Melissa replied.

"Why should I? Because I've taken Henry's shilling?"

Melissa looked at the ceiling and let her breath out between her teeth in a long half whistle of exasperation. I was crossing the line again, pushing her, being insistent. Stealing her act.

She said, "No. But let me tell you one reason why. After the two of you came back from the Little Gobi Desert last time, Henry asked me to check out Bear Mulligan. On the basis of what you told me years ago, I thought I knew all about the case, but I put a couple of bright young associates on it and they came back with all the details. Some of these were new to me."

"Like the baby."

"Yes. But other things, too. Pictures, police reports, medical reports. I hadn't realized how really bad it was, how brutal."

Nor would she ever, I hoped. I said nothing.

Melissa said, "Henry saw all the evidence. He was revolted. Some of the police photographs are very graphic. Plus you're five foot four and Mulligan is six eleven. And you were so young when it happened. Henry is fond of you, so his emotions were engaged. He's a very decisive person. He severed all connections with Mulligan. The Chinese evicted him and his crew from their dig in Hsi-tau and prohibited them from removing any fossils from China. They kicked Mulligan out of the country. His grant was canceled. He'll never get another one from anybody. His career is over."

"That won't be the end of it," I said.

"That's exactly what Mulligan said," Melissa said. "He said he knew you were responsible for it all. He made threats."

"Like what?"

Melissa hesitated, but not for long. "That's not something you need to know," she said.

I already knew. Terror picked me up and shook me.

Melissa left. I went into the bathroom and vomited.

I also knew I was now bound to Henry for life. Nobody else in the world could guarantee my safety. Knowing Bear as I did, I wasn't entirely sure that even Henry and his watchmen could keep me alive and whole. True, they'd be able to see Bear coming from a long way off, but could they get between us in time, and if they did, what good would it do? This monster used to throw three-hundred-pound football players around as if they were Kewpie dolls. There was no doubt in my mind that he could still fight his way through ten ordinary men to get to me and then tear my arms off like a fly's wings, leaving me to bleed to death. Twenty years of bad dreams about Bear congealed into a single clot of dread.

A life of fear stretched before me, a great lion-brown Hsi-tau of emptiness. I could respond to nothing. My brain switched off, function after function, until nothing remained but the pain, the smell, the weight of Bear. The great paintings with which I lived hung on the wall like so many calendar pages. I tried to write. I ended up with two pages of gibberish. I read for a while, or tried to read, but the words did not register. In my subconscious, I was fifteen again, back in the hospital in the Berkshires with a child of the monster growing inside me. I gave birth under anesthetic. They took the child away while I was unconscious. I never saw it. I was told nothing about it, nor did I ask. To this day I didn't even know which gender it was. In my imagination, though, it was a redheaded boy, sixteen years old now, his dementia mistaken for charm, making his adoptive parents proud by breaking the bones of visiting football quarterbacks in some shady village in the Midwest.

When the doorbell rang, I nearly jumped out of my skin. It had never rung before. Henry and Melissa, my only previous visitors, had spare remotes that unlocked my door. I activated the camera outside the door. Daeng, the faithful steward, was smiling into it. I opened the door.

Daeng said, "Henry would like you to join him. He said you should pack a bag for two or three days."

"Wonderful," I said. "What kind of weather?"

"Very warm."

Two hours later, I was flying near the speed of sound at forty thousand feet, out of Bear's reach.

2

THE AIRPLANE LANDED AS THE sun came up on Nuku Hiva in the Marquesas Islands. Mountains wreathed in cloud, green forest, pounding surf, shimmering bays. But where were the canoes filled with dusky maidens and muscular lads in crowns of frangipani that should be paddling out to meet us?

"There is Henry's house," Daeng said over the loudspeakers.

I could see its glass parts winking down below. Tinted pink by the sunrise, it clung to the edge of a cliff.

"Paul Gauguin and Jacques Brel are buried in the Marquesas," Daeng said. "According to Google, the Marquesas are considered the most beautiful of all the Pacific islands."

Ah, so I wasn't the first to notice.

Henry's house was what you would expect—filled with light and dazzling art. I was given a bedroom overlooking the ocean. From its balcony I could see surf splashing twenty feet above the lip of the towering cliff. The surf, Henry told me later, was caused by the South Equatorial Current, which had been smashing into these islands for more than a million years. It had excavated deep caves in the volcanic stone of the cliffs.

There was no sign of Henry. Nothing stirred. I took a nap and went downstairs around noon. Henry, Amerigo, Ng Fred, the English engineer, and an Englishwoman of a certain age whom I had not met were drinking sparkling wine on a terrace. All except the impeccable Ng Fred, who wore a blazer and cravat, were dressed in resort clothes. They had been snorkeling, and could talk of little else. All were pinkened by their morning in the sun. Amerigo was extravagantly glad to see me. Ng Fred smiled in his friendly way. The Englishwoman—big-boned and meager of flesh, sharp Norman nose, sharper eyes, unstraightened working-class teeth, wispy gray chignon in the process of escape from its rubber band—looked me over as if she thought she recognized me from a Wanted poster. Had she been a man she would have been ugly-handsome. She wore perfume that smelled something like witch hazel. Henry introduced her as Clementine Machen.

He said, "Clem is our chief of security. She was in MI5."

Changing the subject as I suppose MI5 people are trained to do, Clementine asked me if I had heard that the Pacific Ocean had been invaded by floating islands of plastic trash—those abominable water bottles mostly—which, if lashed together, would create a single island of debris the size of the United States of America and thirty meters deep.

I said, "No. Somehow I missed that."

We ate lunch. Clementine sat next to me. She commanded many anecdotes, and every story she told me reminded her of something that was even more interesting. She talked, she *looked* like a character out of Oscar Wilde. Her diction was flawless, her delivery fluent, her accent homogenized. Her gruff voice chopped up sentences into words and words into syllables. Her commas, semicolons, and periods were as detectable as the words were audible. On my left sat Amerigo, who filled me in, in whispers, on Clementine's past. Before retiring from MI5 and joining up with Henry, she had had a long career in which she protected her country's secrets and exposed those of her country's enemies. She had outwitted some of the most slippery spies of our times. Her feats and her honors, if lashed together, would probably have been the size of the Shetland Islands. She was a Dame Commander of the British Empire, addressed in Britain as Dame Clementine, though she was just plain Clementine when abroad.

Clementine did not speak of herself or pepper me with personal questions as the Brits are wont to do. She spoke instead of the thing we had in common, i.e., the work. She thought—as did Henry, as would any reasonable person—that there was reason for concern about the security of the operation. It amazed her that we had gotten away with our activities as long as we had. This would not last much longer, in her opinion. We had too much to hide—more than any other conspiracy in history, surely—and every single bit of it was explosive. How, for example, could we possibly keep it a secret that we were going to take off in a spacecraft with tens of thousands of frozen human embryos in the hold, even in the unlikely event that it didn't become known that we had genetically altered those embryos?

If I had come here to escape my anxieties, I had come to the wrong place.

I said, "You seem to know a lot of things. How is it we've never met?"

"I'm the hush-hush department," she said. "Unseen."

"But all-seeing."

"Not quite. But that's the goal."

"How does one go about being all-seeing?"

Clementine neither smiled nor answered. She was the one who had been following me around in Manhattan. Not Clementine in person, of course—her gumshoes. She knew all about Bear, all about Adam, all about everything.

I said, "Are your files going to be encoded in the sphere?"

"What sphere might that be?" she asked.

After lunch we all went upstairs for a nap. Apparently Henry had no urgent work for us to do today. This was a U-shaped house with a courtyard in the middle, two stories high and just one room deep, so that every upstairs room had a view of the sea from the front windows and, from the rear, a view of Tekao, a cloud-ringed peak on the other side of the island. Clementine appeared on the veranda. Her room was next door to mine.

"Lovely mountain," I said.

"Quite," Clementine said. "I understand you like pictures."

She waited to see if I would confirm this report. I nodded.

"There's rather an interesting watercolor of Tekao in my room," Clementine said. "Come over and have a look, if you like."

"Another time, maybe," I said. "I'm worn out."

Clementine raised her eyebrows. Clearly she thought I had misunderstood her invitation. She vanished.

We met again at cocktail time. I drank water, which came in one of Henry's ever-present plastic bottles, and ate some nuts while gazing out over the empty and apparently boundless sea. We seemed to be standing on the only firm ground in the entire world.

I realized that Clementine was standing beside me—that scent of witch hazel again.

"The Marquesas are the most remote islands in the world," she said, "farther from any continental mass than any others."

I said I was not surprised to hear that.

Clementine said, "You played lacrosse for your university, I'm told."

"Ages ago."

"What exactly is lacrosse? Is it like our field hockey?"

"Not really," I said. "It originated as an Iroquois game, very warlike. The ball is in the air all the time. It's yellow and made of hard rubber. You pass it to one another and catch it with a stick called a crosse that has a small net pocket at one end. The players run a lot. It's good exercise, very slimming."

Clementine looked interested. I doubted that she really was. I thought this conversation was a pretext. No doubt she had boned up on lacrosse before she approached me and already knew the answers.

"I gather that lacrosse is quite violent," Clementine said.

"The men's game is very rough. They beat the stuffing out of each other, like the Iroquois used to do. The rules for the women's game were drawn up when ladies still existed. Theoretically, it's a noncontact sport."

"You won some sort of prize or honor for your play, I understand."

"Yes. Nastiest girl."

Clementine guffawed. She laughed like a man who has had a drink or two—loudly and heartily and somewhat longer than necessary.

We remained on Nuku Hiva for five days. Henry had decided that it was time for a tour of the horizon, so the entire enterprise was on the table.

"Our purpose is to simplify," Henry said. "So resist your education."

People flew in and made their reports, then flew out. Among these were the other two engineers, who projected their designs for the spacecraft onto a large screen that lowered itself from the ceiling of Henry's office. The ship they envisaged was a string of spheres that looked something like an ant that went on and on, pods connected by threadlike passageways. The color choice, bad-guys matte black, was a disappointment to me. I had imagined a ship of many Playskool colors, based on my drawings. It took two full days to glimpse—merely glimpse—the many details of this mind-boggling design. Henry understood it in all of its details at first glance, naturally. He critiqued it as if he had designed it himself and made many suggestions for refinements. The engineers argued with none of the suggestions he made.

During a break I asked the Russian engineer why they were so accommodating.

He said, "The customer is always right, and he's paying for everything. Also he's a genius. So why would we object to improvement?"

After the break, Henry announced that he had designed a propulsion system that would somehow draw its fuel from the charged

ARK

particles in the solar wind. A prototype had already been built and was undergoing testing. So far, it worked just fine. The mother ship would carry several compact fusion reactors that would heat and light the ship or even drive it if the other engines failed. The spare reactors could also be used as a source of power if the crew decided to establish an outpost on Mars or one of the moons in the solar system.

Afterward the amiable Ng Fred, who was becoming a friend of mine, asked me if I had any idea what Henry's latest marvel would be worth on the great profit machine that was Earth.

I shook my head. "Do you?"

"About as much as Taiwan," he said.

What did it matter, I asked. Money had no future.

"Sad but true," Ng Fred said.

"Why sad?"

"Because of all things, money will be the hardest to say good-bye to."

"What about humanity?" I asked.

Ng Fred rolled his eyes.

Among those who flew in was the Prof. He did not seem to remember me. In any case, he showed no sign of recognition. His subject was the same as it had been at Amerigo's house on the Hudson, but his conclusions were different. Was it ethical to save a chosen few and leave everybody else to die? Was it OK to alter DNA to produce an enhanced human type? He had pondered these questions since our last meeting. His answer was yes in both cases. If a civilization died, it died as a whole—evolutionary niche, ethics, and all. It was owed no obligation by its survivors apart from their duty to survive. He avoided my eyes while he said these things. This made for a nice moment.

The Prof immediately paired off with Clementine. They sat together like the old friends they appeared to be, and in social moments hung out together, encircled by imaginary Keep Off signs. I hoped they would fall in love, or, better yet, were already in love.

I hoped they would sneak away from the meeting and make out. Alas, nothing of the sort happened, because the Prof flew out that very day.

People came and went daily. Henry owned a lot of airplanes. Finally there was no more business to conduct, and the guest list dwindled to Clementine and me. This wasn't an ideal pairing. Clementine had never really recovered from my rebuff of her invitation to come look at her picture of Tekao. I was not able to forget that she was my personal watcher in the shadows. Henry was still present, but an airplane was due to return that night. He planned to leave the next morning.

He asked if either of us would like to leave when he did. He was on his way to Paris, but the airplane could drop us off anywhere in the world. I opted to leave. Clementine decided to remain—possibly, I thought, to avoid being confined with me in the plane's cabin for the better part of a night and day.

Clementine left Henry and me alone. From the deck I saw her marching off toward the beach carrying what appeared to be a folding easel. Later, I watched again as she toiled back up the steep path that connected the beach to the house. In her voluminous British shorts and thick, folded-over knee socks and her walking boots and her ancient straw hat, there was something touching about her. Maybe it was guilt, but—I didn't know why—I found myself wanting to protect her from her own oddness, to shield her retroactively from the brainless popular girls who must have made her life hell when she was a kid.

At the moment of her return, I was sitting on the deck, writing on a laptop. This was difficult because the sun shone on the screen and I had to keep moving the computer so that I could read what I was typing. Clementine's shadow fell on the screen.

Without looking up, I said, "Thanks for the shadow. I can finally see the screen."

Clementine laughed—that mannish bark of hers. It made me smile and turn around.

ARK

"You don't startle easily, do you?" Clementine said.

I said, "I'm not so sure about that, Clementine."

She was carrying a portfolio and held it open with one finger thrust between the covers. The corners of her mouth were lifted in the semblance of a smile.

She said, "I'm not intruding, I hope."

Actually, she was, and she knew it. I was in the middle of a sentence and its second half was slipping away. But I said, "Not at all. Won't you sit down?"

"I've brought you something," Clementine said.

She laid the portfolio on the table and said, "Since you never came to see the watercolor in my room, I should be very pleased if you will accept this small gift."

She opened the portfolio and showed me the large sheet of paper it contained. I gasped. It was a watercolor of the mountain Tekao, painted by a master's hand.

Clementine said, "Take care, it's not quite dry."

The technique was drybrush. This produces an almost photographic effect. Andrew Wyeth was very good at drybrush. So was the artist who made this painting. It took me minutes of close study before I saw the painting as a whole and absorbed its virtuosity. The signature at the bottom was that of O. Laster, a well-known living painter whose works sold for very healthy prices. He or she (the artist's gender was not known) was a sort of Henry of the arts—unphotographed, uninterviewed, anonymity protected by friends.

Clementine had been watching me closely.

I drew breath to say that I couldn't possibly accept such a gift. I could smell the paint. I lifted the painting to my nose. Clementine watched my investigation with a Holmesian eye.

I said, "Clementine, this is wonderful."

"Thank you."

"You painted it, did you not?"

"I did. This morning."

"Then you are O. Laster."

"You are free to make whatever surmise you wish. Will you accept the picture?"

"With the truest of thanks, Clementine," I said. "It's extraordinary. I will treasure it."

Daeng appeared with a tea tray.

Clementine said, "Tea. Good. I was at a loss for words."

Clementine and I had a pleasant talk over the tea and cakes. Nothing of consequence was said. No personal questions were asked. As we chatted, I invented her backstory—lonely childhood in a vicarage, solitary girlhood, chilblains in an unheated school, honors at Cambridge, unrequited love after unrequited love, finally a home at MI5, and now, rescue from loneliness and obscurity by Henry.

I said, "Tell me, Clementine, why is MI5 called Box 500?"

"My goodness, how do you happen to know that?"

"One of my professors told me. He'd been in the OSS."

"During the 1939–45 war, Box 500 was the London post office box address of the British Security Service, alias MI5," Clementine said. "Why on earth did your professor tell you such a thing?"

"Who knows? Maybe he liked me."

"Of course he did. Have you ever heard of a man called Markus Wolf?"

"I'm not sure."

"During the Cold War he was the head of the East German intelligence service. He was a great spymaster who believed that important targets were vulnerable through the people they trusted, and that success usually came through indirection, almost never by frontal attack. If he wished to know what a politician or a high-ranking civil servant knew, felt, and thought, he did not muck about with corrupting the primary target. Nor did he burglarize his or her office and plant listening devices or cameras or any of that sort of nonsense."

A heavy pause. A keen look. Clementine cocked her great gray head and asked silent questions. She was making a point. Did she have my attention? Did I follow?

"Wolf's method was breathtakingly simple," Clementine said. "He would send a handsome young man to seduce the great man's secretary. This agent would be trained up into a sexual virtuoso in preparation for his mission. Once he was in place, it would be arranged for him to meet the secretary as if by coincidence. Typically, someone she trusted would introduce her to the agent. Romantic gestures would follow—flowers, letters, nights at the theater, intimate suppers, and finally, sex that would drive her right round the bend. Soon she would be doing things with this irresistible sexual mechanic she never imagined existed but was sure would send her straight to hell. And as soon as the session was over, she would long to do them again. Before long, she would be prepared to do anything for her seducer. It is a small step from anal sex or the whip and handcuffs to bringing a few top-secret documents to the next rendezvous. One kind of bondage is very much like another. The way to a great man's secrets is through the orifices of his private secretary. That is what Markus Wolf believed, and he had many disciples."

Clementine delivered this colossal hint in the most ladylike tones imaginable. I had no trouble understanding exactly what she was talking about: Adam. The rush of incredulity that I felt must have shown on my face.

Clementine, frowning, said, "You do understand what I am saying to you, do you not?"

I said, "Clementine, I do indeed understand. Thank you so much for sharing."

She winced at the Americanism.

3

HENRY AND I HAD SPENT no time alone together on Nuku Hiva. On the plane, he decided that the moment had come to tell me something about himself.

I wasn't sure I wanted to hear it. I was already too close to him, I already knew too much. Why did he want to do this? Did he feel he owed me a confidence in return payment for my having told him about my history with Bear? Was it ethical for me to listen to his secret without telling him about Adam? But then, how likely was it that he didn't already know all about Adam?

Henry read the look on my face as easily as Clementine had done.

"It's nothing terrible," he said.

"So I'm not likely to be called as a witness?"

"No one would believe you if you were. Shall I go on?"

I nodded. He went on. When Henry was eight, he had scarlet fever. It was misdiagnosed as a fruit rash and left untreated. It developed into rheumatic fever, which resulted in damage to his heart valves and congestive heart failure.

"The valves were fixed surgically," he said. "I take pills for the congestive heart failure, but it sometimes causes episodes of shortness of breath."

"How short?"

"Short. One moment I'm OK. The next I can hardly breathe at all. Sometimes I pass out. This only happens every five years or so."

It happened to him when he was at Caltech. He was taken to an emergency room and treated with drugs—lots of drugs. The doctor on duty kept injecting new ones until he found one that worked. Henry remained in the hospital overnight.

"I couldn't sleep," Henry said. "At about three in the morning, the routine noises of the hospital faded away, as if someone had turned down the volume all the way. I thought maybe I was dying. Then I began to see things. Very clearly defined, three-dimensional images in living color, as if the things I was seeing were in the room with me."

"People?"

"I saw a person asleep. It was an early human, a caveman— naked, stocky, hairy. For a while, he continued in a deep sleep. Then, as if he felt my eyes on him, he woke up. He opened his eyes and looked straight at me. It was obvious that he saw me as clearly as I saw him. He *recognized* me. He understood that I was a man like himself. I could see it in his eyes. I understood what he was thinking. He wasn't sure that I was real."

"And then?"

"And then he faded out," Henry replied. "Other images appeared—crowds of people, patiently waiting."

"Waiting for what?"

"There were no explanations, just images," Henry said. "All sorts of people, all races, both sexes, clothing from many eras. Soldiers in ranks, wearing the uniforms of different wars—armor, shakos, steel helmets, World War I khaki. They stood absolutely still, absolutely silent, absolutely patient."

"Wounds?"

"None visible."

"Did they see you, like the caveman did?"

"I don't think so," Henry said. "They weren't looking at anything."

"These were long shots or close-ups?"

"Both. I didn't see all of it. It went on forever. I had a sense that there were an infinite number of these silent, motionless people, and I was just being given a glimpse of the multitude."

"What did you think you were looking at?" I asked.

"While it was happening, I didn't think."

"And later?"

"Limbo? The dead waiting for judgment or reincarnation? I wasn't sure. I'm still not sure."

Limbo? Judgment day? Christian soldiers? I couldn't believe my ears.

I said, "Did the hallucinations, or whatever they were, ever repeat themselves?"

"Not the same ones," Henry said.

"How long did they last?"

"All night. I got out of the hospital the next morning and went back to the frat house. The doctors told me to spend the day in bed. Ng Fred was my roommate."

"He knew about the hallucinations?"

"No. Until now I've never told anyone," Henry said. "That evening, I heard music, coming from outside the building."

"What kind of music?"

"A choir—male voices singing, as if a choir were standing under my window. It was completely different from any music I knew— scales and tones I had never heard."

"Did anyone else hear it?"

"No. I said, 'Fred, listen to that.'" He said, 'Listen to what?' A couple of guys came into the room to see how I was. I asked them the same question. They didn't hear the music, either. They thought I was kidding around. The music went on and on, and it was almost too beautiful to listen to. We watched TV for a while and turned out the lights. Fred sleeps like a stone. He dropped off immediately."

I started to ask a question.

Henry held up a hand and said, "Wait. I was lying in the dark,

ARK

trying to go to sleep. All of a sudden, I heard church bells—just a few at first, then more, then hundreds, then many more than that, all sorts, every tone. They were near and distant. It sounded like every bell in every church for miles around was ringing. I knew Fred wouldn't hear them if I woke him up and asked him to listen. I thought, *If this is dying, how kind the Great Genetic Engineer has been to arrange things as he has.* I thought I should call my parents and tell them that I loved them. I had to urinate—all part of the process, a last reminder of my physical self, I supposed. I got up and went down the hall to the toilet. All the while, I kept on hearing the church bells. They drowned out the music. On my way back to the room, I thought, *If I see myself in bed, I'll know for sure.* But as you can see, that didn't happen. Here I am."

So he was. I knew I should say something, but what? I didn't doubt for a moment that what Henry had told me was the literal truth. He really had seen the caveman and the silent armies waiting for the last trump. He had actually heard the ethereal music and the church bells.

I said, "So what do you make of the experience? Was it the drugs, or was the Almighty revealing himself to you?"

Henry said, "Who knows?"

"You don't reject either possibility?"

"No. Which would you choose?"

"The drugs."

"You may be right. But three weeks after that, I saw the solution to the superconductor problem."

"*Saw* it? Like you saw the caveman?"

"The two experiences were quite similar. I was riding my bike, coasting down a long hill, and it came to me in pictures, not as real as the caveman and the soldiers, but pictures nevertheless."

"What kind of pictures?"

"The solution. Equations. Apparatus. The entire instructions manual."

"Has the same thing happened with all your other discoveries?"

115

"Yes."

"Including the Event?"

He nodded.

"This stuff just comes to you?"

"Exactly."

"Did you tell your parents or your teachers about this gift of yours?"

"You call it a gift?" Henry said.

4

BACK IN THE CITY, MELISSA dropped by with some papers to sign. Henry was transferring ownership of the apartment, contents included, to me. Just sign here and here and here and initial in these five places, in blue ink, here's a pen.

I was annoyed. What right did Henry have to inflict such largesse on me?

I said, "Keep the pen, Melissa."

She sighed deeply and said, "What's the problem this time?"

"Same old problem. I can't possibly accept this."

"Of course you can accept it. You've already accepted it. This is a formality. In Henry's mind, it's part of your compensation package. It's his way of telling you he values your services. It's not as though he can't afford it."

"What Henry can afford isn't the point."

"You're right. Take the pen."

"Why?" I said. "Tomorrow we die."

Melissa recoiled. She said, "How can even you joke about that?"

Tears spurted from her eyes and rolled down her cheeks, two thick trickles of mascara. I was astonished: This was Melissa. I sat down on the arm of her chair and put my arm around her. I kissed her cheek, tasted powder and paint, and said, "What is it, dear?"

She waved me off. She covered her face with her hands, as if I might kiss her again. Quite soon, she got hold of herself.

"My kids," she said. "They go to school and every morning after they get in the car and drive off, I know, *know*, that I'll never see them again, that the earth is going to open its mouth and swallow them before the sun goes down. I hate Henry for telling me."

"So do I," I said. "But he may be wrong."

"Like hell he is."

Melissa grabbed her purse and left the room. While she was absent I signed the papers. She returned with her face repainted and immediately spotted the signed documents. She did an about-face, went into the kitchen, and returned with a bottle of wine in her hand.

"A 2000 Pauillac," she said. "It must have come with the place."

We drank the entire bottle in half an hour. Then she gathered up her papers and left.

The wine put me to sleep. I woke up a couple hours later with a cottony mouth and a bad headache. I had nothing in the house that might dull the misery. I stuck my finger down my throat, but it was too late.

I tried to remember where I had hidden my Chef Boyardee cans so that no one would catch me with them. Finally I found them inside an empty canister. After eating a bowl of microwaved spaghetti and meatballs—a sovereign cure for hangover—I felt well enough to go out.

In the cool of the evening I went to the Reservoir for a run. Now that I had been assured that the suspicious characters who haunted me were protectors, I didn't bother to take evasive action. After a week on a tropical island, it seemed strange to be loping along in the midst of dozens of strangers, listening to the clatter of the city. They all looked terribly serious, as people of my age group tend to do, weighed down as they are by the fate of endangered species, the many carcinogens in the air they breathe, the maddening triumphs of politicians and colleagues they loathe, the disillusionments of career and marriage, the guttering candle of the sex drive.

That evening I called Melissa to see if she was all right. She was. I told her about the Chef Boyardee. She actually giggled. In college, we had often pigged out together on the stuff—Melissa preferred ravioli—when we drank too much, etc., on weekends.

The next call was to Adam. I used a special throwaway phone I had bought to call him. I got his voice mail. I left no message.

After a while Adam called back. We went to a violin recital at Carnegie Hall. The artist was a boy virtuoso who played Bruch's ravishing second violin concerto. After the recital we went across the street for coffee. Adam lifted a strand of hair and tucked it behind my ear and touched my cheek with his thumb.

He said, "Shall we?"

I said, "After listening to that music? Are you kidding?"

Adam said, "Your place?"

"No. It's too messy."

"Mine, too," Adam said. "The maid quit."

I said, "I don't like hotels."

He tucked a strand of hair behind my other ear.

"Really?" he said. "I hadn't noticed."

He made calls to three hotels on his cell phone, using speed dial. Apparently he had a list of them programmed in case of need. The third hotel, the same one we had used last time, had a room. It was quite nearby, a godsend after the Bruch. Adam paid in advance with hundred-dollar bills. He had a stack of them—thousands of dollars—in an envelope in an inside pocket of his grungy old suede blazer. That seemed like a lot of cash for a struggling young lawyer to be carrying around, but this was not the moment for suspicions.

We went upstairs. We had the same room as before. What were the odds on that? Adam asked. He was a little too amazed. Was he in fact some sort of undercover operative who had been trained in the art of driving foolish women out of their minds, maybe by Markus Wolf himself? The more I thought of this dispiriting possibility— thank, you Clementine—the more plausible it seemed.

Adam slept, snoring gently, until I woke him up at first light.

He looked at the clock and said, "It's 6 a.m., for Pete's sake."

"Wouldn't want you to be late for court on a Sunday," I said, studying his sleepy face for clues that he remembered his gaffe. None showed.

We ordered a room-service breakfast. Adam paid the bill in cash.

Buttering toast, he said, "By the way, I stopped by your place a couple of times last week and buzzed your apartment. No answer. The second time, I felt somebody behind me and when I turned around, the guy asked me if I knew you."

"What did you say?"

"Nothing. He had me trapped in the entryway."

"He was a mugger?"

"I thought it was a possibility. He held out his hand and said his name, or anyway, a name."

"Which was what?" I asked.

"I wasn't paying attention."

"Did you shake hands with him?"

"No," Adam said. "Why would I do that? It was one o'clock in the morning. The guy was a total stranger."

"Was his manner threatening, or what?"

"Let me put it this way. He was acting like a husband."

"Acting like a husband? In what way?"

"Suspicious, tough, pissed."

"You sound like an expert in husbandly behavior. There are a hundred apartments in that building. How did he know it was my apartment you were buzzing?"

"He was looking over my shoulder while I did the buzzing, so maybe he read your name beside the doorbell."

I said, "What did he look like?"

"Huge, like an NBA center," Adam said. "Maybe three hundred pounds, all muscle, like he'd been lifting weights in prison."

The ghost touched me. My skin shrank. I felt very, very cold.

I said, "Any facial hair?"

"Big red handlebar mustache," Adam replied, talking with his mouth full of toast and drawing in the air a cartoon of Bear's mustache.

FOUR

1

CLEMENTINE SAID, "MY DEAR CHILD, you're having an anxiety attack. Hence the tremor, the twitching eye, the shortness of breath, the perspiration, the fact that the smallest noise startles you, et cetera. Fright often brings on such symptoms."

We were alone together in my apartment. Clementine seemed oblivious to its splendors. No doubt she had become familiar with them while supervising the installation of the cameras and microphones. She was the last person in the world I wanted to talk to, but when I called Henry from the hotel room and told him I was too terrified to go home by myself, she was the person he dispatched to walk me back to the apartment. He himself was too far away to help, exact location unspecified.

Clementine said, "You really should ring up Henry, you know, and report in."

It was easier to do as she suggested than to be stubborn about it. I punched the hot key on the videophone, and two seconds later, Henry's image flashed onto the screen. Wherever he was, he seemed to be in bright daylight. Behind him I could see sunlight bouncing from a windowpane, a bookcase, a table. I squinted, trying to read the titles of the books, as if knowing what was on the shelves would tell me where he was. To a rational mind, it wouldn't have mattered where he was. To my addled brain, in this moment, it was vital, but as luck would have it, I had enough of a grip on myself not to ask.

"You're all right?" Henry said.

"Fine."

"Clementine can stay with you, if you want."

I said, "That really won't be necessary."

"Whatever you say," Henry said. "But pay attention to what she tells you. She knows her business."

Back in the living room, I found Clementine with her cell phone to her ear. I could tell from the signs of delight in her face that she was talking to Henry. When she caught sight of me, she turned her back and murmured a few final words, then hung up.

She said, "Henry tells me you want to be alone. Does that still apply?"

"If you don't mind. I can't write when someone else is around."

"Right. Before I go, we should discuss one or two matters. The first is your protection. A team of ten chaps is assigned to you. They will be in place at all times, day and night. I promise you they will keep you safe. Second, though I don't believe you'll need it, you should have some means of self-defense. Have you ever used a firearm?"

"My father taught me to shoot a .22 rifle. I had a boyfriend in college who liked to shoot rats at the town dump. We went on rat-shooting dates."

"What sort of firearm did you use?"

"A .357 Magnum Smith and Wesson revolver."

Clementine lifted her eyebrows. "You fired it?"

"Lots of times. It was fun."

"You didn't mind the recoil, the report?"

"No. We wore earplugs."

From her large reticule, Clementine produced a semiautomatic pistol. It was stubby and sort of earth-toned. I hadn't known that guns came in any other colors but black and blue and nickel. This one was loaded. Handling the weapon with aplomb, she removed the magazine and ejected the cartridge from the chamber, catching it in midair.

"This is a Heckler and Koch .40-caliber model P2000 SK semiautomatic pistol," she said, handing it to me, butt first.

The gun was very heavy, about the weight of a two-quart milk carton.

"This weapon is the ne plus ultra of handguns," Clementine said. "It makes a very loud noise when it goes off. It holds ten rounds, nine in the magazine, one in the chamber. The trigger is stiff. That makes it less likely to go off accidentally, but you have to use some strength to shoot it. Try. Squeeze, don't pull."

I planted my feet apart, held the pistol in both hands, aimed at a bare spot on the wall, and squeezed, as my gun-nut boyfriend had taught me. The hammer clicked on the empty chamber. She was right. The trigger was stiff.

She took the pistol from my hand and showed me how to load it and unload it.

"Now you," she said.

I loaded and unloaded the weapon several times. It had a nice balance. It smelled like a gun.

Clementine handed me an extra clip. "Wipe the magazine clean with a tissue or cloth before you load it into the weapon. Keep a round in the chamber," she said. "Failure to do this could cost you your life, as the man who is stalking you really doesn't sound like the sort who would give you time to pump a round into the chamber. A single extra bullet can make all the difference, especially if you're hunting rhino, as you appear to be doing. Carry the weapon with you at all times."

She pulled a small shoulder bag out of her own mammoth drawstring purse. "Use this bag as a holster. Carry nothing else in it except the pistol and the extra magazine. You don't want to fumble for it."

"Isn't carrying a handgun illegal in New York?"

"Not to worry. If the target appears, do not hesitate. Do not engage in conversation. Draw your weapon and fire all ten rounds into his chest. Shoot as fast as you can. Then let the magazine drop, thus, reload, and shoot him in the head, twice. Can you do that?"

She handed me the gun. I went through the drill several times.

"Well done," Clementine said. "Practice until it's second nature."

She handed me yet another cell phone.

"Touch zero plus one for Henry, zero plus two for me," she said. "I'll call you on this phone every hour. Remember, fire a full magazine into the torso, then two rounds into the head. That will leave you a reserve of seven rounds in case you need them. If you're outside this apartment, do *not* drop the weapon like Michael Corleone in *The Godfather*. Your fingerprints and DNA will be all over it. Put it into your purse and quietly walk away. Do not run. If you're here, hold on to the pistol in case you haven't quite killed the rotter. Call me immediately. Do not, I repeat, do *not* call the police."

Her jaw jutted. She looked quite grim, but then that's the way she usually looked.

I said, "You sound as if you think I'm actually going to get to shoot him."

"I do hope you will," said Clementine. "I should think it would be quite therapeutic."

As soon as Clementine left, I ran to the computer. I laid the pistol beside the keyboard and wrote far into the afternoon, feeling neither hunger nor thirst. *That* was therapy. My mind was entirely within the story. As she had promised, Clementine called every hour, on the half hour. Time flew, but I was aware of my surroundings. I was alert. Bear could have walked into the room and I would have fired ten rounds into his chest and two in his skull and gone on writing.

Around five, Adam called on one of my throwaway phones. I had a paragraph to finish, so I didn't pick up. A moment later, the phone vibrated again, skittering across the polished mahogany surface of the computer table. I looked at the caller ID. Adam again. But it was the wrong phone. I had never given him the number for this particular one.

I dialed his number. He answered halfway through the first ring.

He said, "Are you OK?"

"Why wouldn't I be?"

"You looked like you thought I was going to throw you out the window when I told you about the guy who was hanging around your door."

"Really?"

"You know you did. And then you go into the bathroom and I hear you vomiting and making a phone call. And the next thing I know, you rush by me without a word and you're out the door."

I said, "So why didn't you run after me, calling my name?"

Adam said, "Because I was stark naked. By the time I got dressed and got downstairs, you were gone. I went to your apartment and buzzed you. No answer. I'm downstairs now. Let me in, please."

"I'm not there."

"Where are you?"

"Hiding out."

"What do you mean, *hiding out*?"

I said, "How did you get this number?"

"I looked up the received calls on my phone and called every number I didn't recognize. You were twelfth on the list."

This was a lie. I had never used this phone to call Adam.

But he was the one who said, "What *is* this?"

He was annoyed. So was I. What was he doing, buzzing my apartment, hanging around downstairs, calling attention to himself, to my doorway, to my absence? Bear was no idiot. He'd read the signs. If I told Adam where I was, Bear would grab him and get the truth out of him and fifteen minutes later be ripping the door off its hinges.

As Adam walked down the street with the phone at his ear, I could hear horns, sirens, loud voices speaking English and a dozen foreign languages, his breathing.

He said, "Meet me."

"I can't," I said. "That guy you saw, the big guy hanging around the doorway?"

"Yeah. What about him?"

"What day of the week was it when you saw him?"

"Saturday night, Sunday morning really. Around one in the morning."

"Thank you," I said. "That's helpful."

"I'm so glad. Meet me now. Right away. Quick."

"No chance."

Adam hung up.

2

THE NEXT MORNING AS THE sun came up, Henry's favorite hour of the day, he and Clementine came to see me. He must have flown back to New York from wherever he had been in order to be by my side. I felt like a fool, but a happy fool. Once again the topic was my safety. Clementine had sent a team of her chaps to Texas to keep an eye on Bear. The chaps reported that he had reserved a seat on a flight from Dallas to New York. He would be arriving at JFK on Friday night. Today was Wednesday. Clementine was sure that her chaps would contain him. They would fly on the same plane with him from Dallas, follow him into the city, and keep him under close surveillance every minute, no matter where he was. I wished I had her confidence in the possibility of managing good outcomes.

"It's our good luck," she said, "that our man must be the most conspicuous stalker on record."

"You'll need all the luck you can get," I said.

Clementine said, "I understand that your Mr. Mulligan is a formidable bloke, but I assure you that our people can deal with him. You'll be all right."

"What about Henry?"

"What about him?" Clementine asked.

"Bear knows what he looks like."

"But not where he can be found."

"Not yet."

Clementine gave me a look of reproof. It was clear that she wanted to say more to me, to teach me the realities, and would do so as soon as we were alone. But before she could say more, we heard a low, muffled sound, like the whoosh of a high-speed train through a tunnel. The noise grew louder. Henry leaped to his feet and ran toward the windows. The building shook itself like a wet dog. The floor rose and fell. Henry stumbled. I ran after him, fearing that the windows would shatter and he would stumble out. I took hold of him. He put his arms around me and squeezed. I had never before felt his body. He was more muscular than I had imagined. I had a strong impulse to kiss him. Over his shoulder, through the windows, I saw tall buildings swaying, shuddering, whipping back and forth—enormous structures that weighed hundreds of thousands of tons. A plume of water was slung from an ancient wooden tank on top of a nearby smaller building. The tank fell apart, staves flying in all directions. Behind me, pictures leaped off the wall. Sculptures and lamps and chairs tipped over. Books spewed out of bookcases. I knew perfectly well that this was an earthquake. But in New York?

And then it stopped. The buildings ceased quivering. They looked almost human, somehow shrunken and chastened, as if they were living things that had been in an accident and did not yet know how badly they had been injured, or whether perhaps they were dead and did not yet know it. Henry and I remained as we were, wrapped in each other's arms. We smiled apologetically into each other's faces and stepped apart. The alarm system rang and rang, because the pictures had fallen off the wall, the sculptures had tumbled off their stands, and the quake had somehow unlocked the doors.

Henry said, "That was interesting."

3

MUCH LATER, WE LEARNED THAT the Manhattan earthquake registered 5.8 on the Richter scale—not catastrophic, but not trivial,
either. On Tuesday, the day before the quake, New York was the
most purposeful city in the world. By Thursday, it was the most
aimless. The earthquake took out the power grid. The great steel
pylons that carried power to the city fell over in a tangle of live
high-voltage cables. Few knew this for sure because, in the absence
of electricity, there was no radio, no television, and after batteries went dead, little or no Internet. Cell phones fell silent at about
the same time. Darkness descended. Computers went down. Cash
registers were inoperable. Bank records were inaccessible. ATMs did
not work. You couldn't use a credit card or cash a check. There was
no place to go and no way to get there except by walking. The pace
of life was reduced from the cultural equivalent of Mach 1 to four
miles an hour. No one had anything important to do. In a community where busyness was everything, this caused a collective mood
swing. The entire population was depressed.

Everything was closed. There was no point in going to work
because elevators weren't running. Even if you climbed a hundred
flights of stairs in the dark and reached your cubicle, you would

still be in the dark. The city had not been destroyed, but the damage was bad enough. Some older buildings shed fragments of stone and concrete. Gargoyles leaped from churches. A few steeples fell over. Many smaller buildings and houses in poor neighborhoods collapsed. A tsunami swept up the Hudson and East Rivers, capsizing ferries and yachts and tugboats at their moorings and flooding streets. Parked cars were swept away. The subways were flooded. So were the Holland, Lincoln, and Midtown Tunnels. Plumbing and wiring was damaged in thousands of buildings. The death toll was small—fewer than a hundred perished, mostly unfortunate souls who drowned in their sleep when rooftop water tanks collapsed.

Traffic came to a stop. There were so many pedestrians clogging the streets and avenues that it was impossible for vehicles to move. Drivers who insisted on trying to weave through the crowd found themselves upside down in overturned automobiles, smelling the gasoline that leaked from the tank. A black market in food and stolen goods organized itself overnight. I lived on what I had on hand—granola, eggs and cheese, bags of salad, bottled water, and my cache of Chef Boyardee.

There were aftershocks. Because our dwellings had generators, Henry and all his people could still recharge their cell phones and computers, so we remained in touch. Henry felt I was living too high above the ground and should move into his house. Melissa and her kids were already in residence. He had invited Clementine to join us. She was on her way to me. She would escort me to his place.

She arrived soon afterward, dressed for whatever might come in whipcord breeches, the usual sturdy boots, and despite the warmth of the day, a tweed jacket with leather elbow patches. Her great swollen reticule dangled from her left shoulder. Somewhere within it, I supposed, was a Heckler and Koch firearm in a larger caliber than I could manage, along with other tools of her trade—certainly a Taser and a blackjack and cans of pepper spray and teargas. No doubt a team of chaps accompanied us, hidden in the crowd.

ARK

As we marched up Fifth Avenue, Clementine's eyes examined every face in the crowd. In no case did she like what she saw. I was fascinated by the overnight conversion of the bustling, self-important citizens of the city into a herd of bewildered mammals, shuffling along with glazed eyes as if the crowd were a single beast thinking a single thought.

When we reached Henry's house, he showed us a large computer map that pinpointed every earthquake, every volcanic eruption, every movement of the poles, every anomaly in the magnetic field over the past several years and compared these to the normal frequency of such phenomena. Clearly, natural disasters were happening much more often and with far more destructive results than before.

"Why has nobody else noticed?" I asked.

"A lot of scientists think something is going on," Henry said. "The Pentagon is sure of it."

"Then why doesn't somebody sound the alarm?"

"They're afraid of panic."

"Go for a walk and take a look. These people aren't panicked. They're stunned."

"It's a local event."

"They don't know that."

"All right, there's another reason," Henry said. "No one wants to be the mad scientist crying that the end is near. What if it's not?"

"What if it is?"

"All the more reason to keep it quiet."

Henry made an impatient little gesture, a flick of the fingers, and an almost undetectable grimace. He wanted to talk about something else.

"What's your feeling about Bear?" he asked.

"My feeling hasn't changed," I said. "Neither has Bear. He's a maniac. He'll keep the promise he made to me in Hsi-tau if he can. But I think you may be the one with something to worry about."

"You think he wants to kill me, too?"

"He wants an eye for an eye. You ruined him; he'll ruin you."

"How?"

"The media, Henry, how else? He wants to take away your anonymity. Smash your mystique. Drive you into the open where ten thousand guns can shoot at you."

Now I had Henry's attention. He said, "How exactly would he do that? What does he know?"

"Quite a lot," I replied. "Think about it. He knows you spend a lot of time in Hsi-tau, that you have a very photogenic yurt compound there, that mysterious circle of unmarked booster rockets probably belongs to you, that you have influential Chinese friends including a general in the Chinese intelligence service, that you have access to one of the most closely guarded parts of one of the most secretive countries in the world. He knows that I hang out with you. You can be sure he knows a whole lot more than that."

"So what would he do with all this knowledge to make trouble for me?"

"Imagine what a journalist could do with it—the secret yurt compound in the Little Gobi Desert, the ferocious chow chow attack dogs, the sinister general, the temptress. Bear probably has pictures of the chows, along with shots of the yurts, of the rockets, maybe even of you."

"He's never photographed me."

"Maybe not personally. But he has all those grad students clinging to the cliff at the dig. What kid would go to the Gobi Desert without a camera that has a zoom lens?"

"All very plausible. Wouldn't murdering you or me affect his credibility?"

"He thinks he'll get away with it—he's sure of it, in fact, because he's crazy. And what's to say he wouldn't? In my case, he got away with it the last time. Serial killers get away with their crimes all the time. Who would suspect that you were the corpse when nobody knows what you look like? Anyway, he can make the same case against you whether he's a murder suspect or not."

"Why do you say that?"

"This is America, Henry. No one is more likely to be believed than a psychopath. And it isn't as if he's a street person. He's a household name among football fans. He's a highly respected paleontologist who has dug up new kinds of dinosaurs and written books about them."

"Everything you say might very well happen, except his murdering you, which I promise you is never going to happen," Henry said. "If he moves against me, we'll have to find a way to cope with it."

I wished I were as confident of my chances of survival as Henry appeared to be. He was shrugging Bear off. He thought he was invulnerable. He had weightier things to think about than sudden death.

"Henry," I said. "Please don't brush me off on this. Give me another moment."

Like the soul of politesse he was, he said, "Go ahead."

"Suppose Bear makes a wild guess and suggests that you're engaged in some super-secret plan to launch a massive privately financed mission into space?" I asked. "Capitalism goes interplanetary. The solar system is about to be ruined just like Earth has been despoiled. Suppose Bear suggests that you are doing this behind the back of the American people, but with the collaboration of the sinister government of the People's Republic of China?"

Henry said, "Go on."

"Imagine the results. The White House would unleash the CIA and the FBI and the IRS and the Justice Department on you. You'd be followed day and night, photographed, wiretapped. Satellites would photograph everything you own and everyone you know. Congress would hold hearings. You'd be subpoenaed. Your choice would be to show up on Capitol Hill and be slapped around on television and the Internet by a bunch of dimwitted egomaniacs, or flee the country, or launch yourself into space."

Henry's eyes smiled. "Is there a sunny side of the street?" he asked.

"The uproar might conceivably turn out to be a good cover story.

It might even solve the cover story problem we've been trying to deal with. It would divert attention from the fact that what you're really planning is the rescue of humanity and the reason for the rescue. That would probably require your telling a white lie or two."

"For example?"

"Like, you're mounting an expedition to survey the moons of Jupiter or the asteroid belt for mining opportunities," I said. "That would be believed—'Greedy trillionaire looks for more treasure at the end of the rainbow.'"

"I'm not that crazy."

"You wouldn't have to actually tell the lie. Just plant the suspicion. The paranoia industry will do the rest. Result: In trying to do you harm, Bear will have done you a favor."

Henry smiled quite brightly and for a moment, locking eyes with me. He was the first to look away. That had never happened before. Was it the advice or the hug that broke the pattern?

4

CLEMENTINE'S CHAPS HAD BEAR SURROUNDED. They thought he had spotted them because he appeared to be wandering aimlessly around the city. Sooner or later, he would make a break for it. In Clementine's view, the sooner the better.

"Why?" I asked.

"Because he's a bother," Clementine said. "A waste of money and manpower. An intruder, not part of the pattern. A distraction from the better things we have to do. Best to get him out of the picture this very weekend and go on with the more important matters."

"How do you accomplish that?"

"We're chewing on that problem."

Next day, as if on a sudden impulse, Clementine turned up at the apartment and asked me to go for a walk with her in Central Park. Not later, not tomorrow, but right now. I was surprised, because while Bear was on the loose in Manhattan, I was under strict orders to stay inside with all doors locked and alarms set.

"Why?" I asked.

"Curiosity," Clementine said. "The crowd grows as the afternoon goes on. Very odd, this mass walkabout. I'd like to study it at close hand."

"Clementine, that's moonshine."

Clementine said, "I have no idea what that means. But oh, do come along. We'll be back in no time."

She walked across the room and picked up my bag with my pistol inside. She was limping. I asked what the matter was.

"It's nothing, really, just a twinge, and anyway I have my rolling chair," she replied.

Clementine's wheelchair was motorized, so I didn't have to push it, just trot alongside as she weaved her way through the crowd. I didn't ask for a fuller explanation. No doubt Clementine had a sound operational reason for riding around in an invalid's chair she didn't need. Her costume had changed slightly. She now wore a floppy blue pancake beret, cocked jauntily just above her left eyebrow. The effect was quite becoming, softening her craggy face and adding a witty touch to the self-portrait.

Near the band shell, a mirror flashed. The pre-Clementine me would have assumed that a woman was fixing her lipstick or a kid was fooling around. The new me was instantly on the alert. I fell back a step or two. This moved me outside the range of Clementine's peripheral vision.

In a controlled but penetrating voice, she said, "Please remain where I can see you." Her head moved from side to side as her eyes searched the crowd for threats. I knew exactly what she was looking for: Bear.

She had baited the trap and I was the bait. The breath hissed from my body.

Clementine was looking to the left when, on the right, about thirty feet away, Bear rose up out of the crowd. This bit of stage business created the illusion that he was being lifted out of the earth like a monster rising from the grave. The mundane truth was that Bear had been sitting on a bench and decided to stand up. He loomed head and shoulders above the rest of the crowd. He wore aviator sunglasses and a baseball cap instead of the usual Stetson. He was dressed in coveralls, a garment he could easily strip off, getting rid of it and the bloodstains that with any luck would soon bespatter it. He was looking straight at me.

Clementine said, "Don't look at him, my dear. Keep on walking, dear. All will be well."

I did as ordered. My Heckler and Koch model P2000 SK swung from my shoulder inside its purse-holster. I knew I could not possibly fire it in this crowd without killing or wounding half a dozen people while missing Bear entirely. Bear knew this, too. He walked toward us, expressionless, the sun behind him. He was in no hurry. He knew as well as I did that escape was impossible. If I tried to hide in the crowd he would simply throw aside the people who stood between the two of us.

Conditions for murder were perfect. He could decapitate me in seconds, throw my bloody head into the crowd like a football, and walk away. No witness was going to volunteer a description of the killer. Not in New York.

Looking straight ahead, talking through her teeth, Clementine said to me, "Steady on! When I stand up, dive to the left. *Dive*. To the *left*."

Bear was now about ten feet away. He gathered himself to make a move. The wheelchair stopped. Clementine stood up. She pointed her pistol at Bear. The crowd saw the gun and parted as if someone within it had stepped on a poisonous snake. I dove to the left as instructed and landed on a prostrate man who recoiled as if I were the viper. I rolled off him onto my knees and drew my weapon. I pointed it at Bear's huge bulk. Even though I was hyperventilating, my hands were quite steady.

"Police!" Clementine shouted in a booming voice. "Freeze!"

Bear put his head down and charged, uttering a primal howl so loud that it must have peeled the skin off his throat. He took one giant step and lifted the opposite leg to take another. At that precise instant, a circular whirling thing like a fisherman's net appeared above his head. It fell onto him. It enveloped him. Two men dashed out of the mob and pulled the net tight. Bear was trapped inside it, as closely wrapped as a mummy. He shouted in rage and struggled mightily, but his arms were bound to his sides and his ankles were tied together. He was still on his feet. The net men gave him a violent push. He fell over backward. Two other men, who were standing behind him, caught him before he hit the ground. Another pair of watchers, each wielding a syringe, injected him in either arm with something that knocked him out almost immediately. The final two chaps in my protection detail pushed Clementine's wheelchair against the back of Bear's knees. His huge body slumped into the chair. They propped up his legs and wheeled him away at a run, with two other men running interference, parting the crowd.

Clementine was now displaying a large gold badge.

"It's all over, ladies and gentlemen," she said. "Move along now."

Someone said, "What'd the guy do?"

Clementine, holstering her weapon, ignored him.

To me, she shouted, "Let's go, sergeant!"

On the way back to my apartment, Clementine talked nonstop on her cell phone, so I was unable to ask questions. As soon as we arrived—or to be more accurate, as soon as she had checked out every nook and cranny of the place to make sure no villains were present—I offered her a nice cup of tea.

"How very kind," Clementine said. "Would you mind awfully if I made the tea?"

"I'd be delighted. I have some cookies. Shall I put them out?"

Clementine said that that would be lovely. She put the teakettle on the burner, and the instant the water boiled she warmed the pot, measured the tea, and let it steep for the precise amount of time required. Then she poured.

"Lovely cookies," she said.

"Wonderful tea," said I.

Clementine beamed. She was truly happy. I was happy for her. Her operation had gone like clockwork. I didn't doubt her competence—how could I after what I had just seen?—but knew that the capture of Bear might have gone less well. I didn't doubt for a moment that if things had gone wrong—say, the net had gone awry—she would have pumped ten rounds into Bear's torso, ejected the magazine, loaded another into the gun, and fired two rounds into his skull—unless he killed her with his bare hands while she was reloading.

And now that she had captured the monster, what was she going to do with him?

"That thing your men used to immobilize Bear," I said. "What was it?"

"As you saw, it's a net," Clementine replied. "It doesn't merely entangle, it entraps. It was designed as a humane way to subdue a violent subject who might also be insane. Bleeding hearts don't much care for it because they don't understand its underlying ethical principle, but as you saw, it's quite effective."

I said, "Obviously. I never imagined that Bear could be subdued."

Clementine sipped her tea and made no comment. Plainly, she had never doubted that anyone, no matter how fearsome, was unsubduable.

I asked her what would happen to Bear now.

"There are a number of options," Clementine said.

"Such as?"

"We might do the French thing and drop him off a bridge in dark of night, still wrapped up in his net," Clementine said. "Or give him a stern talking-to and send him back to Texas."

"Not the latter, if you don't mind."

"I was joking. But his situation will be explained to him."

I said, "You're not concerned about legal difficulties?"

"Of what kind?"

"A case could be made that he was kidnapped."

"Quite so," Clementine said. "But Mulligan is not the most credible of accusers. He intended to commit murder. He came all the way from Texas to New York on at least two occasions, with murder as his purpose."

"He had every right to be in New York."

Clementine's eyebrows rose. She placed her empty cup in its saucer and put the cup and saucer down on the table. The look she gave me was alight with false good humor.

She said, "My dear child, you are the most determined devil's advocate I have ever encountered. What do *you* recommend doing with this psychopath?"

"Let me put it this way," I replied. "I wish your men had missed with the net."

"Really? May I ask why?"

"So that I could have had the pleasure of watching you shoot Bear ten times in the heart, then twice in the head."

Clementine's eyes brightened, as if, to her surprise, she was beginning to like me. She looked at her watch.

She said, "I really must go. Thank you for the delicious tea."

I said, "You will let me know what you decide about Bear?"

"That rather depends on what's decided, doesn't it?"

"It depends on no such thing, Clementine. I do not wish to live in uncertainty."

She said, "Of course you don't. I recommend you to remain inside this apartment for the time being. You won't encounter Mulligan if you do go out, but he's not the only madman in New York."

She nodded briskly. I did the same in return.

I cleared my throat and said, "I know it's bad form, Clementine, but I do want to thank you and your chaps for what you all did today. It was the most amazing thing I've ever seen."

With a thin smile that told me she didn't doubt my amazement for a moment, Clementine murmured, "Not at all. Truly our pleasure."

With a stronger smile and in a stronger voice, she added, "I'm sure the chaps would thank you for the opportunity. It's good for them to have a bit of fun. Relieves the tedium."

Out she went, cell phone at her ear. There was a spring in her step.

5

AIRPORT SERVICE WAS RESTORED AROUND the middle of the second
week. As soon as it was possible to take off, Henry called. He was
terse. The car would come by for me in an hour. Bring clothes for
two climates. We were going to visit a factory of Ng Fred's in Mongolia, then make a couple of other stops. There was much to be
done, and it had to be done quickly.

In Hsi-tau, after a night's sleep, Henry and Daeng and I boarded
a small high-winged propeller plane. The pilot was Mongolian—
epicanthic eyelids, leathery blank face, horseman's physique. We
flew west along the border between China and Mongolia—brown
mountains dusted with snow, little brown dust storms on the floor
of the desert. A sepia sun shone through a scrim of dust particles.
The plane was brown, too. The instruments were labeled in the
Cyrillic alphabet and the instrument panel itself was marked CCCP.
Apparently the plane was Red Army surplus, therefore an antique
that had been maintained by Russian mechanics. We turned north
toward the mountains, into Mongolia. Suddenly the plane was being
knocked around the sky by wind shear. The flimsy aircraft pitched
and yawed and plunged and climbed. I am as fatalistic as the next
woman, but the prospect of crashing on this moonscape and lying

in the wreckage with a couple of broken bones until I died of thirst and shock made me reach for an airsickness bag. There was none.

At last we landed bumpily in a small flat valley between two low mountains. A spring bubbled from one of the mountainsides. Its waters, the color of weak tea, flowed into a trough and then into a catch basin. I walked over and washed my face.

Henry had vanished. The pilot, working alone, was tying down the plane, which was rocking in the wind that whistled down the narrow valley. There was absolutely no other sign of life.

Daeng said, "Follow me, please."

The ground was rough. Stones rolled under my foot. I turned my ankle and gasped. Daeng, pretending not to hear, led me into a cleft in the mountainside. After only a few steps we were in darkness. Daeng produced a flashlight, and walking backward, shone it at my feet. We turned a corner. Bright lights switched on. A squat Mongolian who had been standing guard in the dark let us in. He wore night-vision goggles and carried an automatic rifle. An ornamental hatchet, ancient weapon of the horde, was tucked into his belt.

I followed Daeng through the dazzling light down a long corridor, then down a long steel ladder to a gallery that ran along all four walls of an enormous cavern. A sphere that looked to be about a hundred feet in diameter hung from the ceiling. I recognized it from the engineers' drawings as a component of the spaceship. Henry and Ng Fred, as tiny from the distance as toy soldiers, stood below it. We went down in an elevator and joined them. Up close, the sphere seemed enormous—much larger than I thought it would be when I saw the designs that the three engineers had shown to Henry a few months before.

Ng Fred seemed happy enough to play tour guide. As he talked, we walked across the factory floor together. It was a long walk. The place looked to be at least a square mile in extent.

I said, "Did you make this cavern?"

"I wish I had," Ng Fred said. "It's an old mine. The Russians rebuilt it as an underground factory when they were running Mon-

ARK

golia. They didn't have time to use it much before the Soviet Union fell apart. After they left it was just sitting here, so we bought it."

Henry disappeared again, cell phone pressed to his ear. A gondola dangled from cables. Ng Fred, affable as ever, and I got into it and were lifted inside the sphere.

Dozens of workers, all of them young Chinese women, clung to the sphere's curved interior surface—installing wiring, plumbing, insulation, and other things I couldn't identify. They wore harnesses that were suspended from long cables.

Why women?

"They're just better than men at this kind of work," Ng Fred replied. "What they're putting together here is the most sophisticated flying machine ever assembled by human beings, but most of the work is done with bare fingers and thumbs. Men's fingers are too big. The detail and the repetitiveness drive men crazy. But the ladies have no problems. To them it's the same as making running shoes or sewing on buttons or assembling wristwatches. That's the kind of work most of them used to do in other factories. They're faster and better than machines. Don't ask me why or get political about it. It's just a fact of nature."

"Where do you find the workers?" I asked.

"In my other factories, mostly. Some recommend their sisters or cousins."

"And you have enough left over to run the other factories?"

"There are lots of sisters and cousins in China," Ng Fred said. "For this job, we accept only very healthy women twenty-five or younger who weigh ninety pounds or less and have an IQ in the 110s. A lower score means the worker is not smart enough, a higher one that she's too smart. If they gain five pounds, they go on a diet. If they can't lose the weight, they're history."

The women were young and lithe and agile and completely absorbed in their work. Most were too far away for me to make out their faces. Almost the only noise was the whir of power tools or the occasional tap of a hammer. There was little or no chatter. They were making steady, visible progress. Watching them was like waiting for the hand of a clock to move. Each little job had its frozen moment. Then the minute hand moved. Everything changed ever so slightly, and when the hand moved again would change once more.

I asked Ng Fred what he was going to do with the sphere after the women had completed it.

"They'll take it apart, then put it back together again," he said. "Then they'll do it all over again. They've already done this once."

"Why?"

"Training. They have to be able to assemble it with their eyes closed. It's like a prefabricated house. Each part is numbered and is added in a predetermined sequence. Next time they'll do it while wearing space suits. Then they'll do that again. Finally they'll do it for real—in orbit, in zero gravity. By that time, they should be able to do it without thinking, or almost."

I said, "Why use women instead of men, apart from the fact that their fingers are smaller and they're more patient?"

"Those factors are reason enough," Ng Fred said. "But they weigh less than men and eat less than men, so we can lift more of them into orbit as payload and take care of them better at less expense."

"How many women equal how many men in ounces and pounds?"

"Do the math. The average Chinese male at age twenty-five weighs around a hundred and thirty pounds. These women weigh ninety pounds or less. For a hundred workers, that's a total difference between male and female of plus or minus four thousand pounds. The dividend is forty-four more women than men for the same dead weight."

Henry arrived from wherever he had been and listened in on the rest of Ng Fred's lecture. Fred painted with a broad brush. First, a large space shuttle would be placed in orbit with the materials for a bare-bones sphere in its cargo bay. Fifty women would live in a second shuttle and assemble the sphere. When the sphere could support life, they would move inside it while completing its construction. The shuttle would return to Earth to pick up another load. Another sphere and another work crew would be placed in orbit nearby. The combined crew would assemble the second sphere. When that task was completed, the first crew would return to Earth. Another would take its place and continue their work, joined in time by a third crew.

As more spheres were constructed and equipped, the number of workers would be increased because there would be living space for them in the spheres. Construction crews would be rotated. Some of them would assemble spheres. Others would load cargo. Finally, the ship would become a unity through the connection of several spheres. The propulsion system would be installed. The fusion plant would be loaded and activated. At that point, the flight crew would be ferried to the ship, along with any others who might be taking the voyage. The frozen embryos that were going to replace *H. sapiens* would be loaded into a sphere of their own, inside a device that would keep them alive and intact, theoretically forever, at a temperature of approximately minus 321 degrees Fahrenheit.

"What happens to the women who built the ship?" I asked.

"The best of them would go along, to maintain the ship," Ng Fred said.

"That should foster competition."

"That's the idea."

"Do they know the truth about the flight?"

"They know it will be a long flight—longer than a human life. Before liftoff they will know everything. We don't lie to our people."

"How many will remain aboard?"

"A hundred or so."

"What about the rest?"

"They'll go home," Ng Fred said. "There's no room for them."

"How do you replace workers as they die?"

"That will be taken care of."

"How? Are you going to breed them to the flight crew?"

"We're going to let them make their own arrangements," he said. "Polyandry is the likeliest outcome. Would you be affronted by that?"

"Not in the least," I replied.

Like most of the women I knew, I had been practicing polyandry all my life without calling it by its proper name.

We spent the night underground. The guest rooms were utilitarian: small, ship-shape, each with its own shower and toilet, computer, and refrigerator. A fact sheet in several languages was provided. The purified water for the scores of people who worked and lived here came from the mountainside spring and was continually recycled, as was the vast amount of urine produced by the workers. The refrigerator contained only juices and bottled springwater. The factory was a drug-, alcohol-, and tobacco-free zone. A fusion reactor, one of Henry's smaller models, provided electrical power. The sheer efficiency of the whole installation calmed the mind and lifted the spirit. This surprised me. I had always despised the collective, and here I was, admiring with all my heart the only one I had ever seen close up.

That night we dined with the workers in their cafeteria. Chinese songs played on the sound system—greatest post-Mao hits. After dinner, Ng Fred sang along in a jovial bass-baritone. I joined in with my quavering alto on the two or three songs I knew. Daeng and a tall, anorexic man in a chef's toque came out to listen. The workers hesitated to join in.

"Sing, sing!" boomed Ng Fred, waving his arms like a conductor.

Daeng and the chef added their voices. Daeng sang countertenor beautifully in perfect Mandarin, no surprise, and the chef's tenor wasn't bad, either. Henry did not utter a sound, but regarded the four of us with guileless affection. Never in my life had I been happier, and while the music and the company had something to do with this, the factory was the real reason for my joy.

Those pretty little women, hanging as if weightless from spiderwebs inside that sphere and doing their work in silence, had gladdened my heart. There really was going to be a ship, and if we had time on our side and a little luck, life really was going to go on.

6

HENRY AND NG FRED STAYED up all night, talking about technical matters. The next morning, Henry cut the trip short—a phone call from Amerigo, he said. Something urgent. Would I mind a stopover?

Amerigo came aboard the Gulfstream in Milan. His face was grim. His charm was absent.

He said, "This is serious, Henry. One of my people, a doctor who has worked with us from the beginning, has smuggled several embryos into the plant and placed them in the freezer with the enhanced embryos."

"Why did he do that?"

"He sold passage for the embryos to couples who want their DNA to survive the Event. Apparently they were rich couples. The price was five million euros per embryo. That included mixing the sperm and ovum in vitro."

"This fellow knows the truth?"

"He deduced it," Amerigo replied. "He's greedy, but he's not stupid."

Henry closed his eyes and tapped his fingers on the arm of his chair. This was the equivalent of a loud, foot-long curse from an ordinary person.

He said, "You have removed these bootlegged embryos, I assume."

"We don't know which ones they are, Henry. Maybe the doctor doesn't know himself. He labeled them in the same way as all the others and dropped them into the inventory in different slots on different dates. We don't know exactly how many he smuggled in, and he won't tell us. For all we know, it could be hundreds."

"Did you try checking out his bank deposits?"

"Yes. Clementine's moneyman couldn't find any, apart from his salary. This guy is from Calabria. He could have given every member of his family a million or two in cash to hold for him. They'll never tell anybody outside the camorra."

"Did he enhance the embryos first?"

"No. I think sabotage was one of his motives."

"Explain."

"He knows that these specimens will pollute the experiment. If they survive and mate with enhanced individuals, they'll produce a hybrid. It will mate with other individuals. That will introduce aberrant genes into the gene pool. It's impossible to know what the effects might be over time. Certainly not what we intended. If you mate a nymph to a mortal, you might get Achilles. But not always."

"Why would he do this?"

"For the money. Why else? Maybe he's religious and thinks he's protecting God's work. Maybe he's like a computer hacker and did it for the hell of it. But the obvious is usually the explanation. So it's probably the money."

I said, "Wait a minute. 'God's work'? You really think that was his motive?"

Amerigo said, "Why not? The world is full of religious people. Some of them are crazy. The question is, what do we do now?"

"Correct me if I'm wrong, Amerigo," Henry said. "The sequence of preservation is as follows: All water is removed from the embryos to avoid the formation of ice crystals in their cells. Then they are placed in plastic containers and cooled until they are chilled enough to be stored in a tank filled with the vapor of liquid nitrogen, which freezes them to a temperature of minus 196 degrees Celsius."

"Correct."

"They cannot be thawed and refrozen?"

"It's considered unwise. Too much handling."

"How many survive storage?"

"Sixty to eighty percent of our embryos should be viable at voyage's end."

"So it's possible that all the intruders would die en route."

"Or they could all survive. Either outcome is statistically unlikely, but not impossible."

"What are the stages of thawing?"

"The embryos, still in their containers, are removed from the tank and warmed at room temperature, then placed in a water bath at a temperature of thirty-seven degrees Celsius. When completely thawed, the embryos are removed from the containers, and then incubated for two days to determine if they are alive."

"How do you know they're alive?"

"If the embryo was three weeks or older when it was frozen, it will have a beating heart even though it's small enough to pass through the eye of a needle. If younger, there are other indications."

Surely Henry already knew the answers to the questions he was asking Amerigo. I couldn't understand why he was asking, and from the look on Amerigo's face and the cautious tone of his voice, neither could he. Henry moved in mysterious ways.

"Can its DNA be decoded after thawing?" Henry asked.

"Yes. But the problem of too much handling would arise again."

"But that aside, it's possible to differentiate the intruder embryos from our embryos at the moment of thawing."

"Probably. Whether the crew will remember how to do it at the end of such a long flight is another matter. Maybe the crew will have forgotten the English language and can't read the instructions."

"So if you forget all the maybes, where are we?"

"The question remains," Amerigo said. "Do we destroy the embryos or not?"

Henry said, "I think we've got to start all over again. Freeze a new batch."

"What about the embryos we've already got?" Amerigo asked.

"Let them be," Henry replied.

FIVE

1

THE NEW YORK I CAME home to no longer knew all the answers. It was tentative, watchful, apprehensive. So was I. I sent a text message to Adam. He answered instantly. We arranged in ten words or less to meet at ten o'clock.

"Where?" he queried.

I was tired, I was thinking of something else, I wanted sex. Without thinking—or so I told myself a nanosecond later when I realized what I had done—I gave him the address of my new apartment.

I had imagined Adam walking in, stopping in his tracks, and crying "Wow" when he saw the apartment for the first time. He did not disappoint me. As he stepped into the hallway, the door closed itself behind him. He looked up. The Hopper stared back at him. He actually leaped in his skin as if he had been startled by a loud noise. He stared back at the painting for what seemed a full minute, and then took in the other objects in the hall. Without so much as a look at me, he strode into the living room, and then, uninvited, into all the other rooms. He stopped in front of every picture, taking inventory. Adam knew pictures. He knew exactly what he was looking at.

He said, "This is a Dante Gabriel Rossetti. What *is* this? Are you apartment-sitting or what?"

I said, "I'm glad you like it."

He walked into my office, the last place I wanted him or anyone else to go. I had framed Clementine's watercolor and hung it in this room. He walked up to it, nose almost touching the museum glass, and studied it for long moments.

"This is an original O. Laster," he said. "Where did you get it?"

"It was a gift," I said.

"A gift," he said tonelessly. "What about the rest of this stuff?"

I said, "Cut it out, Adam."

"It's a simple question."

He sounded like a husband accusing his wife of adultery. I said, "Here's a simple answer. It's none of your business."

Adam's face was clenched. He looked like he would never smile again—at least not at me.

He said, "Tell me the truth. Are you some zillionaire's squeeze or what?"

I said, "That does it. Out."

I pressed the remote. The door opened. Adam left, walking heavily on his heels as if he wanted to punch holes in the carpet. At the door, he stopped, turned around, and gave me what I thought was a good-bye look. There was no love or understanding in it. Sadness, deep and dark, enveloped me.

I sobbed—just once, but from the bottom of my being, as if I loved this man. I didn't, but I knew that something irreversible had happened. It had happened before with other men who didn't like surprises, so I knew the signs, the look, the feeling. I thought I'd never see this man again.

2

I HAD HAD NO SERIOUS exercise in several days. This had a bad effect on my mood. I wanted to run, but lacked the pluck to go to Central Park. I used the treadmill, but it was like prison exercise, no substitute for the smell and sound and jostle and memories of the park.

One afternoon the phone rang while I was on the treadmill. I saw who the caller was but answered anyway.

"Clementine here," said the husky voice. "I was wondering if you might be able to stop by my office. It's not so very far from you. The chaps will lead you to it. Or we can come to you."

"Who is 'we'?"

"A person Henry wants you to meet."

"When?"

"Would five o'clock be convenient?"

"I'll be there. What is this person's name?"

"He's a lawyer," said Clementine. "Nice chap. American. Do be sure to take along the phone you're using now, so the chaps can ring you up."

I wore jeans and running shoes to the meeting. As always, the doorman was holding his cell phone to his ear as I got off the eleva-

159

tor. He spoke a word into it and tucked it away. Almost immediately, my own phone rang.

A slow male Southern voice said, "As you go outside, ma'am, please turn right, then right again on Fifty-seventh Street, then left on Seventh, then left on Fifty-fifth." I did as I was told. After walking a block and a half on Fifty-fifth Street, a man beside me said, "Next building on the left, please, ma'am." He went inside with me and rode up with me on the elevator. He then walked me to the door of an office and pressed a buzzer. The sign on the door read Grendel Associates, LLC.

The bright-eyed sexagenarian waiting in Clementine's office was no longer young, but not yet elderly. His hair was white and well cut, a bit of pink scalp peeking through. He wore a good suit and shirt and tie and lace-up shoes with a mirror shine. He stood up, spare and tall and not at all unhandsome.

"May I introduce Mr. Elway Scott?" Clementine said. "He has a few questions about Mr. Mulligan."

I said, "He does? Who is he?"

"I am an attorney at law, engaged by Mr. Henry Peel."

"If Henry wants me to talk to a lawyer," I said, "what's wrong with the lawyer I know?"

Clementine said, "Melissa has recused herself owing to your friendship."

"Strange reason," I said. "What's this about?"

"Your Mr. Mulligan," Clementine said.

Elway Scott handed me a business card—heavy stock, engraved, not embossed. He was a partner in a firm called Scott, Elway, and Starke.

With a toothy smile, he said, "Shall we begin?"

I made a gesture of indifference—*why not?*

"A couple of weeks ago, a man named Francis P. Mulligan was delivered by Good Samaritans to the emergency room at Lenox Hill Hospital on Park Avenue, near Central Park," Elway Scott said in a drawling, old-money voice, speaking as smoothly as if he were reading the words off a teleprompter. "The Samaritans, who identified themselves as tourists from London who were stranded in New York by the earthquake, stated that they had discovered Mr. Mulligan, who was a stranger to them, in a state of unconsciousness in the park. Because Mulligan was such a large man, they borrowed a wheelchair to get him to the hospital. They had promised to return this item to the invalid who owned it, and who was waiting on a park bench for their return. Whereupon they disappeared.

"The emergency room staff," Scott added, "revived Mr. Mulligan, but not without difficulty. He had a large amount of a powerful antipsychotic drug in his system.

"Some time later, Mr. Mulligan woke up with a roar, and though he was under restraint, somehow got to his feet, and with his hospital bed strapped to his back, slammed the doctor who was treating him against the wall, knocking him unconscious, and then, with two nurses in flight before him, charged down the ward, upsetting carts, overturning several dispensing machines, and in general terrifying patients and staff. When the police arrived, he was slamming the bed into the wall in an apparent attempt to free himself. Two police officers who attempted to subdue him were injured. They called for backup, and after more humane methods failed to do the job, the police fired Tasers into Mr. Mulligan's body. Three Taser darts were necessary to subdue him.

"The cops placed the unconscious Mulligan in a straitjacket and shackles and transported him to Bellevue Hospital, which was better equipped to deal with him. There, he was medicated and placed under heavy restraint.

"When, after Mr. Mulligan had become somewhat calmer, two police detectives interviewed him," Scott said. "He told them, in the presence of a staff psychologist, that he had been strolling in Central Park, minding his own business, when a woman wearing a floppy beret rose up out of the wheelchair in which she had been riding and pointed a large brown pistol at him. He had no doubt that she intended to shoot him. He had no idea why she was pointing a gun at him. He assumed she was a maniac. Fearing for his life, and seeing no way to flee through the heavy crowd without causing the woman to open fire and perhaps kill innocent persons by mistake, he ran toward her, intending to disarm her, or failing that, heroically absorb the bullets that might otherwise have wounded or killed innocent bystanders.

"At that moment, someone threw a net over him and injected him with a drug that rendered him unconscious."

Scott paused to drink a little more water.

"Mr. Mulligan then stated that he had reason to believe that his assailants were in the pay of Mr. Henry Peel," he said, "and that you, my dear, were responsible for the attack. You had, he stated, poisoned Mr. Peel's mind against him by telling outrageous lies about him. This had resulted in the abrupt withdrawal of Mr. Peel's support for his, Mr. Mulligan's, extremely important dinosaur dig in Mongolia, and in his ignominious expulsion from China by friends of Mr. Peel's in the Chinese secret police. He stated that you and Mr. Peel are intimate friends, and that he is going to sue Henry Peel for every penny he has and also file charges of assault with a deadly weapon and attempted murder against you. And that, my dear young lady, is why I am here. To help you."

He and Clementine looked at me like a couple of bright-eyed old parrots hoping for a cracker.

I said politely, "Help me in what way?"

"With advice, with guidance," he said. "It's easy to put a foot wrong in this kind of situation."

"What kind of situation would that be, Mr. Scott?"

"Surely you see the potential for embarrassment, or worse, for yourself and others."

"Surely you're not suggesting," I replied, "that the police or the hospital or anyone else could possibly have believed Mulligan's story."

"No," said Scott. "They took it for the ravings of a deranged person. That is not the point. The point is that this man Mulligan does not intend that it should end with the police. A jury might very well believe the story. It is, after all, largely factual. Worse, it is one hell of a story for the media. It will be published. Your picture and the most intimate details of your past and present life will be splashed all over television and the press. It will cause a sensation. You are known to the public, and you are also, if I may say so on such very short acquaintance, most photogenic. You have a reputation as the author of daring books. In terms of journalistic appetite, that's an irresistible combination. The media will follow up. They will find out more. It will be extremely unpleasant."

Scott's voice did not change in any way as he spoke these words, nor did the urbane expression on his face.

"You seem to be very well informed, Mr. Scott," I said. "I assume that you are aware of the history between Bear Mulligan and myself?"

"I am, indeed," he said. "I have read the record. It was a revolting crime. But the charges against Mulligan were dismissed. In the eyes of the law, therefore, he is as innocent as a newborn babe. In the eyes of the media, the allegation of rape and his exoneration, not to mention the drama in Central Park, are grist for the mill—just another compelling reason to do the story and make the profit. That is the reality with which we must deal."

"The reality is that Bear Mulligan is a monster," I said. "He's a psychopath. He always has been. What happened in Central Park happened because he had threatened to tear my head off and he had come there, stalking me, to do exactly that. He was entirely capable of doing it in the presence of hundreds of witnesses, crazy enough and strong enough to do it. He intended to do it. He was on the point of doing it when Clementine's people did what they did to stop him. That's why he was there. That's why they were there."

Scott sighed. This was the first sign he had given that he was not utterly imperturbable.

"I accept that to be the truth of the matter," he said. "However."

"However what?"

"Even if Mulligan is all the things you say he is, even if he did intend to murder you in cold blood, he is in fact also a former All-American football player, much beloved in Texas and remembered by football fans everywhere. He is also a distinguished paleontologist who has made important discoveries, written books, appeared on television, and lectured all over the country. In his way, he too is very photogenic. These facts are stored in the mother memory to which all journalists have access. They will be stimulated to recover these data and turn them into money. It is their nature."

"Why do you keep on telling me there is no hope?" I asked.

"If I thought there was no hope, I wouldn't be here," Scott said.

Scott shot his cuff and looked at his watch.

"I must run," he said.

He smiled at me—big square, well-kept teeth, avuncular twinkle, eyes on my chest. Then he said, "May I have your answer before I go?"

"What is the question?"

"Shall we work together on this problem?"

"I'll think about it," I said.

"Fine," Scott said. "Perhaps we can chat some more over dinner tonight. I know a nice quiet little place just around the corner."

I said, "I think we've chatted enough for one day, thank you."

Scott looked through me as if I were someone who happened to be on the same elevator as he was. Clementine opened her eyes wide, cocked her head, looked annoyed. I was *such* a bother.

Downstairs, the chaps awaited—one in the lobby, one on the sidewalk, one across the street. Now that I knew they were there, I was a camera, searching the blurred crowd and pulling Tom (*whirr-click*), Dick (*whirr-click*), and Harry (*whirr-click*) out of the multitude and into focus.

3

AS I WALKED WITH THE crowd, I called Melissa. When she picked up, I heard her kids having a fight in the background. She sounded disheartened. Ordinarily I would have shouted something encouraging over the din and hung up, but I needed her counsel. I asked if I could come over.

"You do hear what's going on here?" she said.

"Yeah, but I figure you'll have sent them to their rooms by the time I get there."

"You should be so lucky."

By the time I got to her apartment, the kids were in angelic mode. We knew one another well. I had been their babysitter of last resort ever since they were born. On Melissa's instructions, they called me Auntie. They were as beautiful as Greeks on an urn and painfully bright—no surprise considering who their mother was and the fact that Melissa wasn't the sort of girl who married stupid, homely men. We ate kiddies' macaroni and cheese for dinner. If you put ketchup on it, it's almost as good as Chef Boyardee. The kids cleaned their plates—a peace offering to their mother, I supposed. She responded in kind by not insisting that they eat their salad.

Dutiful kisses for Auntie followed, real ones for Mom. Then the kids disappeared into their rooms.

Melissa knew all about the capture of Bear Mulligan and his plans for the future. I told her about Adam, including his neurotic break on seeing the apartment for the first time. To my surprise, this was news to her. She listened attentively, asking nudging little questions from time to time. She didn't ask why I had been crazy enough to invite Adam into the apartment in the first place. Some things are too stupid to be mentioned.

"I've got to say you're worrying about the right things," Melissa said when I had finished. "This guy—Adam?—doesn't sound like a share person."

"He's pretty square."

"Then he'll be easy to replace. He's the least of your worries."

She was right, of course. For Melissa, that was not enough. Without skipping a breath, she told me the reasons why she was right.

"First of all, the story is false. You and Henry are not sexual partners."

"You're absolutely sure of that?"

Melissa snorted. "Yes, I am," she replied. "The story will be published. Elway Scott was right. It's irresistible."

"I've always gotten along fine with the media. Mostly, they're nice people."

"This time you're not going on a book tour."

"So what are you advising me to do?"

"Shut up and weather the storm," Melissa said. "Neither confirm nor deny anything. Do not speak a word to the media. Confide in no one—no one—about anything. Avoid cameras if you can, but don't cover your face like a perp when the media starts camping outside your building."

"How would they find it?"

"They have ways. If Adam is pissed enough at your alleged infidelity, and he certainly sounds like the type, he could give a reporter the address, plus a glimpse of the splendor in which you live on

Henry's nickel. A virtual tour of the apartment would be grist for a week's stories. 'Artist's impression of love nest.' If Adam keeps his mouth shut, they might follow you."

"In spite of Clementine's chaps?"

"The chaps don't have enough nets to capture this particular plague of locusts," Melissa said. "Those people are like the secret police—no warrants required, no limits, no consequences, no conscience. Show trials are their bread and butter."

"Maybe I'm the one who should go away," I said.

"Not a bad idea," Melissa said. "You could move to Nuku Hiva if it gets too bad. Or Hsi-tau. The chow chows would deal with the press. Bear is banned from China, but if he does find you and you want the creep shot or locked up forever, General Yao is your man. You could finish your novel in peace and quiet."

"And celibacy."

"Celibacy worked for Catherine of Siena."

From the lobby of Melissa's building, I called Adam. There was no harm in finding out if he was still mad. He knew my voice at once. He acted as if nothing had happened.

I decided to be charming, too. I said, "What are you up to?"

"Waiting for the phone to ring," he said. "Please hold. I have to make a call."

He was back on the line in thirty seconds.

"Same hotel, as quick as you can get there," he said. "They upgraded us to a suite."

"Lovely," I said.

I set off into the night, the chaps trotting along behind, beside, and before me like so many chow chows.

4

THE STORY BROKE. BY EVENING Henry and I were the stars of a thousand blogs. By the following morning it had spilled over into television news and the few newsprint tabloids—now weeklies distributed free of charge from unlocked sidewalk boxes—that had survived the rise of electronic journalism. No broadsheet newspapers remained except as websites—digital ghosts of the glorious old trollops that in their day had rubbed printer's ink into their victims' wounds.

The story and its biases were pretty much as anticipated. If you want to sell gossip, you can't go wrong by going after a trillionaire. Bear was the victim, Henry the villain. "Who is the real Henry Peel?" asked the Kens and Barbies of cable news. If he was human enough to have a paramour, he was their kind of guy—like Citizen Kane, like Jack Kennedy, like all those lucky stiffs who took their pick of the chicks. Vintage pictures of Bear in his football uniform and in the Stetson and ostrich-skin cowboy boots he wore when digging up fossils made the point that he was a real all-American. Jumpy old film clips of his comic-book exploits in championship games and his big, charming postgame aw-shucks grins for the camera certified his credentials.

Clementine and I had not spoken since the encounter with

ARK

Scott and I wondered if we would ever speak again, but she duti-
fully informed me, in a curt phone call, that a mob of journalists
had gathered at the entrance of my old apartment. The chaps were
keeping an eye on them, so if the swarm showed signs of changing
location, I would be informed.

Henry did not call. Who knew what he thought?

Adam didn't call, either. We had been together almost every
night, all night, for the past week and a half. During our last rendezvous, at the usual hotel, I had presented him with my O. Laster
watercolor. I wrapped the wonderful thing in layers of brown paper
and carried it to the hotel on my lap in the back of a taxi.

He opened it at once, not pausing to read my Hallmark card, ripping paper and throwing it all over the room like a small boy in a
Christmas-morning frenzy. He knew it was a picture, of course, but
what picture? I had such a lot of them. When he saw that it was the
watercolor, he let out a yelp.

He said, "I hope you don't imagine I'm going to say I can't possibly accept such a gift."

What could I do but look pleased? Not that Adam noticed. He
rushed to a wall, took down the lifeless hotel-room print of a quaint
covered bridge that hung there, and replaced it with Clementine's
watercolor. He backed rapidly away from it, eyes fixed upon it, arms
extended as if dancing with the invisible woman of his dreams.

The picture changed the room, as if it had somehow let in more
light. Because so much drabness surrounded so little color, the
opposite ought to have been true, but there you are. And there we
were. We went to bed with the lights on, so Adam could keep looking at the picture. I didn't really mind sharing.

In the morning, earlier than usual, Adam took his painting off
the wall and left. As we parted, he gave me a regulation farewell-my-
lover look of affection and remembered pleasure, but what he was
really remembering was the watercolor.

He said, "Thank you, my love. This is the nicest thing anyone
ever gave me. I'll never let it go."

Was he saying one thing and hoping I thought he was saying another? Was he saying good-bye? Was he faking it? Had he faked his jealousy? Was the answer all of the above?

Bear's lawyers applied for a writ of habeas corpus. He hadn't been charged with a crime because the chaps had prevented him from committing one, but he was still under observation at Bellevue. A Solomonic judge released him when he volunteered, through his lawyer, to pay for the damage he had done to hospital property and leave New York at once and never return. The blonde with the décolletage and the microphone who interviewed him as he emerged from the courthouse treated him like a teddy bear.

"How do you feel after your ordeal, Professor Mulligan?"

"Kinda dazed, to tell you the truth. This whole thing has been a big old bad dream."

"So what's next?"

"The airport and the first plane back to Texas," Bear said. "I've learned one thing for sure: New York ain't no place for a country boy."

"Tell me, professor, what brought you to New York in the first place?"

"I thought I might be able to help folks out—the earthquake and all."

The camera watched him out of sight. He was wearing his big Stetson, and that plus the high-heeled boots added enough to his height to push him well over seven feet, dirt to dandruff. Somehow the producers resisted the temptation to play Willie Nelson singing "Red Headed Stranger" as America's most picturesque homicidal maniac walked into the sunset.

5

HENRY CAME BACK. HE ALWAYS did. He was in his bodhisattva mode, tranquil and disconnected from all unpleasantry. He said nothing about the media storm. Plainly he was not in the least interested in it. I felt a pang of irritation and envy that he should be so detached while I was so entangled.

Preoccupied as I was by my plight, I missed the first few words that Henry spoke to me. I vaguely realized that he was talking about the embryos. I thought he said something about Amerigo. By the time I started paying attention, he was four or five sentences into his opening paragraph, and I just couldn't figure out what he was trying to tell me.

I said, "Henry, forgive me, but I've lost the thread. Can you please start over from the beginning?"

He stopped in midword.

"Sure," Henry said. "I was saying that I wanted you to consider a proposal that may strike you as being, well, a little odd."

Was this a Jane Austen moment? Surely not.

I said, "Not to worry, Henry. Go right ahead."

"When I was small, my father used to call me his messenger to the future," Henry said.

"How nice."

"He was a nice man," Henry said. "When Amerigo told us about the doctor who sold passages for embryos aboard the mother ship, I realized that every man wants a messenger to the future. That includes me. I'm not quite sure how to put this to you, but what I'd like to propose to you is that you and I provide an embryo—actually more than one—to sail with the others on the ship."

I said, "Henry, you take my breath away. How long have you been thinking these thoughts?"

"As I said, ever since Amerigo reported the sabotage," he said. "I've hesitated to bring it up because I'm uncertain about the ethics of the thing."

"What ethics?"

"It's a selfish act, maybe even an abuse of power."

What was a selfish act? Impregnating me? I had no idea what to say.

Henry, watching whatever was going on with my face, said, "Wait a minute."

"Gladly."

"Don't misunderstand me," Henry said. "I'm talking about in vitro fertilization."

Of course he was. How could I have imagined otherwise? I visualized the procedure—ova and sperm stirred together by a lab technician, life awakening, cells multiplying.

Clearing my throat, I said, "Why me?"

Henry grinned. "Because there's no other possible candidate."

What did he mean by that? I decided not to ask.

I said, "This is sort of sudden, Henry. If you don't mind, I'd like a little time to think it over."

SIX

1

THE THOUGHT OF CONCEIVING YET another child I would never know or see was not a happy one. Supposing I lived long enough, would I be as haunted by him or her—or them, since Henry had spoken of producing more than one embryo—as I had been by the lost child that Bear had left behind him along with my broken bones? I had a thousand questions. Why hadn't I asked a single one?

I couldn't deal with this. I needed to get my mind off it. I needed a break. I tried six or seven times to call Adam but got his voice mail. Finally I decided to go hunting for him in SoHo. He seldom left his neighborhood at night. I knew his favorite places. I would surprise him—just bump into him. I packed an overnight bag. I had a plan.

The BMW that Henry had loaned me when last we visited Amerigo in his mansion on the Hudson was still parked in the basement of my building. I had supposed that someone would collect it and return it to its owner, but no one did. Although the car had been sitting there for more than a month, it started right up. The chaps spotted me at once and followed me down the West Side Highway in a bulbous, midnight-blue sedan. When I pulled into a parking lot, the sedan pulled in behind me. Adam's building was a block or two away from the parking lot. I walked to it, chaps lurking along beside and behind, and rang the buzzer. Adam's distorted voice issued from the ancient, crackling speaker.

I said, "It's me."

A long, long silence ensued. Finally Adam buzzed me in. At his door, I had to ring again. A delay ensued. I put my ear to the door—no sounds within—and counted to fifty, telling myself that I would walk away if I got to fifty—make that a hundred—and the silence remained unbroken. At the count of seventy-nine, he opened the door, but left it on the chain. Through the crack, I could see two-thirds of his face. He needed a shave. His hair was tousled. His eyes were resentful. Clearly he was angry again.

Finally, abruptly, he slammed the door. The End? Apparently not. The chain rattled. The door opened completely. Adam's lips were compressed into a thin line, his eyes were averted. Based on his behavior the last time he got jealous and underwent a personality change, I had expected accusation, anger, a tantrum. What to make of this sullen passivity? Since eye contact didn't seem to be on the menu, I looked past him into the apartment—chaos in the living room, and beyond it, the kitchen sink full of dirty dishes, garbage can overflowing, pizza boxes and empty bottles and cans everywhere. Where were the roaches, the rats that ought to have been nibbling on this mess? On the telephone he had been wonderful. Now he was crazy again. Something had happened between the call and this moment.

I said, "Have you ever considered getting professional help?"

"*I'm* the one who needs a shrink?" Adam said.

"I meant a cleaning woman."

"I told you. She quit. The earthquake shook her up."

Progress. He was talking, volunteering information—looking at me, even. Pretty soon he'd start yelling. Before that happened, I wanted to get him out of here. Adam was fully dressed—quite becomingly dressed, as usual, in khaki shorts and old boat shoes with untied laces and no socks and a black muscle shirt.

I said, "Look, we can't stay here. Let's find neutral ground and talk this out."

"Talk what out?"

"The vicissitudes of life," I said.

"Why do you think everything is a joke?"

"I don't. Come on, let's go for a ride."

"I don't want to lose my parking space," Adam replied. He had shifted from sneer to sarcasm.

"That's OK," I said. "I've got a car."

"Rolls-Royce or Lamborghini?"

I said, "BMW. Let's go."

He shrugged—what did it matter?—and followed me down the corridor to the elevator. He even pushed the button for the lobby. This wasn't much of a gesture, but it was a start. I didn't ask him to drive. Whatever feeble control I now had, I meant to keep. Besides, I had a destination in mind.

When we crossed the Triborough Bridge and got onto the Hutchinson Parkway, Adam said, "Where are we going?"

"What time do you have to be in court tomorrow?"

"Tomorrow is Sunday. Remember?"

The midnight-blue sedan was still following us. Probably another one just like it was a half mile ahead of the BMW. The chaps never slept.

I said, "Do you know how to turn on the radio?"

Adam switched it on. The satellite station it was tuned to played nothing but songs of the 1940s—Crosby, Sinatra, Margaret Whiting, Doris Day before she sounded like Doris Day. It was sweet. Cheek-to-cheek music. We didn't talk. Adam didn't ask where we were going. The miles flew by. Somewhere between Lee and Lenox the headlights illuminated a sign for the resort hotel we were headed for. I made the turn and in minutes we were parked by the front door. Adam stayed in the car while I went inside, taking the car keys with me so he couldn't flee. They had a room available—a very nice suite, in fact. Adam was still in the passenger seat when I came out to fetch him. I didn't see the chaps, but that didn't mean they weren't there.

The suite *was* lovely. It smelled of dried rose petals and potpourri. The owners had gone to a lot of trouble with authenticity. Within these walls it was 1890 again. A young waiter with twenty-first-century manners brought the bottle of prosecco and the plates of smoked fish and salad I ordered. The wine was too cold, Adam said. It seemed fine to me, but I just smiled.

He showered first. When I emerged after mine he said, "Is this when we have our fight?"

"Tomorrow," I replied.

Because of the aphrodisiacal effect of anger, the night was somewhat pornographic. In the morning, the promised denunciations flew. It wasn't much of a quarrel, but it did the job. Even while it was going on I didn't know what it was about, really, but I knew a valedictory when I heard one.

After breakfast, I don't know why, we went for a walk in the woods. The path followed a shallow brook that ran over a series of granite ledges. The path wasn't wide enough for two people to walk abreast. Adam went ahead. The laces of his scuffed old boat shoes whipped around his bony ankles at every step. His khaki shorts were a size too large for him and he had to keep pulling them up because he wore no belt. After half an hour or so, he stopped, and without turning around, waited for me to catch up. At this point the brook ran through a narrow ravine, its waters bouncing off smooth round stones and throwing up mist.

He said, "So what's the truth?"

At that moment, a black bear, large and glossy, emerged from the underbrush on the opposite side of the ravine. The wind was in my face, so I guessed the animal didn't smell us or just didn't think that human beings were much of a threat. The bushes parted again and a roly-poly cub emerged. I poked Adam and pointed at the bears. He didn't look. He was waiting for his answer.

"Bears," I whispered.

By the time Adam turned around and looked, the bears were gone—they had just faded back into the woods as if they had never been there.

ARK

"The truth about what?" I said to Adam's back.

"Come on," he said, turning around. "Let's get it over with."

"OK. The truth is that the world is going to come to an end and this will happen quite soon."

"Cut it out."

"I'm serious. The end is near."

"What's the use?" Adam said. "You can't be serious about anything."

"You want truth? You're a lawyer. Cross-examine."

"How can I cross-examine someone who invents bears as a way of changing the subject?"

"Are you asking if you can believe what you read in the newspapers?"

"Yes."

"The answer is no."

He said, "Then you don't know Henry Peel?"

"I didn't say that."

"Henry Peel didn't bestow on you that apartment or its contents or the BMW?"

"I didn't say that, either."

"Will you say whether you're screwing Henry Peel?"

He uttered these words with a twisted, man-of-the-world smile.

I said, "Nor will I say that."

Adam said, "In other words, the answer is yes."

"Wake up, Adam. I won't say it because you have no right to ask."

"Oh, really?"

"Really. What licenses you to police my life?"

"The crimes you commit."

I said, "Oh. I wondered."

Adam said, "Oh, the hell with it."

He kissed me. It was a gesture, not an impulse. I didn't kiss him back, just let it happen. The lust was lost and gone forever.

Nevertheless I said, "What would you say to spending another night here?"

"If we're going to do that, maybe I should buy some clothes," he said.

I picked them out for him at a local Geoffrey Beene outlet. Without protest, Adam let me pay for his new khakis and polo shirts and a belt, plus underwear and a sweater and a new pair of Top-Siders, as if I had all the money in the world, or at least a credit card that a trillionaire covered for me. Which I did.

Our second night at the hotel was chaste. We dined, we drank, we were kind to each other. We slept in the same bed. It seemed strange without the usual aromas. Around midnight the crystal chandelier rattled. The bed shook. I thought the tremor was a local event. My earthquake research had informed me that there are dormant faults—big ones—under Massachusetts. We got up at five and drove back to the city. When we pulled up in front of Adam's building, he made no move to kiss, touch, or even look at me. He just sat there expressionless, staring through the windshield.

I said, "Hey."

Eyes averted, Adam said, "Hey."

No tears, no last look, no rueful smile. He just got out of the car and closed the door behind him. I watched him walk across the sidewalk. He wore the shorts and muscle shirt he had worn on the way up to the Berkshires. He left the things I had bought for him in the trunk of the car. On the way uptown I stopped at a trash can and got rid of them.

2

NOT LONG AFTER MY WEEKEND with Adam, Clementine called and invited herself to tea. I was somewhat flustered. Naturally she would want to pay her watercolor a visit. What was I supposed to tell her when it wasn't where it ought to be? If Clementine asked what had happened to the painting, I would have no choice but to tell her the truth—if only because she probably already knew it.

In any event, Clementine was the soul of good nature. She ate two pieces of butter cake and small-talked like a schoolgirl. Finally she touched the corners of her lips with the square linen napkin and put down her cup.

"Lovely tea," she said. "Now, I do have something rather important to tell you."

I waited.

"We feel that the Mulligan situation has stabilized somewhat," Clementine said. "He's back at his university, lecturing and basking in the injustice that was done to him. All very reassuring, but of course he's a psychopath, so one can't afford to be too tremendously reassured by appearances. We'll continue to keep a close lookout."

"I'm glad to hear it," I said.

Clementine said, "There's one more thing. It's a bit disturbing. Shall I go on?"

"Please do."

"We have been making inquiries. Our operation is still in early phases, I'm afraid," she said. "But we may be on to something. Your broken arm and the manner in which it was inflicted have fascinated me. Mulligan did it deliberately, I gather?"

"Yes. He snapped it over his knee."

"The pain must have been excruciating."

"It was."

"Have you any theory as to why he did it?"

"Apart from the fun of it?"

"Yes. Did you think it had a practical side effect?"

"It rendered me unconscious."

"So you don't remember the rape itself?"

"I'm not sure what I remember."

"One doesn't," Clementine said. "Rapists nearly always rape again, you know, and many of them tend to ritualize their methods. They do the same things over and over again in exactly the same manner so as to perfect the thrill. Of course this is never entirely possible, which is why they keep on raping."

Where was Clementine going with this? I asked her the question.

"It occurred to me that Mulligan might be that sort of rapist," she replied. "If he raped again and broke another arm or two or three or more, the police who investigated the crime would note the detail."

"Supposing the rape was reported," I said.

"Yes, or a body found. I have a strong feeling that there were bodies. You had a lucky escape. Perhaps you were the first and he hadn't yet fully established his modus operandi. If we can establish that Mulligan was a serial killer, the problem would go away forever."

I saw. I said, "You're telling me that you have a hunch."

"A wild surmise, you might say," Clementine replied. "But many crimes, if not most, are solved by the follow-up to what you've just called a hunch."

"And have you found evidence that matches your hunch?"

"Not yet. We've made a list of places to which Mulligan has traveled, and sent inquiries to the police in all those places, on the chance that there might have been matches in terms of broken arms connected with rapes when he was in the neighborhood."

She paused for effect.

I asked, "And have the police replied?"

"Not yet. But they will. I know a good many of them personally, so they won't ignore the request. Not that most of them would ignore it whoever was asking. To an honest copper, a crime committed five thousand kilometers away or ten years in the past is as much a personal concern as a crime committed ten minutes ago in his own precinct."

She had more that she wanted to say. This was written all over her face. I waited for her to say it.

"Let me ask you this," Clementine said. "Do you doubt that Mulligan would have put an end to you if he had got his hands on you that day in Central Park?"

"No."

"And why do you think he wished to kill you?"

"Hatred. Disgust. Revenge. Madness."

"All those reasons were no doubt valid," said Clementine. "But that wasn't his real purpose."

"Then what was his real purpose?"

Clementine leaned forward in her chair. "He was tidying up."

"You're losing me."

"Think about it," said Clementine. "You were probably his first victim. If he killed all the other women he raped and broke their arms as he broke yours, you're the only living witness to his identity. You can link him to his method. You are a danger to him. He doesn't want to get caught before he gets it right, don't you see."

I saw.

3

IT TURNED OUT THAT THE tremor in the Berkshires originated in Iceland. A moderate earthquake occurred in the countryside about a hundred miles from Reykjavík. Houses were destroyed. Sheep were asphyxiated, but no human beings died. No one, not even Henry, knew how long these small mercies would continue. Few besides him took any great interest in this pox of seismic events. As a result of its long experience with the deity, humanity tended to look upward for doomsday—a giant meteor like the one that supposedly wiped out the dinosaurs, or maybe a black hole that would eat the universe, compress it to the size of a molecule or something even smaller, then free it from gravity and let loose another Big Bang.

It took me three days or so to realize that Adam was gone forever. He wasn't gone from my mind, and I bore him no ill will, but wherever he was now, he was doing me no good. Mentally, I put him in the ground and covered him up. And after that, like a young widow passing cookies at a wake, I might have returned a certain kind of look if one came my way. None did. The whole world was leaving me alone with a vengeance.

Then the refrain: Henry called. He asked the usual question. I said of course I could fly tomorrow.

"Where we're going, it may be a little cooler than New York," he said. "There may be a dinner party."

Henry was already there. Or on his way there from somewhere else.

My mystery destination turned out to be Paris. The house to which I was driven was in the Marais, between the Place des Vosges and the river. It was very early in the morning, before first light. When I rang the doorbell a tall young African, thin as an eyelash, wearing a silk dressing gown, let me in frozen-faced, then disappeared. I waited fifteen minutes for him to come back. This didn't happen. Supposing that the African had gone back to bed, I wandered deeper into the house. I heard someone coming down the stairs. Henry intercepted me in the orangery, in which actual orange trees and other exotic plants grew in wooden tubs. He seemed glad to see me and led me into the garden. It was lovely. Dew sparkled on the flowers. Whimsically pollarded hedges made me smile. Fountains played, dispersing a faint aroma of chlorine. Birds sang. The day was bright and breezy. The sigh of traffic on the quais was muted because it was so early in the morning.

After changing into jeans and sneakers, Henry and I went for a walk along the river. We sat down on a bench just beyond the Pont de la Concorde.

Henry said, "Have you decided?"

"About the embryo?" I asked.

"Yes."

"Something about it troubles me," I said.

"Specifically?"

"Are you planning to enhance this embryo?"

"Interesting question," Henry replied.

"Because if you are, Henry," I said, "I don't see the point of the exercise. The child won't be the child we made."

"Children," Henry corrected. "Amerigo's people can produce a large number of embryos in vitro."

I said, "Won't they be all alike?"

"They'd be siblings, not clones."

"But Amerigo's people would manipulate their DNA?"

"You're still troubled by that?"

"Henry, I will never cease to be troubled by that," I replied. "I think it negates the entire purpose of the enterprise."

"So you're saying no?"

"I'm saying you should reconsider."

"What if that means the embryos aren't strong enough to survive? Or if they do, they'll live a life of slavery to the enhanced?"

"That's a leap."

"You think so?"

Henry frowned, for him the equivalent of a shout. The two of us fell silent.

How many lovers' quarrels is it possible to have in less than a month? Answer: It depends on how many lovers and how many issues you have. Adam and I had put an end to the best sex either of us had ever experienced with the exchange of two monosyllables. Now Henry and I seemed to be free-falling toward another sad ending while talking our heads off. Adam had been my lover, and I had loved his body, but I say again, I hadn't loved him and never could have. It had never crossed my mind that he and I might produce a child, or that either one of us would want it to survive if we did. On the other hand, Henry was not my lover and I had never let myself feel physical attraction to him, but I loved him. In fact, I was an inch away from being in love with him. Having a child with him, even though it might be conceived in a laboratory, and even though I would never see it and would never know what happened to it, would be a wonderful thing. The two of us would be joined together in the child, and in its children. I wanted to protect it, I *had* to protect it. This was something my blood instructed me to do.

Nevertheless, my impulse, all but irresistible, was to just say yes. I resisted it.

"This is getting us nowhere," I said. "I'm going for a run."

Henry said, "Does that mean the discussion is over?"

"It means I need time to think. Running helps me think."

"I'll come, too," Henry said.

We ran all the way to the Eiffel Tower, crossed the Seine on the Pont d'Iéna, and ran back along the Left Bank. There were people everywhere. No doubt the chaps encircled us, but as usual they were unseen. As my body warmed up and my mind calmed down, an inexplicable mixture of worry and happiness flooded my being.

I was hungry by the time we got back to the house. We had both broken a sweat. The morning air was damp and chilly. A sharp wind blew. I shivered.

Henry said, "You should take a hot shower."

"Then what?"

Henry wiped his sweaty face with his bare forearm.

"Let's see what the day brings," he said.

I saw him again at breakfast, served by the anorexic young African who was now dressed for company in a black jacket and striped pants. While Henry ate, he read *Le Monde* on an iPad. Once or twice he read excerpts aloud, translating them at sight into English. The tableau was Victorian—Father reading the paper in a good loud voice, Mother smiling happily as he shared the most interesting bits with her.

Finally, Henry shut down his iPad and said, "Shall we wrap this up?"

Wrap what up? The question of the embryo? Breakfast? Everything? Of course I knew exactly what he was talking about.

I said, "Henry, I'm truly torn."

"I know," he said. "Do you want more time to think?"

"I don't think time is going to be my friend in this situation," I said. "May I ask you a question?"

He didn't say no.

I said, thinking of Melissa, "Suppose I just can't do it. Then what happens?"

"In what sense?"

"If not me, who?"

Henry was surprised by the question. What's more—talk about breakthroughs—he made no effort to conceal his surprise.

He said, "There are no backup candidates."

"There aren't? Why?"

He didn't answer—not even a change of expression, not even a shrug. For better or worse, I was the lucky girl. I could not understand this choice, but I did not press the issue. Sometimes even I know when to shut up. Maybe Henry himself didn't understand it, on the conscious level. Maybe he had made up his mind about this in the same way he invented things that shook the world. It just happened. Now, clearly, the moment had come for me to say yes or no. I told myself I was making too big a thing of this, that my moral objections were a pretense. When it came right down to it, scruples had seldom applied to much of anything in my life or as far as I could see, in anyone else's. Whatever they might blame for their errors and misfortunes, people did what they wanted to do.

The fact was, I *wanted* to do this even though my every corpuscle advised me not to do it. Choose life was the law of the blood. Live forever somehow, anyhow. The embryos, messengers to the future, could in theory live forever, or until they were thawed, warmed in a bath of water, and commanded to wake up. And then they would be fertile and multiply, carrying Henry's DNA and mine, mingled forever, into whatever future awaited them and our ghosts.

I knew this was malarkey, of course I knew, but speechless as a maiden in a bodice ripper, I gave Henry my answer by touching his hand and sweetly nodding my head. I had tears in my eyes. In a love story, Henry would have kissed me. No such luck. Nevertheless, I had been chosen by Mr. Darcy out of all the girls in the world.

Later that morning we flew to Milan, where in Amerigo's laboratory a young doctor harvested my ova—he didn't tell me how many—and passed them to his assistant, who carried them off to their rendezvous in the petri dish.

SEVEN

1

IT TOOK CLEMENTINE MANY MONTHS to nail Bear Mulligan, but in the end she managed it. She found seven cases in six different places of very young women who had been raped and murdered while Bear was known to have been in the vicinity. All had compound fractures of the left arm.

"Two in Venezuela, one each in Arizona and Colorado," Clementine told me. "Three in China—two in Beijing, one near Hohhot in Inner Mongolia. The murderer's DNA was found at the crime scenes in the U.S. and Beijing. The specimens match Bear's DNA."

To deliver this news, she had invited me to tea in her offices on Fifty-fifth Street. She seemed to be alone in the large suite, but maybe she wasn't. The doors of all the other offices were closed. Phones rang, but only once before they were answered by man or machine. One of the smaller offices had been converted into a cozy sitting room, with soft lighting and floral slipcovers on the chairs and sofa. Although it was December, the thermostat was set at no more than fifty degrees Fahrenheit. You could practically see your breath. I shuddered. Clementine wore a blouse with short sleeves.

"This might be upsetting, but you should be aware of the facts," Clementine said between bites of cake. "Both American victims quite strikingly resemble you. The others were about your size and slim, like you. And as young as you were when you were attacked."

"What happens now?" I asked.

"Ah, that is the question," Clementine said. "The cases are cold. The evidence is circumstantial, however unequivocal it might be. A clever lawyer—and America teems with them—might get the charges thrown out."

"What about Venezuela?"

"Just as chancy for quite different reasons. Another lunatic is in charge there."

"Then nothing will happen?"

"Actually, something *is* happening," Clementine said. "Mulligan has been soliciting funds for his research ever since Henry pulled the rug out from under him. No luck until a couple of weeks ago, when an obscure foundation in Liechtenstein offered him a modest grant. It's not a great deal of money, only a couple of hundred thousand euros, but enough for a summer's dig."

"What sort of dig did Bear propose?"

"He thinks he has a line on *Gigantoraptors*. As I understand it, this was a very large, feathered, carnivorous dinosaur that resembled a bird. An adolescent specimen that stood thirty feet high and weighed three thousand pounds was discovered, but no fossil of an adult has yet been found."

"Where does Bear propose to look for this thing?"

"China. Inner Mongolia, actually. Not so very far from Hsi-tau."

"I thought Bear was banned from China for life."

"Indeed he is," Clementine said. "But he's been in touch with General Yao, who is said to be willing to reconsider his case."

Our eyes met. Nothing resembling a clue showed in hers. A beautiful big-eared, blue-eyed, plump Siamese cat that had been hiding behind the sofa emerged and leaped onto Clementine's lap.

To the cat she said, "Hewwo, tommykins."

"Meet my friend Dickens," she said, tickling the cat's throat. "I understand Mulligan means to fly to Beijing over the holidays," Clementine said. "No doubt General Yao will weigh all the facts and render a fair decision."

Dickens was sniffing Clementine. It meowed, then meowed again, louder. To the cat, Clementine said in plain English, "You want a treat, do you, you incorrigible tomcat?"

The cat meowed again.

Clementine got out a box of chocolates. The cat went crazy when it smelled it. Clementine chose a chocolate with a soft white center, and holding it above her head, out of Dickens's reach, broke off a piece, and fed it to him. She popped the rest of the chocolate into her own mouth.

"They have a bit of catnip in them," Clementine said. "They're not good for him, you know. But he's mad about chocolates as long as they're not awful sticky caramel. Aren't you, Dickens?"

2

MY NOVEL WAS PUBLISHED. OWING to my fifteen minutes of tabloid infamy, the mainstream media paid more attention than usual. At first, all was routine. I read in bookstores as usual and chatted with readers and made the rounds of the television and radio stations. On camera, every interviewer asked the same five questions—all of them variations on "What is Henry Peel really like?" I replied in many different ways and at various lengths that it was my understanding that Mr. Peel was a very private person. Was the novel really a roman à clef about Henry and me? I was not offended by these brainless inquiries. The interviewers were just practicing their profession. So was I. It was fun to bob and weave and change the subject and slip the title of my novel into the conversation. They held up the book for the camera and voiced the title and my name with admirable diction. From my publisher's point of view, and mine too, this was the whole purpose of the exercise. The book sold approximately three times better in its first week than any other I had ever published.

Early one morning toward the end of the second week of this publicity whirl, I did a gig on the *Samantha Slye Show*, a morning cable program watched mostly by stay-at-home moms. Samantha, known for her off-the-wall questions, ambushed me by holding up an advance copy of one of the more brazen tabloids. Page one featured a photo of Adam and me, intertwined and kissing outside a midtown hotel—our hotel—whose sign showed clearly in the background. Superimposed on this picture was a smaller one, about the size of passport photo, showing the two of us walking toward the camera with our arms around each other. We were quite recognizable. The headline, in big comic-book type, read:

"EXCLUSIVE!! She cheated on Multi-Trillionaire!!"

Samantha Slye said, "Some girls have all the luck. Who *is* that dreamboat?"

I didn't answer.

Samantha said, "Are you going to identify this guy or not?"

I shook my head no. The director fed Samantha another question. I could hear the crackle of his voice in her earpiece.

"Is the man you're kissing Henry Peel?"

I shook my head no.

"Is he as yummy as he looks?"

I shook my head yes.

Samantha giggled. This was fun. She went with it. The producer kept feeding questions into her earpiece, each one a little raunchier than the one before. In response, I nodded, shook my head, or deadpanned while looking straight into the camera. The dumb show went on for many minutes.

Next day on my dressing room they hung a star. Clips from the show were all over the screen. I was offered the opportunity to appear on other shows, many of which wanted me to reprise the nod-and-shake routine. I said no to that, but they had me on anyway. The tabloids reawakened like a plague of mice smelling peanut butter. Cash prizes and new cars and trips to the Caribbean and television appearances were offered to anyone who could identify Adam. For the most part, the regular press confined itself to brief allusions in book and TV columns, but it was all grist for the mill.

"If this keeps up," Melissa said, "this book is going make you more money than you ever dreamed."

We had met for lunch in a way-downtown restaurant. It was a hangout for the Wall Street crowd, men and women both wearing drab suits and bright ties, so it seemed safe enough. Melissa was known here. The maître d' gave us a table up front, the better to showcase her looks. Media overexposure notwithstanding, no one gave me a second glance.

The babble of the lunchtime crowd was deafening. I asked Melissa a question.

Melissa said, "What did you say?"

I raised my voice. "Where did they get the picture?"

"Who?"

"The rag. Who gave it to them?"

"How would I know?" Melissa said. "Do you have any suspects in mind?"

The answer was yes, but they were all unlikely. I named them: the chaps, who probably had more pictures of me in more compromising situations than you could shake a stick at. Clementine. Adam. Adam's other girlfriend, if he had one, and with his looks and mechanical aptitude, how could he not have one or more extras? A private detective hired by persons unknown may have been the photographer, I said.

"Any other suspects?"

"The hotel doorman. A paparazzo who got lucky."

Melissa said, "You left out the CIA."

I said, "Come on, Melissa, help me out. Couldn't someone have been following the chaps while the chaps were following me? A private eye would notice that I always had the same entourage."

"Who had a motive to put a private eye on you?" she asked.

"Who knows? Maybe I had a rival for Adam's affections—a wife, a jealous girlfriend."

"A gay lover?"

"Adam's too slobby to be gay. He's only got one blazer."

ARK

"What does it matter?" Melissa asked. "Why should you care? Chances are you'll never know. The paparazzo who got lucky is probably the culprit. He saw a sex scene unfolding in front of his eyes and took a picture of it, having no idea who you were or how much money he was going to make. Mere coincidence."

"Why are you talking to me like this?" I asked.

"Because I don't understand what you're complaining about. That picture has made you millions. If you ever do identify the paparazzo, you should buy him or her a nice new camera."

This conversation, remember, was being carried on in screeches. A beefy man at the next table, emphatically not a chap, was listening to every word. He watched me intently, as though reading my lips. The beefy spy's luncheon companion, also beefy, had his back to me. I stopped talking and pointed a thumb at the eavesdroppers. Melissa paid the check.

Outside, Melissa held up a languid hand and immediately a cab pulled over with screeching tires as if the driver had been waiting all his life for a passenger like her. As we drove away, I looked out the back window and saw the eavesdroppers hailing another taxi. A greenback fluttered in the uplifted hand of the one who had had been studying me. Their rumpled suits were too small for them. They must have gotten into the restaurant the same way they hailed a cab. Apparently the chaps on watch found them dubious, too, because when at last a taxi stopped, two of them stepped in front of the beefy men, blocking them off from the cab, and two other chaps jumped into it.

When we arrived at Melissa's building, she asked me to get out with her and come upstairs. I asked her why.

"There's something I want to put into your mind," she replied.

When we were inside Melissa's office with the door closed, she put on a serious face.

"Sit down," Melissa said. "This isn't going to be girl talk."

I sat. She did the same—back straight, feet on the floor, knees together like teacher's pet. For a long moment, she looked out the window, as if gathering her thoughts. This was something new. Melissa never groped for words. Sentences and paragraphs—whole legal briefs—flowed from her lips as if accessed by the click of a mouse. Why the hesitation? If she had ever worried about giving offense by being too frank, I hadn't been present. Something serious was afoot.

Finally I said, "Melissa, speak. What's this all about?"

"Men," she said.

"Is *that* all?"

"It's not funny. Parts of this are not going to be very enjoyable."

"Which parts?"

"This part," Melissa said. "You never told me how you met Adam. I'd like to know."

I filled her in: the call from my old boyfriend, the chance meeting in the gallery, the trophy bride, the dinner party at the Italian bistro, the talk about lacrosse, the convertible with the clockwork top, and—up to a point—the denouement.

"None of this seemed at all contrived to you?" Melissa asked.

"It seemed more like fate at the time," I said.

"An old boyfriend blows into town and passes you on to his buddy, who turns out to be a sexual mechanic, and a raving paranoiac like you thinks it's fate?"

The Melissa I knew so well was alive and well and functioning.

"Where was your old boyfriend from, if he was from out of town?" she asked.

"Washington."

"And where had Adam lived before he allegedly moved to New York and hung out his shingle?"

"Washington."

"And that rang no bells?"

I said. "Melissa, just tell me what you have to tell me."

"Clementine was supposed to do this," Melissa said, "but she thinks you don't trust her in spite of all she's done for you."

"She's right. On the other hand, I love you like a sister, but I don't know how much longer that's going to last."

"Whatever you say. Clementine put the chaps on Adam. He's not who he says he is."

"What man ever is?"

"Listen," Melissa said. "This isn't a run-of-the-mill impersonation by a guy who wanted to get laid. His real name is James J. Morrison—J. J. to his friends. He didn't go to Syracuse. He didn't play lacrosse. The real Adam did do all those things before he was killed in an automobile accident in Los Angeles ten years ago at age twenty-two."

"The 'real Adam'?"

"Your Adam, the imposter, took over the dead man's identity. According to Clementine, spooks steal the names of the dead all the time. They prefer the ones who die young. The system doesn't know they're dead, so the spooks get all the documentation—birth certificate, Social Security number, passport, diplomas, everything. Your guy is not a lawyer, but the good news is, he's married to one, and she apparently understands that he sometimes has to do distasteful things for his country, like screw other women cross-eyed. They have two kids."

"I don't believe it," I said.

"Which part?" Melissa asked.

"That any wife would share Adam with anybody."

"J. J."

"He may be J. J. to her. He's Adam to me."

I said, "So what are you telling me? Adam was CIA?"

"Apparently not," Melissa replied. "Clementine's friends in Langley assured her he's not one of theirs."

"Wouldn't they look her in the eye and say that even if he was? Especially if he was."

"They might. But Clementine doesn't think so."

"So who does Adam work for?"

"Clementine's not sure. Most likely it's the FBI, but not necessarily. The possibilities are almost infinite. The Department of Homeland Security has more spooks than it knows what to do with. Result, they're always looking for something to do."

Melissa was here to give me the facts, not offer me comfort. Nor did she volunteer an explanation. Whoever sicced Adam on me was trying to get to Henry.

I said, "Wait a minute. Adam never asked me a single question about Henry until the story broke in the media. Then he broke up with me. So in what way does the theory that he was after Henry make sense?"

"It was Adam's handlers who fed the pulp fiction about you and Henry to the tabloids," Melissa said.

"How do we know that?"

"Clementine hands out very impressive bribes."

"She bribed the CIA?"

"No, dear. She bribed people at the tabloids. It was Adam's friends who took that photo of you and Adam."

"They did? They exposed their own agent? That's so weird it doesn't even happen in books."

"I'm quoting Clementine," Melissa said. "Maybe spooks are even stranger than we think. Maybe they're stupid. Maybe they don't know what they're doing, just like everybody else. Who knows?"

"Does that include Clementine?"

"You're entitled to your opinion of Clementine. But don't let it fog your judgment."

"I'm not the one with the foggy mind," I said. "Maybe Adam does work for the CIA or something worse. Maybe the weirdos he works for ordered him to do what he did to a lonely little writer living in New York. But the idea that they'd then put his picture in the paper and show him to the world while he was carrying out his secret mission is preposterous and you know it, Melissa."

Melissa gave me a lingering, lawyerly look, but no spoken answer: I was a sad case. She knew the facts. If I wouldn't accept them, she understood. I was besotted by Adam, a woman in lust. I was beyond reason. After giving me this moment to cool off, she drew breath to go on with her report.

Before she could speak, I said, "I think there's a far simpler explanation. I think the chaps took the pictures and Clementine gave them to the tabloid. Clementine wanted to bust up the operation before Adam and his employers got any closer to Henry. I think Adam's wife saw the pictures in the rag like everybody else, and gave him an ultimatum—get rid of the home wrecker or get divorced. He chose her and the kids over giving her every cent he owned and living in an efficiency apartment on peanut butter and jelly sandwiches for the rest of his life."

"According to Clementine, the wife knew exactly what he did for a living."

"Come on. I saw how he behaved when he dumped me. The pictures were the reason. I know how he behaved at the last and how he behaved before that. If ever I saw a man doing something he didn't want to do, it was Adam walking out on me. He was under duress."

"So what are you saying, that he loved you?"

"I never thought so for a moment. But there were things we liked about each other."

"I don't doubt it," Melissa said. She shrugged. "Suppose you're right?" she asked. "Whether his wife or his boss gave the orders, his cover was blown and he got out of town."

My throat was dry. I cleared it and said, "Does Henry know all this?"

"Clementine briefed him this morning. He was not pleased."

"Why?"

"Because, sweetie-pie, you're the apple of Henry's eye even if you were too wound around James James Morrison Morrison Weatherby George Dupree to notice. That's why."

Melissa looked at me as though it was time for me to get a grip on myself and breathe a sigh of relief on hearing the whole truth about the confidence trick that had made me, briefly, the least frustrated woman in New York. Frankly, I would just as soon have gone on living in ignorance.

I said, "If you knew all this, why were you playing that game with me in the restaurant, talking about Adam as if you didn't have a clue?"

"Sorry about that," Melissa said. "Those thugs at the next table were probably Adam's buddies."

"Who told you that?"

"The chaps. They called me on my cell and warned me I was being followed while I was walking to the restaurant."

"Then why didn't you warn me? We could have gone to the ladies' room if you were afraid they were going to read your lips."

"Gosh," said Melissa, "why didn't I think of that?"

"That does it," I said, and left.

Alone in the elevator, I imagined what Adam's life must have been like when he was J. J.: the nice brick house in a Virginia suburb with a tree in the front yard that got a little bigger every year, just like the children; the refrigerator with the kids' drawings and photos stuck to it by magnets; the two green cars that ran on electricity generated by coal-fired plants; the freshly shampooed wife dashing off to work in her lawyer's togs; the blond noisy kids spilling out the front door; dad loading them into the car and telling them to fasten their seatbelts and stop fighting. He'd have one of those inner-sanctum Washington photo IDs hung around his neck on a chain of steel BBs.

Across the Potomac, as he approached the capital in traffic that barely moved, he'd see the sound stage for a Cecil B. DeMille epic that was the federal city. He'd do this every day, except on weekends when he coached soccer and the days when he was ordered to New York to commit the unspeakable acts I remembered so fondly.

3

I TOOK THE SUBWAY TO Chelsea. My idea was to count my memories as a way of purging them from my mind. It was three days before Christmas. The sun was bright, the weather was cold. Though it hadn't yet snowed in the city, the air smelled of snow. As I walked to the station, the sidewalk shook. Everyone knew at once that it wasn't a train. They stopped in unison, as if choreographed, and looked downward at the pavement. After a beat or two, the concrete shook again, harder. Then it stopped. The crowd waited attentively for another sign that something was awakening deep in the earth, and when nothing further happened, walked on. Was this just another aftershock, or had fifty thousand people been buried alive in Turkey? No one seemed to care one way or the other.

In the gallery where Adam and I first met, the big paintings of galaxies had been taken down and replaced by sweet little water-colors. Most were awful. I wasn't really looking at the pictures, just walking by them in a daze and glancing at them for something to do. One of them caught my eye. I didn't realize what I had seen until I was three or four paintings beyond it. I spun around and went back to it. And there it was, the O. Laster watercolor.

I felt a surge of anger. The bastard had sold it! He really was as bad as Melissa said. Was anything about him as it should have been? Had he read my novels and read up on paintings as part of his cover? What other evidence of his perfidy still awaited discovery? But wait a minute. What else could he have done, poor guy? How could he have explained the picture to his angry wife? He had no choice but to get rid of it. Maybe he had spent the proceeds at Costco on a ring to give her as a peace offering at a candlelit dinner.

I asked the price. The clerk said, "You do understand that it's an original O. Laster." I just stared at him. This caused him to dislike me. He looked up the price and when I told him to wrap it up, said, "If you want the frame, that's fifty dollars more."

I paid with a credit card, thus purposely leaving a record of the transaction that Adam's handlers could easily retrieve. From my Visa bill, I hoped, they would be able to deduce that I knew all about J. J. Would they let me live in possession of this classified information? Would I be hit by a car as soon as I went outside, or would the end come more suddenly—a poison pinprick as I ran around the Reservoir, a bullet behind the ear in a check-out line?

Back in the apartment, I hung up the watercolor in its old spot on the office wall. If Clementine ever came again for tea, there it would be, and there would I be, sadder but wiser.

EIGHT

1

AS HENRY ATTEMPTED TO EAT his sliver of fruitcake at Christmas dinner, he answered Clementine's questions about earthquakes. She and I had been invited to the glass house in the Grenadines for the holidays. Doors and windows were open, admitting the sea breeze. Brilliant sunlight flooded the dining room.

Millions of earthquakes occur each year, Henry said, though only a million and a half or so are recorded. Those registering from 8 to 8.9 on the Richter scale, called great earthquakes, had in the past occurred at a rate of one a year. Every twenty years or so, a great quake measuring between 9 and 9.9 was detected by seismographs. No quake as strong as 10 on the Richter scale had ever been recorded.

"So what is your estimate of the force of the ultimate earthquake you predict, should it actually occur?" Clementine asked.

Her eyes shone. She was an interrogator by nature and training, and therefore she loved questioning Henry, who came as close to having all the answers as anyone since Euclid.

"Conceivably, 20 or more on the Richter scale," Henry replied.

"And what does that mean in comparative terms to your 8 to 10 on the Richter scale category of earthquakes?"

"The energy released by a category 20 earthquake would be equivalent to the detonation of several trillion tons of TNT," Henry said, "or about the same force as a meteor five kilometers in diameter crashing into the planet."

"Unimaginable," Clementine said.

Henry, who had imagined the apocalypse in detail, gave her one of his faint smiles.

Clementine was just back from a mission to Hsi-tau, where she had met with General Yao. She had hit it off with one of the chow chows. She and the dog that had been assigned to protect her were great friends now. I asked Clementine if she had tested the relationship by removing her protective identity badge. Of course she had. The chow had been quite happy to smell the real Clementine.

"Of course," said Clementine with a fond smile, "he could also smell the identity disk in my bag."

She had painted a watercolor of the dog, which had posed for its portrait like an angel.

Neither Henry nor I volunteered a new subject, so Clementine kept talking about dogs.

"Have you ever wondered," she asked, "how we and dogs got together in the Paleolithic, and why we formed such an enduring friendship?"

"Yes," I said, "My theory is that the dogs helped us hunt down Neanderthals and eat them."

"What a perfectly outrageous idea," Clementine said.

"Maybe, Clementine, but think about it. We know Neanderthals were cannibalized, and we're the logical suspects."

From deep inside her, Clementine made a sound of disgust.

"In what way does that incriminate dogs?" she asked.

"It would explain why dogs are so fawning. They're our partners in original sin."

"You do go too far," Clementine said. But she stopped asking questions.

Henry was gazing out to sea. He had long since tuned out. Now he excused himself in an almost inaudible voice and went away. Clementine gazed in fond admiration at his retreating figure.

She said, "I have what might be called a Christmas gift for you. General Yao informs me that Mulligan's DNA matches evidence collected at the scene of all three rapes in China. The Chinese act very quickly in such matters. Mulligan has been sentenced to life imprisonment without the possibility of release. He is in a very secure, very remote prison in Hsi-tau."

I kissed Clementine on the cheek. She looked as though she wanted to kiss me back, but exercised self-control.

She chattered on. Clementine knew all sorts of things—such as what each of the gifts in "The Twelve Days of Christmas" symbolized in English folklore. There was a reason for her encyclopedic bent. As a schoolgirl, she had made a business of studying up on out-of-the-way facts.

"Because I wasn't pretty, I strove to be interesting," she said, "but of course it was hopeless. I was avoided as the most boring girl at school."

I asked how she knew that. She listed the cruelties that had been visited upon her by the blackshirts in the sixth form. By the time she flew back to New York on the fifth day of Christmas (the five gold rings are a code term for the first five books of the Old Testament), I was learned in her miseries. It turned out we had a good deal in common. Any two people plunked down together on an uninhabited island might have made the same discovery, but the important thing was that we made friends and closed our eyes to each other's peculiarities.

On her day of departure I walked her down to the airstrip. I carried her easel and paint box. On the tarmac, we kissed each other on both cheeks. I told her I sincerely hoped neither of us would be buried alive before we met again. Clementine considered this, then laughed for the first time in my presence. It came out as a series of yips that must have been much imitated at her school.

"Look after Henry," she said. "He seems to be on the verge of something."

Henry was breakfasting on the terrace and fiddling with his laptop when I got back to the house. He lifted a careless hand. I gestured in return and sat down opposite him at the table. Since Christmas dinner, he had been hiding out, and mostly had not even joined Clementine and me for meals. Clementine assumed he was thinking great thoughts in his solitude.

Finally he looked up. "Clementine told you the news from China?" he said.

"If you mean Bear's fate, yes."

Although I had questions—where exactly in Inner Mongolia was Bear imprisoned? what would his life be like? might General Yao, at some future moment, decide to swap him for a Chinese spy held by the CIA?—it seemed inappropriate to ask the questions or to thank Henry for putting the man who wanted to murder me away for the rest of his life. Justice had been done. That was enough.

Henry said, "Would you mind going back to China for a few days? There's something I want you to see."

We left the next morning. In Hsi-tau I was assigned to my usual yurt and chow chow. After more than three years, the dog and I knew each other pretty well, but if the animal recognized me, it didn't let me know. Looking over the pack, I wondered which one was Clementine's chum. It might even be my friend.

On my way to the big yurt for dinner, I saw Chinese soldiers lounging around their armored vehicles. I smelled their cigarette smoke before I saw the men. Inside, General Yao gallantly kissed my hand and gave me a mock-flirtatious look. He had brought a gaggle of cooks and waiters and all the other necessities for a Chinese banquet. He was attentive throughout the evening, transferring delicacies to my plate and making small talk. His subject tonight was the New York theater. He read all the reviews online and knew far more about it than I did. He was shocked by my ignorance. How could I live in a theatrical paradise and pay so little attention to it? One day he would come to New York and we would go to all the best plays together for at least a week, matinees and evening performances.

I would emerge reeducated, hungry—insatiable—for more theater. He had a hundred different smiles and let me know with one of them that this promise was double entendre.

When dinner was over, General Yao dismissed his aides, and he and Henry talked very intently in English. Their voices were low. The exchange lasted no more than five minutes. I listened in, of course, but I missed most of what they were saying. Both men seemed tense, even uncomfortable with each other. As was so often the case, Henry's mind seemed to be elsewhere.

At last the conversation ended. General Yao turned to me with his smoothy's smile and once again bowed over my hand.

"Until tomorrow, then," he said.

What was going to happen tomorrow? No one told me. I smiled and said good night. Henry saw General Yao to his car and didn't come back.

At first light the following morning, General Yao called for us in an unmarked helicopter. It was the biggest helicopter I had ever seen. Its twin rotors created a pall of brown dust as it landed. The chow chows' frantic barking could not be heard above the noise of the machine. Henry watched the landing impassively. He had done everything impassively for many days now—few words, no smiles, hardly a gesture. Something was eating him, but who knew what?

We flew much lower in the giant helicopter than we had done in the rickety little brown airplane Ng Fred had sent for us the last time we went on a field trip. The passenger compartment of the ship wasn't insulated against noise. The *whack-whack* of the rotors was deafening. After maybe an hour, Yao got to his feet and pointed out the window. When I didn't respond right away—what could there be to look at in this wilderness?—he touched the skin under his eye with a fingertip to indicate that I should take a look. I did as suggested, and there below us was a vast prison camp surrounded by a high fence that enclosed a great many buildings. Hundreds of human beings, all dressed alike in blue, marched across its open spaces in long columns, like worker ants. The helicopter flew lower and circled. The ants, apparently under orders to pretend that this intrusion wasn't happening, did not look up. Soon they were hidden in a cloud of dust. The helicopter was now flying so close to the ground that I could see the faces of the guards in the watchtowers. They too were ignoring us.

The helicopter hovered. General Yao put his lips close to my ear. I felt the warmth and moisture of his breath.

"Mulligan," he shouted, pointing.

I looked hard and sure enough, there was Bear himself, standing on a rooftop with his red hair blowing in the wash of the chopper's rotors. He now had a red beard to go with his mustache, and the beard was windblown, too. Bear was in chains—not shackles but actual chains, very heavy ones, secured by padlocks. Like the rest of the prisoners, he wore a blue uniform. Four smaller men in brown uniforms held his arms. Half a dozen other guards surrounded them. Bear struggled, silently roared. It was a version of the theater scene in *King Kong*. The guards beat him with truncheons. He shrugged off their puny blows. In his mind he was still the lord of the jungle. He had not yet realized he was now an ant and could never change back into the invincible creature he used to be. He glared upward. Could he see my face in the window? One of the guards struck him in the small of the back with a baton. Bear paid no heed, but continued to snarl at the helicopter. Would he leap upward, take hold of the helicopter, and smash it into the ground? Evidently the pilot had a similar thought. Abruptly, the machine climbed to a much higher altitude. Hundreds of kilometers of empty desert surrounded the camp in all directions.

"No escape possible," General Yao shouted in my ear. "Finished." I wondered.

2

NG FRED GREETED US AT our destination, a factory in the middle of nowhere. Unlike the underground installation I had visited earlier, this one was a complex of enormous structures made of corrugated metal. Two tremendously long concrete runways dwindled into the distance across the perfectly flat landscape. Ng Fred tugged at my arm. Henry was in the act of disappearing with General Yao into the building. Ng Fred, hurrying after them, rushed me through the door.

What I saw when I stepped inside astonished me. Five spaceships stood on their tails, their noses a few feet short of the ceiling two hundred feet above. They had stubby wings, two amidships and two at the tail, but they couldn't possibly be airplanes, nor did they resemble any flying machine I had even seen in reality or the movies. Two large engines hung from either side of the tail. The ships had no windows. Painted on the fuselage was a picture of our blue planet, wreathed in white clouds. There were no other markings—no flags, no lettering, no numbers.

Henry, still locked into his silence, gazed wordlessly at these wonders. He seemed to be as spellbound as I was, even though he had certainly seen these extraordinary objects many times before.

He had invented them—no one else who ever lived could possibly have done so. They belonged to him. They had been conceived in his brain and built with his money.

"Shuttles," Ng Fred said. "Very new. We call them Spaceplanes."

Hearing Ng Fred's words, General Yao nodded—one curt bob of the head. It was inconceivable that he had not already seen pictures of these craft, taken by spies he had planted in the factory. Yet he seemed to be taken aback by the reality. The astonishing quickly became the familiar. By the time we completed our guided tour of the Spaceplane, its mystery was dispelled. It was just another wonder of technology, its eventual development foretold by the first stone tool. If mankind lived on, this machine would metamorphose over time into marvels that no one, except maybe Henry, could begin to imagine.

The Spaceplane was designed to carry two hundred passengers or six hundred tons of cargo. It would lift the components of the spheres and the scores of women who would build them into orbit. Fifty people could live aboard for weeks without resupply. Resupply by another Spaceplane would be a routine exercise.

"The ship requires no booster rockets," Ng Fred said. "It will take off from a runway like an airplane, climb to the upper edge of the atmosphere, and then accelerate and escape Earth's gravity. It will attain orbit at a distance of about five hundred miles from the planet. When its mission is achieved, it will return to Earth, land like an airplane, and be ready for turnaround just as quickly as an airplane—quicker, because it will not require refueling."

"One moment," General Yao said. "What powers these engines?"

"A new kind of propulsion devised by Henry."

"What kind of propulsion exactly? Fission, fusion, charged particles, antimatter as in *Star Trek*, what?"

"That is proprietary information, General Yao. I'm sorry."

"What's its top speed in space?"

"I'm sorry, General. I can't tell you that."

"What is its range?"

"Or that."

Yao fairly quivered with indignation at having these doors slammed in his face.

"You are a citizen of China," he said to Ng Fred. "You felt no duty to inform your country of what was going on here?"

"We're not in China, General."

The two Chinese were speaking to each other in English—General Yao, I think, because he wanted Henry to know how insulted he was, Ng Fred because speaking Mandarin would double the affront.

"You have not tested this ship in space," Yao said.

"No," Ng Fred answered. "But we plan to do so soon."

"You *hope* to do so soon. How many have you built?"

"Seven. Two more are in production."

"Each one costs approximately what?"

"Ten billion dollars."

"So Henry has spent ninety billion on this ship?"

"So far, not counting development costs, yes."

"Why build so many before you have tested even one? It's not like Henry Peel to be so incautious."

"We are confident the product will perform as designed."

"I'm touched by your faith," Yao said. "You have trained the necessary pilots?"

"It's a drone."

"The pilot flies it by remote control?"

"It is controlled by a computer."

"From what location?"

"The Spaceplane can be controlled from any point on Earth, or in space."

"Will it be controlled from China?"

Ng Fred did not answer the question. I found this puzzling, but not so puzzling as General Yao found it. He seemed to be positively bewildered. He had been a silent partner in the enterprise from the beginning. Why this sudden stonewalling? General Yao fairly quivered with resentment.

At this point, Henry spoke his first words of the day.

"Seen enough?" he asked.

"Actually, no," General Yao said. "Nor heard enough."

Henry said, "General Yao, I hope we can speak plainly to each other, and that you will speak plainly afterward to your government."

"That is also my hope, Henry," General Yao said. "Who asks the first question?"

"Go ahead."

"Why have you not told us before about the existence of this Spaceplane?"

"It was and is a trade secret."

"The People's Republic of China is not a competitor. Far from it."

Henry replied, "This assembly plant is not on Chinese soil."

"It would not be on Mongolian soil in the absence of China's good offices in your behalf."

"That's debatable," Henry said.

Yao said, "When you deal with China, you must trust China as it trusts you. You are not a sovereign state even if you have more money than most countries."

Henry said, "General Yao, what point are you making?"

General Yao said, "I will come straight to it. I have made the point once before. If you insist on testing this vehicle, or anything like it, without giving notice to the rest of the world, and especially to the Americans, who may very well regard your Spaceplane as a new Chinese weapons system, you will seriously embarrass the People's Republic of China and endanger its national security. My government cannot permit this to happen."

General Yao rose to his feet. "And now I must go," he said with no hint of his usual urbane smile. "Do you need a ride home?"

"Thank you," Henry replied. "We can manage."

He wasn't smiling, either. He had the look of a man whose thoughts are far, far away.

Yao left, striding purposely. Lately, everyone seemed to be doing this.

I said, "What was that all about?"

"I'm not sure what Yao wants," Henry said.

"How about a couple of Spaceplanes?" I asked.

"What would they do with them?"

"Hijack the mother ship?"

"Why would they do that?"

"To load the party leaders on board. To make the escape from this planet an all-Chinese affair—nobody but the Han in the next world."

Henry widened his eyes. He fought a smile and lost. He laughed— just a couple of half-smothered snorts, but a laugh just the same.

"No wonder I love you," he said, shaking his head. "You're the most creative paranoiac I've ever known."

No wonder I love you? Is that what he had just said? If so, he gave no sign of remembering it.

"What's so paranoid about it?" I asked. "Henry, think about it. Are you not the Henry Peel who invented swarms of fighting hornets to repel boarders from Earth who might try to take over the mother ship?"

"Yes," Henry said.

"Then what does this scenario change?" I asked. "A smart pirate—General Yao, for example—might reason that it would be a lot easier and cheaper to capture the Spaceplanes while they're still on the ground. Or is *that* paranoid?"

Henry said, "I'm listening."

"Suppose Chinese special forces decided to slip across the Mongolian border in the dark of the moon and take possession of this place and the underground factory? How would you stop them?"

"How could I?"

"What about the chaps? Aren't they all former Delta Force and the British equivalent and whatever?"

"They'd be outnumbered," Henry said. "Besides, if we fought off the commando raid, they'd just bomb the factory."

"What, and blow up their only chance for escape?"

This was not a direction in which Henry wanted to be taken. He held up a hand: *Enough.*

"If that was the intention, why would Yao tell me about it?" he asked.

"Maybe he *was* trying to warn you."

"Why?"

"Friendship?"

"Please."

"All right, then. He wants something."

"Are you saying he wants to go along on the voyage?" Henry asked.

"You said it first," I said.

Ng Fred, who had been listening, joined in.

"She has a point," he said. "Maybe Yao does want to go on the voyage. Maybe the party leadership wants to go along, too. But maybe they're not quite that farsighted. Maybe Yao is telling us something else."

"Which is?" Henry asked.

"The Spaceplane is a revolutionary weapons platform. What would the White House do if it found out such a thing existed and this factory was in Saskatchewan and belonged to a Chinese?"

We all knew the answer to that question.

Henry stared at each of us in turn, and then climbed into his shell and pulled it shut. Emerging from it after a very long minute, he asked Ng Fred questions about the Spaceplane. Except for the two that were still under construction, the ships were ready to fly.

Ng Fred was, of course, telling Henry things he already knew. Nevertheless, Henry listened attentively—as if, like a normal human being, he simply wanted reassurance.

But this was Henry. Why would he need reassurance?

NINE

1

AT ONE MINUTE AFTER MIDNIGHT on New Year's Day, the first of the Spaceplanes was launched. It positioned itself at the equator over Borneo, then climbed straight up to the edge of the atmosphere, broke free of Earth's gravity, entered space, and settled into orbit. The launch was observed by American, Brazilian, Chinese, European, Indian, Japanese, and Russian satellites. It lacked the flaming exhaust that had been the signature of every other space vehicle ever launched by man; in fact it seemed to have no exhaust at all. Despite this peculiarity, it was treated as a commonplace event by the news media, which reported that China appeared to have launched a vehicle of some kind into high Earth orbit. The media's nonchalance came as no surprise. Thousands of man-made objects already circled the planet. One more caused no excitement just because it didn't have a flaming tail. The Chinese government maintained its customary silence. The following midnight, and for the next three midnights after that, another Spaceplane was launched, so that by the end of the week, five of the craft were in orbit.

This did create excitement. No nation had ever sent so many objects into space in such a short period of time. It suggested a new dimension of power. The cost alone boggled the minds of media pundits. What were the Chinese up to? Were these spacecraft manned? Were they headed for the other planets or perhaps for the stars? Or were the Chinese about to plunge the world into darkness and silence by destroying every communications and intelligence satellite in orbit except their own? Was this a prelude to war, or as many hoped even in America, the longed-for event that finally put an end to American supremacy on Earth and in space? The Chinese remained silent.

A week passed before a hitherto unknown public relations firm in Ulan Bator issued a press release in Khalkha Mongolian announcing that the launch of the Spaceplane fleet was the work of a Mongolian corporation whose name translated as CyberSci, Inc., which would soon launch a separate, larger spacecraft constructed from components carried into orbit by the Spaceplanes. No press conference was called. Neither Henry's name nor that of any officer of the corporation was mentioned. Only the most rudimentary technical details were disclosed.

Media investigations uncovered no further information. CyberSci, Inc., had no office or telephone number or Internet address anywhere in the world. Neither the Spaceplane nor its propulsion system had been patented in the United States. It was possible that the system had been hidden in plain sight by patenting each of its thousands of parts in many different countries. Multinationalism had gone multiplanetary. CyberSci was holding its secrets close.

Meanwhile, the two remaining Spaceplanes were being loaded with components of the mother ship. By the end of the second week, they too launched themselves into orbit. The Spaceplanes they replaced returned to Mongolia, landed in darkness, and fifty young women filed aboard each of them. Within minutes, these workers were in orbit. A couple of days later, after they had had some experience of weightlessness, twenty-five women emerged from each Spaceplane. They wore bright red space suits. The space suits were much trimmer than the puffy Michelin Man costumes of earlier space walkers—so close-fitting, in fact, that the lithe figures of the nubile females who wore them could be discerned by the cameras. They immediately set to work. While one twenty-five-woman team unloaded the long strips that would form the outer shell of the spaceship, the other team fastened them together. All this was photographed and broadcast to Earth. After three hours of work, new teams replaced them. The women worked with choreographed precision, as if they were a synchronized swim team and space was a vast Olympic pool.

By the end of the third week, the first segment of the sphere that would be a segment of the mother ship looked in magnified television images like a crescent moon. The first one hundred workers returned to Earth. This time the Spaceplanes landed in daylight, in full view of the dozens of spy satellites that were watching. A second shift of workers took off immediately. Henry saw them safely into orbit, then departed, taking me with him but leaving Ng Fred, the nuts-and-bolts man, in charge of the routine. We had been in Mongolia, and the women had been in space, for three weeks.

The little brown airplane flew Henry and me back to the yurt compound. Why we traveled in such an archaic device was known only to Henry, but after watching the otherworldly perfection of the Spaceplanes and little else for twenty-one days, it was a comfort of sorts to be riding in a rickety machine that barely held gravity at bay.

General Yao awaited us at the yurts. He regarded us with cold eyes. I guessed that he hadn't had a pleasant visit to Beijing. His insignia of rank had not changed, so for the time being at least he was still a general and a free man. Henry offered a friendly nod. It was not returned. The dust of Hsi-tau saved the moment by going up my nose and causing a paroxysm of sneezing. Henry and Yao, distracted from their staring contest, watched sympathetically.

Henry said, "I think we'd better get her inside."

"Excellent idea," said Yao.

Inside the big yurt, Daeng materialized and poured tea into translucent porcelain bowls. I expected Yao to wave his bowl away, but etiquette prevailed. Would it be the polite thing for a Chinese to wait to arrest or shoot his host until after drinking his tea? I had a feeling we might soon find out. We were in one of the most out-of-the-way places in the world and nobody except Ng Fred knew we were here. It was not inconceivable that Henry and I, and maybe Daeng as the only witness, might, at the very least, soon be joining Bear in chains. Henry seemed unperturbed by these possibilities. When he had emptied the bowl and handed it back to Daeng, Yao looked directly at him for the first time.

"First of all, Henry," he said, "I offer you congratulations on your great achievement."

"Thank you, General Yao," said Henry, "but others deserve most of the credit."

"Nonsense."

Henry looked interested, but nothing more than that.

"You have stolen a march on the world," Yao said. "Including your friends. The result is that you have very few friends left in China. Perhaps only one."

As if he were the inscrutable Chinese and Yao the impetuous foreigner, Henry remained opaque. His expression was attentive, serious, pleasant. If he was apprehensive about what was coming next, as I certainly was, he gave no sign of it.

"Serious violations of Chinese law have been committed," Yao said.

He enumerated them. The list was long—the smuggling of matériel into China itself and across Chinese territory, many unauthorized intrusions into Chinese airspace—in fact, practically every act, large or small, that Henry had committed on Chinese soil—including bringing me and many other foreigners to Hsi-tau, a restricted security area, without visas.

Yao continued. "You have, in addition, installed on nearby foreign soil advanced ballistic missiles that threaten military and civilian targets within China—weapons that could be launched at a moment's notice. You did this under the pretext that they would be used peacefully to launch objects into space for scientific purposes and with the promise that any results would be shared with China. Now you have deployed advanced spacecraft into orbit that have obvious military capability, and you are building a space station that has the capacity to launch a devastating attack on China. You kept the existence of these spacecraft a secret from us. China asks itself what your true intentions have been and what they are now. It is clear that it cannot rely on your assurances in the future."

As General Yao went along, his voice became louder and his military bearing more noticeable. He was standing at attention, boot heels together, shoulders back, face frozen. He had not removed his cap.

"I now come to the most serious of the infractions," General Yao said. "You have manufactured your Spaceplanes, your booster rockets, and the components for your space station on foreign soil with Chinese labor. The work now being done in space is performed entirely by Chinese workers. Nearly all of these workers are young women. Without official permission or knowledge, they were removed without proper documents to a foreign country, and later sent into space without regard for their safety or good health."

The period after the last sentence was all but visible as it fell from Yao's lips. Had he in fact come to the end? Henry waited, in case there might be more. A full minute seemed to pass.

Henry said, "Let's sit down, shall we?"

He indicated a chair. General Yao sat down in it. He crossed his legs. He removed his cap and placed it on a side table. His gleaming hair was as perfectly combed as if he had just risen from a barber's chair. Daeng entered with a tray of tinkling glasses and a bottle of champagne in an ice bucket. Apparently we had something to celebrate.

Yao drank a single glass of champagne. Henry had his customary tablespoonful. I managed with a shaky hand to drink half a glass. As if stepping out of one movie and into another, the general stopped being the avenging angel and became his old flirtatious self again. He was entirely at ease, chatting me up about my book.

"I'm on page one hundred and thirty-two," he said. "I wish I had read more, so that I could discuss it more intelligently, but thanks to Henry's merry pranks, I have had little time for novels lately. So far I like it tremendously. The man-woman scenes—perhaps I should say the woman-man scenes—are most enjoyable."

"You're very kind," I said.

Yao said, "Tell me, my dear, do you write on a computer?"

"I'm afraid so."

"I wish I had known. Certain young friends of mine who are very good at that sort of thing could have hacked into your computer. I could have read your book as you wrote it, as people did with Charles Dickens in Victorian times."

This banter continued for minutes, shutting Henry out of the conversation. At last Yao looked at his watch, put down his glass, and rose to his feet.

"Forgive us," he said to me. "Henry and I are going to have a private word. It's been a pleasure to see you again, dear lady."

He made an after-you gesture to Henry, and then followed him to the opposite side of the yurt. Yao put a hand on Henry's shoulder, a distinctly un-Chinese gesture, and peered into his face. He spoke softly. I caught the murmured words.

Yao said, "So, my friend, what shall I take with me back to Beijing?"

Henry reached inside the neck of his shirt and pulled out a tiny computer flash drive that hung around his neck on a thread. He took off this necklace and handed it to Yao, who unbuttoned his collar and strung the thing around his own neck. They shook hands. Yao's grip seemed positively fervent.

Henry walked him to the door. Through the open door I glimpsed troops snapping to attention. Moments later, engines started. Tires crunched. Yao and his escort drove away. Would they creep back in the night, drug the chow chows again, and pounce on me, asleep or awake?

I needn't have worried. An hour later, Henry and I were airborne. The skies were as empty as usual, and the ground below as lifeless. It seemed like the last place in the world that anyone would go in order to save the world. No doubt that was why Henry had chosen it.

Daeng woke me at four in the morning with the announcement that we were on our final approach to Andrews Air Force Base. Henry was already awake. He was wearing a shirt and tie and shined shoes. Suspenders—suspenders!—held up the trousers of a dark suit. After the plane taxied, he stood up and put on the jacket. The change from his usual nerd attire could not have been more dramatic if Henry had appeared in the saffron robes of a Buddhist monk. The plane taxied to a gate. Henry got off. He was greeted by a marine in dress uniform who accompanied him to a waiting helicopter with *Marines* painted on its fuselage. Evidently Henry was going to call on the president.

I flew back to New York in a smaller plane. After completing his business in Washington, Henry flew on to Brussels, Moscow, and Tokyo, though I did not deduce these destinations until later in the week, when CyberSci, Inc., announced in a press release—in English this time—that it had granted licenses to the governments of the United States, the European Union, Russia, Japan, India, and China to manufacture replicas of the Spaceplane and the space vehicle that was presently being assembled in orbit by the company's construction teams. Blueprints and full technical information had been provided to all these governments. No license fees had been charged, nor would any be charged in the future. Each of the governments had solemnly promised, in writing, that the technology would be used for peaceful purposes only.

In the next news cycle, Henry Peel was identified by senior officials in the White House as the inventor of Spaceplane and also of the ship that the space maidens in red were putting together in orbit. Experts at NASA and the Pentagon calculated that it would cost trillions and require many years to manufacture the Spaceplanes. Commentators who had their doubts about plutocrats bearing gifts speculated that Henry's largesse might lead to the bankruptcy of the United States treasury, if not that of every other country he had just visited.

Notwithstanding this risk, every world power that had received the plans would have to build the hardware and launch the ships because none of them could suffer another country to possess such a novelty without matching it ship for ship .

TEN

1

BEAR'S LAWYERS FILED LAWSUITS IN federal court in Washington, D.C., and the world court in The Hague, demanding that Cyber-Sci, Inc., Henry Peel, et al., be ordered to cease work on an experiment to produce thousands of genetically engineered embryos in a secret laboratory near Milan, Italy. The lawsuit charged that Henry intended to implant these embryos in the wombs of unsuspecting surrogate mothers, most likely in secret camps in Mongolia. The babies that resulted would be a new human type intended to be as much superior to ordinary human beings in intelligence and physical stature as people were to chimpanzees.

The lawsuit got some of the details wrong or simply invented them for effect, but there was truth enough in Bear's charges. His timing could hardly have been better, coming as it did after the outing of Henry as the inventor and financier of the Spaceplane and whatever it was that his space maidens were assembling in space. The awe and admiration that this feat had inspired was replaced in the news media overnight by almost universal schadenfreude. The mighty had fallen. How wonderful! A cordon of demonstrators formed around Amerigo's factories to prevent removal of the monsters. The media went berserk. A plot was afoot to take over the world, and the most elusive trillionaire genius in history was behind it. No wonder he had lived in secret. No wonder no one knew what he looked like. This explained why Henry had hidden himself from the world, why he had escaped being revealed as a villain of technology for such a long time, why he had masqueraded as a benefactor of humanity.

Ng Fred called me. He couldn't locate Henry. He didn't use Henry's name. He used pronouns only. Would I tell *him* to call Ng Fred as soon as possible? I took the message, but told him I had no more idea than he did where *he* might be or when he might reappear.

"If he gets in touch with anyone, it will probably be you," Ng Fred said. "Tell him to call me immediately. Tell him that before you say hello."

Days passed. An 8.4 earthquake occurred in Tierra del Fuego. The shock caused a tsunami that engulfed the Shetland Islands and shook loose enormous fragments of ice from Antarctica. Once again great numbers of penguins and seals set sail on a melting floes, followed by a squadron of television camera crews in chartered airplanes. Two days later, a dormant volcano in the Japan Alps erupted, destroying several remote villages and asphyxiating scores of tourists at nearby ski resorts.

Dead people, cute threatened animals! For the time being at least, the news media forgot all about Henry's crimes against evolution. Besides, there were no pictures, there were no quotes, there was no proof of Bear's allegations, and as far as anyone knew, Henry was a figment of the world's imagination. Nothing was happening, there was nothing to report, so how could you make this interesting, let alone exciting, for more than a day or two? On the other hand, the stranded penguins, being swept toward certain destruction as their melting icebergs approached the Tropic of Capricorn, touched millions of hearts. Rescue missions were proposed. Donations flowed. Cascades of fish and several veterinarians and many journalists were dropped from chartered airplanes. Ships steamed at high speed toward the floes, hoping to intercept them and save the penguins before they were destroyed by the sun and warm water, and tow them back to Antarctica.

2

IT WAS EARLY EVENING WHEN the phone rang, the wrong time of day for Henry to call, but when I switched on the videophone, his image appeared. He looked restored, somehow—happy, even relaxed. Stifling the impulse to ask where he had been and why he had been there, I told him about Ng Fred's call.

"He told me to give you the message before I said hello. Hello."

Henry's image nodded. Message received. Footnote understood.

His voice said, "Hello. Would it be convenient for me to come over for dinner?"

He was in New York? I told him to come over.

It was a rush—several different kinds of rush—to open the door and see the original Henry standing there in his customary Nikes and jeans and untucked T-shirt and Yankees cap instead of the bespoke suit and tie and burnished shoes he had been wearing the last time I saw him. Had he been anyone else, I would have kissed him. Apart from that brief waltz when the earthquake rattled Manhattan and one other quick touch of the hand, Henry and I had never touched each other's skin. We hadn't even shaken hands on first meeting. We had conceived children without touching each other. What Henry's own impulses in this department were, sup-

234

posing he had any, I could not guess. He seemed glad to see me, but looked at me, I thought, as if he knew me only from a photograph and was measuring the reality against the image.

The conversation was slow at the outset—nonexistent, in fact. I thought Henry wanted to say something, but what? His hand lay on the tablecloth. To my own surprise, I reached across the space between us and touched it with a fingertip. I applied a little pressure, whitening the skin. He didn't seem to notice.

I thought, *Wake up.* I said, "What about the news from Milan? Where are our children?"

He didn't seem to be startled by the question. "They're safe," he said. "They're healthy."

"They're still on Earth?"

"Yes. In Milan."

"How many are they?"

"Just two," Henry said. "A boy and a girl."

"Were there others?"

"Yes, several. They weren't viable."

"You mean they weren't the kind that can be enhanced?"

"No. Enhancement was never considered in their case."

"Why not?" I asked.

"Because by then there was no more enhancement."

"No more enhancement. You didn't tell me that."

A silence. I said, "Why?"

"Bad manners," Henry replied. "Reluctance to admit such a big mistake."

"What changed your mind about enhancement?"

"Two things," Henry said. "Your moral disgust over the idea, and the sudden realization that two of the embryos were our own flesh and blood, yours and mine. I came face to face with the personal. I had to admit to myself that I wanted them to be like us, not wake up after a sleep of a thousand years as something else. Objectivity went out the window. Emotion ruled."

"That took you by surprise?"

Henry paused before he answered. It wasn't one of those mental disappearances of his that made you think he was going to step out of this world like a visitor from a parallel universe who suddenly remembers that he has an urgent appointment back home.

At last he said, "No. I just understood that I was wrong. Apart from everything else, it made me realize that time was getting away from me."

I said, "Time is getting away from everybody."

Before I could say more, Henry held up an arresting hand. He then looked into my eyes and said what he had come to say. He was perfectly composed. There was no preamble or epilogue, no explanation. He just spoke his piece.

His exact words were, "I have always wanted to make love to you."

I gasped, actually gasped. I was flabbergasted, not that he wanted to make love—why shouldn't he?—but that he actually said so. My response was not in question, but for the moment I was deserted by the power of speech and gesture. I stood up. I crooked a finger at Henry and left the room like a sleepwalker. He followed.

It was in no way strange to wake up the next morning and find him asleep beside me. It was still early. Just enough light came through the windows to make him visible. He slept on his right side, facing me, with his arms outside the covers. He looked like the proverbial little boy, a lock of hair on his forehead, eyelashes on his cheeks, the white outline of his drugstore wristwatch on the tanned skin of his wrist, his breathing only just audible. The shadow of a beard had grown on his chin overnight. He smelled different naked—a trace of sweat on his skin, a trace of soap, a trace of the two of us; on his breath, a trace of espresso. I wanted to wake him— dimpling the back of his hand with the same fingertip as before, but first I wanted to study him in his sleep a little longer.

However, he woke up.

As soon as his eyes were open, I said, "Why did you wait so long?"

"You seemed to be elsewhere involved."

"Why would that stop you?"

"I'm not a poacher."

Was that why Adam got his picture in the paper? I didn't ask. Henry's face revealed nothing.

I said, "Tell me, really. How long has this been on your mind?"

"Since you solved the riddle of the sphere that first day in Central Park," Henry said.

"You're serious?"

"Absolutely."

"It wasn't my bottomless eyes, my glowing face, the wind in my hair, my graceful carriage?"

"I have eyes to see with. But that's when it started."

"So you were looking for a marriage of true minds?"

"That and getting naked."

After a while we showered together as if we were living in the age of innocence and this was the first morning of the honeymoon, and we had come to each other the night before as virgins dying of curiosity. It was a large glassed-in shower, as spacious as an ordinary bathroom, a multifunction water joke with all sorts of showerheads and nozzles spraying water from all directions. I had never been able to figure it out. It was no mystery to Henry, who knew exactly which knob controlled which showerhead.

In his backpack Henry had brought a toothbrush and an electric razor and a clean T-shirt and socks and underwear. One does like a confident man. Because my hair was soaked, it took me longer to get dressed.

When finally I emerged from the bedroom, I found him strolling around the house, looking at the paintings. He was drinking coffee. He gave each picture at least five minutes of scrutiny, as though looking within it for other, concealed paintings. When I stood beside him, he put his arm around me. He kissed me on the forehead. We continued the tour in this fashion. All the while, he never took his eyes off the pictures.

I said something to him and he said, "Hmmm?"

We had breakfast. It was Sunday. The city was quiet. I played with the illusion that we could go window-shopping if the spirit moved us, or walk out for lunch at a nice little restaurant somebody had recommended. As if Henry had issued a command, no earthquakes or volcanic eruptions were reported. Nothing rumbled beneath the sidewalks of New York except the subway. The phones did not ring. Henry showed no disposition to leave. We watched a movie, putting it on hold a couple of times to fool around. We turned on the music and danced, for heaven's sake. He was a good dancer. We had a long, long talk. Suddenly Henry was so domestic, and so was I, that it wouldn't have surprised me if he had suggested a game of gin rummy in front of the fireplace, or asked for a liverwurst sandwich on rye with lots of ballpark mustard and a slice of red onion and a glass of beer for lunch.

Or proposed marriage—Ng Fred for best man, Melissa as maid of honor, Clementine frisking the guests, the last of the Duchins conducting the orchestra, no strobes or klieg lights because Henry had bought up every camera on the planet.

At eleven that night, when it was eleven in the morning of the next day in Mongolia, Henry's phone rang. It was Ng Fred. Henry listened to what he had to say, then made some calls. After that, he told me what was happening.

"He says Beijing is sending a delegation to the Spaceplane plant. Can you be ready in fifteen minutes?"

"Five," I said.

I packed a bag. Henry never bothered with luggage. He had jeans and T-shirts and sneakers and baseball caps and razors and toothbrushes stashed on all his airplanes. The car took us to the airport. We flew eastward, into the darkness of other time zones, and met the sun again somewhere over Afghanistan.

As we approached the factory in Mongolia, we watched from fifty thousand feet as a Spaceplane launched. It rolled along the tarmac of the long runway, then lifted off, then climbed to an altitude so far above us that we could only see it on a monitor. There, it seemed to pause for an instant before it accelerated and vanished.

3

THE DELEGATION FROM BEIJING ARRIVED at noon exactly aboard a large military transport. Dozens of men filed off the plane, each with an identical laptop slung across his shoulder and an identical briefcase in his hand. Their somber suits were identical. They formed up in ranks on the tarmac like terracotta soldiers and waited impassively for whatever was going to happen next. It was obvious even to me that these men were not bureaucrats, but troops disguised as bureaucrats. That the deception seemed to be designed to be detected gave the masquerade a certain extra frisson.

Ng Fred, who had gone out alone to meet the delegation, was escorted inside the plane. Long minutes passed before he reemerged, accompanied by General Yao, who wore a light gray suit with a red tie and a matching pocket-handkerchief that mimicked, not to say mocked, the space suits the world had been seeing on television.

We met in a small, unadorned room with a concrete floor and unpainted drywall partitions in which the nailheads showed. The only furniture was a plain, cheap table that teetered because one of its legs was slightly shorter than the others, and several uncomfortable folding metal chairs. Henry omitted the customary hospitable tea. General Yao didn't bother with the usual smiles and flirtation.

Smiles were totally shut down, handshakes perfunctory. The general's was positively flaccid. Henry and I sat on one side of the table with Ng Fred. General Yao and two other men—obviously army officers in civilian clothes but not the ones I had met before—sat on the opposite side. Never before had I known Henry to place a table, other than a dining table, between visitors and himself.

In a cold voice that also was new to me, Henry said, "We are surprised to see you, General Yao."

"And I am surprised to hear you say that, all things considered."

"What is the purpose of your visit?"

"We wish to interview the Chinese citizens who are employed in this place. Each of them individually."

"Then you should address your request to Ng Fred, who is in charge."

"Come, come. You are the man in charge."

"There will be no point in proceeding, General, if you begin by doubting my word."

The two men, who had always before treated each other as fraternity brothers, now behaved as if they had never met. The change couldn't have been more complete if it had been rehearsed. For all I knew, it *had* been rehearsed.

General Yao said, "There will be no point in proceeding unless I am addressing the actual principal."

"I say again, you should talk to Ng Fred," Henry said.

"What is the role of the woman?" General Yao asked.

"She is my adviser."

"If you have no interest in this matter, why do you need an adviser?"

"General, once again—talk to Ng Fred."

"You are placing Comrade Ng in a difficult position. He is a Chinese citizen. In your case, the violations of Chinese law that have occurred here are serious crimes, but as a foreigner you might in certain circumstances be spared harsh punishment. In Mr. Ng's case, however, the same offenses might very well constitute treason."

"We are in Mongolia, General. Chinese law does not apply here."

"Wherever he might happen to be, Comrade Ng is a Chinese citizen and his family and property are in China," General Yao said. "As a matter of protecting his legal interests and rights, I decline to regard him as the principal in this affair. If you continue to insist that I must do so, and Comrade Ng supports you, I will understand that you are, in fact, the principal and he is obeying your orders."

His words were meant to chill. In my case, they succeeded. What was happening began to seem real. This, at last, was the smiler with the knife I had always assumed lurked within the actor I had previously known. Without his ingratiating smile, Yao looked more than ever like Zhou Enlai. Henry's face was as stony, his voice as frigid as Yao's.

With formality, Henry excused himself, rose from his chair, and left the room. Yao exhibited no surprise. I followed Henry. So did Ng Fred. Henry and Ng Fred were walking fast. Our footsteps echoed in the vast building. The workers who usually crowded the factory floor had disappeared. It was the same in the next building and the one after that—not a human being in sight. Birds fluttered among the rafters, the only signs of life in a space that usually teemed with workers. It was the lunch hour, but no clamor issued from the cafeteria. If Henry and Ng Fred knew what was going on, as surely they did, they offered no explanation to me, let alone Yao, for whom this charade had been arranged.

In Ng Fred's office—deserted like the rest of the factory—we drank green tea drawn from a large thermos bottle. One wall was filled with small video monitors clustered around a much larger one. Not a word was spoken by any of us. Henry and Ng Fred were silent, presumably, because they were waiting for something to happen. I kept quiet because I had no idea what was coming next and was trying not to think about it. On one of the monitors I watched the bureaucrats, who were still waiting in formation on the tarmac by their airplane. They weren't talking, either.

Henry's cell phone rang. He looked at the caller ID, then let the phone ring seven more times before picking up.

He said, "Henry here."

He listened to the caller, and without saying anything more, switched off.

"Gotta go," he said to Ng Fred and me. He pointed a finger at the monitors. "Feel free to tune in."

Henry left us. Ng Fred clicked a remote. Henry and Yao appeared in split-screen view on the large monitor, marching toward each other along the catwalk. Like Henry, Yao was alone. When Yao and Henry met, the relaxed body language I remembered from their other encounters had been restored. Henry indicated the many doors lining the catwalk and in dumb show, invited Yao to choose one. A moment later they reappeared on another screen inside yet another small, utilitarian office. Ng Fred switched the image to the large screen. He touched another button and we heard what they were saying.

Yao said, "Alone at last."

Henry said, "Shall we get down to it?"

"Please."

Henry said, "What do they want?"

"Everything that's already in orbit," Yao replied. "On the ground, the factories and everything under construction, plus the girls and Ng Fred to run things. China's flag on the existing Spaceplanes."

"Is that all?"

"No, the list is long. They want a Chinese quota on the crew of the eventual mission. They want Chinese embryos chosen by China, Chinese only, in their own freezer. You may be interested to know that specimens of Chairman Mao's semen have been preserved."

"What else will they demand if I'm dumb enough to give them these things?"

"Use your imagination. Meanwhile, you've been given an opportunity to negotiate, so negotiate. It would be better to give them something instead of giving up everything."

"I've already given them a trillion dollars' worth of data."

"An appetizer."

"And if I don't give them anything more?"

"They will take what they want. I know you've taken the precaution of operating outside China. However, power still comes out of the barrel of a gun. There are three million soldiers in the People's Liberation Army. If even a very small percentage of these soldiers march across the border, Mongolia can't stop them. It won't even try. The United States will not intervene, since it doesn't need you or another disastrous war in Asia, and it doesn't have the cash. In its hubris, America may not recognize the reality, but it is impotent in this situation. You have given it everything it needs except time—time to build its own Spaceplanes, mother ship, and all the rest. China's position is the same. One power or the other must seize your property in order to rule the future."

Henry said, "So what do you recommend?"

"As I just said, negotiation."

"Why should they negotiate with me instead of just taking what they want?"

"For one thing, it would be quicker and cheaper. For another, the world might come to an end sooner than they think and they'd be stranded. You could blow up the factories and go into orbit, or to another galaxy, aboard the last Spaceplane. Or the end might not come despite the horoscope you have drawn up for humanity, in which case the invasion of a peaceful neighbor would become a serious embarrassment."

"What odds are being quoted in Beijing that the end is near?" Henry asked.

"The materialists, the scientists, say a thousand to one against," Yao replied. "They think you're delusional. The astrologers and the feng shui masters are divided on the percentages, but the pessimists are in the majority. There's some sort of problem with the magnetism of the planet, so the feng shui masters can't get the precise compass readings they need to make a valid judgment. If you can invent a super-compass and make a gift of it to the Party, our leaders' hearts might be softened."

Henry had taken with him the thermos from Ng Fred's office. Now he drew two bowls of tea and handed one to Yao. They sipped while they took a break.

Yao asked about Amerigo.

"Is the poor fellow in jail?"

"No," Henry replied—just the one word.

"I'm glad to hear it," Yao said, without asking for more information. "He's a harmless soul. And of course it would be a great bother for you if he were locked up."

Henry made no reply to that observation. The two men finished their tea.

Yao put down his bowl and said, "This is the offer I am instructed to present to you. CyberSci, Inc., will enter into a contract with the government of China to manufacture any or all of the items it has licensed China to manufacture. It will also give the young women who return from orbit the opportunity of joining the Chinese space program. It will train additional *taikonauts* and also train Chinese people chosen by the party to be trainers."

"Even if these terms were acceptable to us," Henry said, "we would not be able to start work on any such contract for several months, perhaps for a year or longer."

"You mean, until you complete your own mother ship?"

"We cannot interrupt our own work."

"Then you are saying no?"

"I'm saying two things. One, we're busy. Two, Ng Fred is the CEO of CyberSci. I'm just a customer."

Yao let a long moment pass. Then he said, "I'll deliver your message. The offer is not what my principals were hoping for."

"Sorry about that," Henry said. "But that's all there is."

"Whatever you say. But speaking as your friend, Henry, I hope you won't be adamant about this. Sometimes a sweetener, offered at the right moment and in the right spirit, can change minds."

Henry returned to Ng Fred's office. The three of us watched the monitor as General Yao and the bureaucrats got back on their airplane and it took off. Ng Fred made a telephone call and spoke a sentence in Mandarin. Soon afterward, the workers spilled out of hiding. The buildings filled with the sound of voices speaking Mandarin. This stirred the myriad birds perched in the rafters in our building.

The human beings looked up at the birds and clapped their hands in unison. The birds formed into a Gobi-brown cloud—there were many, many more of them than had been visible earlier—and fled through an aperture in the peak of the building in a long, thin stream, as if poured from a spout.

"The workers don't like the birds," Ng Fred said. "Neither do I, and I'm not the one who has to clean up after them."

4

HENRY SAID, "ARE YOU IN any way religious?"

We were lying in bed, in the dark.

"Are you kidding?" I said. "What about you?"

"My parents were Methodists," Henry said, "but I always thought that to them, Christianity was a code of behavior, not a matter of prayer and hope of heaven and fear of hell."

"They sound like sensible people," I said. "Why did you ask me such a question?"

Henry replied, "Because I think Mongolia would be a good place for us to get married, and I wanted to warn you that the eyes of God won't be involved."

"Are you sure of that?"

"This is a Buddhist country, and Buddhists attach no religious significance to marriage."

"So?"

"To them, it's a secular thing—something of this world, therefore illusory," Henry said. "Buddhism doesn't require anyone to get married, or stay single, for that matter. You can be blessed by a monk for good luck afterward if you want, but that's up to you."

I said, "Henry, did you wake me up to tell me you're a Buddhist?"

"No, to see how you felt about getting married in a godless country," Henry replied. "The Buddhist ceremony requires the man and the woman to make certain assurances to each other in the presence of others, but no clergy is involved. I think it would be good to do it that way."

"I agree. Let's do it."

"Would tomorrow be soon enough? It's customary to put on some clothes and have witnesses present."

It seemed strange to me to be having a conversation like this in the dark. We couldn't see each other's faces, so how could we know what was really happening between us? Henry must have had similar thoughts, because he switched on a lamp. This enabled him to see the tears in my eyes.

He said, "I'm serious."

"I know. You don't think we're rushing into this?"

"Hardly. We've had a long engagement."

The next morning, accompanied by Ng Fred and Daeng, we flew to Ulan Bator. Arrangements had been made. A large black car met us at the airport and took us to a government building. I wore the nicest dress I had brought with me. Our witnesses, besides Ng Fred, were the pilot, a Chinese woman called Li-li, and Daeng. An official who spoke English listened while we exchanged vows as prescribed in the *Sigalovada Sutta*, the Buddhist text that pertains to the happiness visible in the present life. We had memorized the words on the plane.

Looking into my eyes, Henry said, "I promise to love and respect my wife, to be kind and considerate, to be faithful, to confide responsibility to her in domestic matters, and to provide gifts to please her."

Looking into his eyes, I said, "To my husband, I promise to perform my household duties, to be hospitable to my in-laws and friends of my husband, to be faithful, to protect and save our earnings, and to fulfill my responsibilities lovingly and conscientiously."

Ng Fred produced rings—plain gold bands Henry must have

bought in New York, or who knows where. Henry and I exchanged them. Chastely, Henry kissed his bride.

The official spoke a few words in Khalkha Mongolian. Ng Fred interpreted and told us what to say in response. The official filled out our marriage certificate, writing everything in Cyrillic letters except our names, which he copied in Roman letters from our passports. It was evident that Henry's name meant nothing to him. We were just a couple of wandering Americans who thought we were Buddhists, getting married in the wrong country. He signed and stamped the certificate and handed it over. Ng Fred paid the fee. The thing was done.

This was my thought: Nobody had ever spoken lovelier vows. They left Henry and me feeling that for once between the two of us, nothing had been left unsaid. I could see this in his eyes, and I tried hard to make the same thought visible to him.

ELEVEN

1

IN THE TIME THAT FOLLOWED, I learned a lot about Henry that I hadn't known before—chiefly, that he liked to talk in the dark. Our deepest conversations occurred when he woke from a dream. In many of his dreams, Henry found himself in a metropolis that resembled a city he knew, yet was not quite itself. The light was dim, as if bathed in moonlight alone. Either electricity has not yet been discovered in this place, or knowledge of it has been lost. He stands just outside a crowd of strangers who shun him. He speaks to them. They hear him but do not reply. He's not inaudible or invisible to them—they just don't want to have anything to do with him. They are like people waiting for a bus that's late. Where is it, they think in unison. Is it coming or not? Suddenly the crowd parts and a kind of Quasimodo, squat and ugly and unwashed and dressed in rags, leaps out and wraps his arms around Henry. He is tremendously strong. Henry tells him to let go, but like the original Quasimodo, the creature is deaf. Henry struggles, but struggle is hopeless. Quasimodo's arms are a vise that keeps on tightening. There seems to be no limit to his strength. Henry realizes that there can be no escape. The creature is never going to let him go. What is this thing? Death? Fate? Madness? Henry's intelligence? The dream faded to black before Henry found out.

We made love and went back to sleep.

After the wedding, Henry moved into "my" apartment. Apart from a couple of brief, long-ago experiments while I was still learning the dos and don'ts of intergender relationships, I had never before lived with a man. Having a husband around the house was far nicer than I had supposed. It turned out that Henry had lived here by himself for a couple of months, so he had no adjustments to make to his surroundings apart from having me around. Except for my closet, the place was as he had left it. I wondered if the original bed, his bed, had been replaced, and if not, what had gone on in it before he started keeping himself only unto me. Judging by his vigor, the answer was, Quite a lot. I had no wish to know who the lucky girls had been, and Henry asked me no questions about my past. Adam was never mentioned by either of us. Henry and I were hardly ever apart. We didn't hang out together when we were at home, but I caught glimpses of him and heard fragments of his voice as he talked on the telephone. Months after the novelty had worn off, we made love many times a day, whenever the idea came to one or both of us.

Everyone came to dinner—Amerigo and Garbo, Clementine, the three engineers, Ng Fred and his wife, who bore a striking resemblance to a great beauty I had seen in several Chinese movies. It turned out that she and the gorgeous actress were one and the same woman. Like Ng Fred, she spoke American English. Her American name was Gwen. She had been raised in Santa Barbara. How she and her children had gotten out of China was not explained.

Henry's Rule Number 1, "Make no fuss," was strictly observed throughout the evening. The food and wine were no better than usual, but how could they have been? No announcement of our union was made. None was necessary. Ng Fred already knew the facts. Everyone else saw the rings. No one remarked on them.

A couple of times a week, Henry and I actually went to restaurants where he was a familiar but nameless figure, a very generous tipper who always paid cash. Sometimes we even went to the theater. We walked a lot in the evening, and gradually I learned the faces of the chaps who accompanied us. It was easy. Four of them always sat, two by two, at nearby tables in restaurants or in the seats behind us and beside us in theater, while two remained outside, one on the front door, one on the back. We ran in the park every morning. The chaps ran with us. In the wee hours, we swam in the pool in the basement of our building while the chaps patrolled the perimeter.

There were reasons why Henry's anonymity endured. Some people didn't believe he existed, but was a phantasm invented by the dark side for its own hidden purposes. Because of the constant feed of images from orbit, he was much discussed on talk shows and in social conversation. He and I overheard people talking about him in restaurants and theater lobbies. Most seemed to like the idea that they might walk right by Henry, look right at him, and never know who he was. Even if they suspected that Henry was who he was, restaurateurs and waiters who graciously accepted his crisp tax-free banknotes had no motivation to tip off the paparazzi. Hanging out in public with me was chancy, but the possibility that someone might recognize me as the scarlet woman of the tabloids and realize that Henry must be Henry didn't seem to worry him. Or if it did, he never said so or behaved as if it was anything to worry about. The real reason that he was spared the burden of celebrity may have been a simple one: Despite his wealth, Henry was perceived to be a nice guy who had done what he had done on his own, by using his head. He had every right to put on airs, even to make a spectacle of himself, but he had never done so. His inventions were regarded by most people as good deeds. Room-temperature superconductors and a virus-free Internet and fusion power and the Spaceplane and the greatest show in orbit had made everyone's life more interesting, and if he made a lot of money out of them, what was so un-American about a guy taking his cut? Henry's latest thing, the construction of whatever he was building in Earth's orbit, clearly had benevolent purposes even if he hadn't yet revealed them. Who knew what he had in mind this time? Maybe a ship would go forth and in due course return from the other planets, or even the stars, laden with treasure like a Spanish galleon. If so, he was far more likely than any imaginable government to share the loot.

The media might not have shared the good impression of the masses, but the spectacle of the space maidens going about their mysterious work in their bright outfits was a better story. Henry had the power to shut off the cameras and stop the flow of information and the Niagara of money that the images from orbit generated for the television industry. The media did not want that to happen. In the end, the uproar over the enhanced embryos was a two-day story. Henry was not hiding out in the White House or the Pentagon or some imperialist corporate office. He just wanted his privacy, and the fact that he was just about the last man on Earth who had any privacy didn't seem to bother the common man at all.

2

IT TURNED OUT THAT THIS idyll of wedded bliss was an entr'acte. After months of silence from China, Beijing carried out the threat that General Yao had delivered when he and his soldiers in disguise visited Ng Fred's factory in Mongolia. A no-holds-barred story in *People's Daily* awakened the sleeping scandal of the enhanced embryos. The paper alleged that the hidden purpose of Henry Peel's work in progress on the fringe of outer space was to build a spaceship whose mission was to rescue a group of multinational capitalists, who were secretly financing it, from a catastrophic worldwide earthquake that was expected to cripple civilization, cause billions of deaths, and make the planet Earth inhospitable to life. The secret plan of the capitalists was to return to Earth as soon as it was safe to do so and impregnate such women as had survived the catastrophe with the genetically engineered embryos recently discovered in Italy. The goal was to establish a new political and economic order imposed by the Übermenschen that would be the product of these technological rapes. The helpless survivors of the apocalypse would be enslaved, and in the dark age to follow, would be bred selectively, like livestock, to ensure an adequate supply of slave labor.

People's Daily quoted from the report of a commission of one hundred distinguished scientists that had been convened by the ruling body of the country, the Politburo Standing Committee of the Communist Party of China. The scientific commission was called, inevitably, the Commission of One Hundred. It included not only Chinese scientists, but also scientists and academics from several other countries, including Asian, African, Latin American, and European nations and the United States. All affixed their signatures to the report, and on the day after it was made public by *People's Daily*, many of them fanned out to appear on television and websites in their own countries to explain its details in the local language. The scientists described in detail the catastrophic effects of the hyperquake and the role of the core of the earth in generating it. Their vision of the Event was remarkably similar to Henry's—as of course it would be, since they were at long last considering the same data. Some were certain that the hyperquake would occur soon. Others believed that it was unlikely to take place in the lifetime of anyone now alive. Most agreed that it was inevitable. The consensus of the media, which polled the scientists, was that the odds were fifty-fifty and that X-Day, as journalists immediately named it, would occur sooner rather than later.

This scenario was the paranoia industry's dream come true. Not only was the world going to come to an end and the accursed United States of America along with it, but the planet that the human race had abused so shamelessly was going to strike back and destroy its tormentors. At bottom, an international capitalist conspiracy was the villain of the piece, and Henry, the capitalist whom the masses had loved, was exposed at last as the villain of villains.

The *People's Daily* story pulled no punches. The thesaurus remained the bible of the Reds. Ng Fred was described as the notorious lackey of U.S. imperialism, Amerigo as the infamous international drug peddler, Clementine as the ruthless spymaster and tool of the CIA, Melissa as a Wall Street pettifogger, myself as the notorious courtesan and pornographer. Even the poor Prof was described as an agent provocateur and infiltrator of academia. The engineers were also named, along with others.

The problem was that the underlying facts, if not the frosting about the multinational capitalist conspiracy, were accurate enough. Henry and the rest of us had been doing exactly what the story said we were doing, i.e., building a ship in which a sample of humanity of our own choosing might escape extinction. We had been doing so without revealing our intentions.

Melissa was consulted. She addressed Henry and me as if summing up for a jury that held Henry's life in its hands. She was eloquent, she was sincere, she offered many examples of Henry's honesty and probity, his constitutional inability to lie, cheat, steal, or act dishonorably in any way. Every potential juror in the world had believed that until today. I would have preferred that she had gone into the bathroom, closed the door, and screamed into a towel.

As it was, she demonstrated how impossible it was to defend Henry and the work he was doing now that the seeds of doubt and anger had been sown.

3

ONCE AGAIN, THE PLANET INTERVENED within the week and killed
the story. A cluster of twenty-one separate earthquakes occurred
almost simultaneously in the Pacific Ocean along the Solomon
and Bismarck Plates, north of New Guinea and close to the equator. None registered less than 8 on the Richter scale. The strongest,
centered in the Bismarck Archipelago, was measured at 9.6, roughly
equivalent to the energy released by the explosion of forty billion
tons of TNT. It was the strongest earthquake ever recorded by scientific instruments. Thousands perished. Tsunamis swept over the
Bismarck, Solomon, and Admiralty Islands, as well as others lying
hundreds of miles from the epicenters. Waves surged inland in
New Guinea. Dormant volcanoes erupted on many islands, and
new volcanoes rose from the sea. A pall of ash obscured the sun,
moon, and stars. Parts of northern Australia were underwater.
Fishes from the Great Barrier Reef washed ashore in New Zealand.
In New Zealand itself, Lake Taupo and several other formerly qui-
escent volcanoes erupted on both the North and South Islands.
In Japan and Alaska, more volcanoes were ignited. In Singapore,
Jakarta, Manila, and Hong Kong, the windows of skyscrapers—
often every window in the building—were shattered by the shock

waves that these events generated. On the island of Hawaii, Mauna Loa, Mauna Kea, and Hualalai belched gas and ash and lava. In the Marquesas, long-dead volcanoes also awakened, and surf overflowed the cliffs and flooded Henry's house, among many others. In New York, ten thousand miles from the epicenters, buildings quivered. People walking their dogs in the dark felt the tremor and as memories awakened, stopped in their tracks, waiting for something worse to happen. Dogs in their hundreds of thousands barked and howled and whined from one end of Manhattan to the other. Rats and mice and squirrels fled. Pet cats escaped en masse, so that lost cat posters fluttered from every other lamppost in the five boroughs.

Henry slept through the first part of this news. I watched the live feed—raw unedited footage of events being photographed as they happened and were transmitted via satellite to the network. The images began to come in at about four in the morning. By that time I had been watching with the sound muted for four or five hours. Several moments passed before I realized that the images had changed. I clapped on a headset and listened. Watching raw video can be disorienting because there is no voice-over. Nobody in a suit and tie stands in front of the White House telling the world what's what, as the soundless images tumble across the screen. Cameras were turned topsy-turvy as their operators fell over backward as the ground heaved beneath them or they were trampled by the crowd. Sometimes they got back on their feet and refocused the cameras, sometimes not. The sky was a funny color, tropical blue brindled in hellish red and black. Many of the pictures were aerial shots. Once in a while images taken from space were intercut. The screen then filled with ocean panoramas in which great columns of black smoke, filled with the boiling blues and yellows of burning gas, burst from the surface of the water and rose thousands of feet into the air in a matter of seconds.

My God, I thought—of course that's what I thought—*it's all over.* I didn't scream—not because my brain and nerves did not instruct me to do so, but because I could not let myself wake Henry, the hater of fuss, with a shriek. Instead, I ran to the bedroom and laid a cold hand on his face. He opened his eyes, registered what he was half-seeing in the unlighted room, and laughed. I understood why: I still wore the headset, but nothing else except the afghan I had wrapped around myself to ward off the chilly draught of the air-conditioning. Henry reached for me. I wanted to play Indian princess? Fine, he'd be the cowboy. I leaped back, avoiding his encircling arms.

"Henry, wake up."

"I'm wide awake."

He reached for me again.

"No, come quick. Something is happening."

He followed me into the television room. He turned up the sound. In seconds he put together the horrific jigsaw puzzle that was flashing piece by piece onto the screen. I wanted to ask him for confirmation that the end had come, to cry out, *Is it happening?*

"I don't think so," he said calmly.

"Then what is it?"

"It's a local event."

Local? Had he said that the Pacific Ocean was about to be flung into space like a mouthful of spit, I would have been more ready to believe him.

I said, "How do you know?"

"Because nothing is happening here, or anywhere else except in one chain of islands."

Henry produced a cell phone and punched one of its keys. Ng Fred's voice said hello. Henry put the phone on speaker so that I could hear what was going on.

Henry said, "Fred—are you aware what's happening in the South Pacific?"

"I'm watching. What is it?"

"Not It," Henry said. "Not quite, not yet."

Ng Fred said, "You're sure?"

"Aren't you?" Henry asked. "But be alert. I'll be there tomorrow afternoon."

Soon afterward, we were flying toward Mongolia.

In the weeks that followed, aftershocks by the hundreds came one after the other—strong around the epicenter, mild to imperceptible elsewhere. Temperatures dropped throughout the world by an average of 1.5 degrees Fahrenheit and continued to fall, yet the rain was warm. It was also gritty. You could feel it, and see the volcanic dust in the rainwater that swirled in the gutters. The sky was one big bruise. The sun was blurred. Curiously, media panic notwithstanding, not many people looked up. They just went about their lives as if they thought these signs would soon go away and everything would be normal again.

Few wanted to think about the implications of twenty-one simultaneous earthquakes, no matter how many excited scientists and highly paid alarmists were shouting at each other on television. A minor earthquake that turned off the electricity for two weeks might cause mass catatonia in Manhattan—but Micronesia? The twenty-one quakes—now called the "cluster quakes" by the media—hadn't happened in New York (or London or Paris or Beijing or Moscow). They had only happened inside a television set, and inside the box they remained. Rescue missions were dispatched. Checks were written, schoolchildren drew pictures, politicians harrumphed, the truly disturbed sought therapy. This particular moment of excitement was over. On to the next.

From my point of view, the principal benefit of this mass repression of reality was that the media hubbub about my husband died. He simply disappeared from the airwaves. One moment he was the villain of the hour, the next he was ectoplasm. *People's Daily* continued to denounce him, but the rest of the talking heads appeared to have forgotten that he had ever been the subject of commentary. I wanted to believe that the slander died because Henry was and always had been above suspicion. Ng Fred believed that the propaganda failure had robbed the Politburo Standing Committee of its pretext for launching a raid into Mongolia and seizing the factories and human assets of CyberSci, Inc. Henry disagreed. He thought that Beijing would either invent another reason or else just do what it wanted to do in the knowledge that it was too powerful to be challenged.

"The world is looking the other way," Henry said. "It's a good moment for the Chinese to act. All they need to take possession of everything we own in Mongolia is a couple of platoons of commandos. It would be over in minutes, without firing a shot. We're not going to resist and get our people killed. They don't want to kill them. They know that the human assets are at least as valuable as the equipment."

"To you, maybe," Ng Fred said. "But one thing China has got plenty of is people. I can assure you that shots *will* be fired—one at least, two if you also happen to be here when it happens."

Henry didn't argue the point. I hoped this meant that he didn't intend to be in Mongolia when the raiding parties arrived.

I said, "What about the Mongolian government?"

"They won't make a sound," Ng Fred said. "Number one, they're not crazy. Number two, they've already got their money and Beijing will let them keep it if they mind their own business. Number three, you should forgive me, all this stuff belongs to an American capitalist whose body can't even be identified."

Ng Fred's summing-up brought a faint smile to Henry's lips. It tied my insides into knots and made my mind go dark with fear. At night I dreamed, by day I imagined, one of General Yao's genteel young officers firing a pistol into Henry's brain.

Henry continued to behave as if he were going to live forever. We coupled, we talked in the night. Henry waited, or so I thought, for the idea that would calm the situation. Meanwhile he ordered the work to proceed at even greater speed. One hundred additional women were almost at the end of their training. In a matter of days they were lifted into orbit. There was plenty for them to do, and plenty of room for them. The original space maidens had by now assembled two complete spheres and the command module. Two other spheres were under construction. One was almost complete, the other in an early stage. Two new Spaceplanes were almost ready to fly. The circle of booster rockets, rendered obsolete by the Spaceplane, still brooded near the Chinese frontier.

4

ON JULY 11, THE NORTH Magnetic Pole jumped 376 miles in a single day and relocated itself in northern Siberia. On the same day, the South Magnetic Pole moved about 150 miles across Antarctica. Earth's magnetic field weakened dramatically. In what-if interviews with scientists, the media raised the possibility that cosmic radiation might now penetrate the planet's enfeebled magnetic field and fry life on Earth. Although nobody could explain why or how this happened, heavy snow driven by high winds fell a few days later in belts of the Northern and Southern Hemispheres, stretching from the poles to Seoul in the north and Rio de Janeiro in the south. In Siberia, Scotland, and Canada, as much as ten feet of snow fell. It melted quickly—almost instantaneously, in fact, as might have been expected in midsummer. As usual, most of the public showed little curiosity or concern. Quirks of nature were nothing new. To most human beings it didn't matter much where the North and South Poles were located. They didn't believe in X-Day. The media warned that it was coming; therefore the media would soon report that there was no danger.

5

ONE NIGHT, THE PHONE WOKE us up at 3 a.m. Henry put it on speaker.

Ng Fred's voice said, "They're here. Fifty men. Special forces."

"Have you completed the checklist?"

"Everything's in position, Henry."

"Our people?"

"They're OK so far. Don't come."

"I'm going to make the call now," Henry said.

He got up and walked briskly out of the room. I followed, switching on lights as I went. After the click of each switch, Henry's pale body would take shape, then stride through a doorway into another dark room. I caught up to him in the television room.

The screen blinked on and the familiar image of the mother ship and its attendant Spaceplanes appeared, space maidens busily fitting the pieces of the puzzle together. Henry switched channels and we were looking at a Spaceplane—behind it, the moon. A satellite, bristling with antennas, floated in the foreground. It was marked with the roundel of the People's Republic of China, a red star with a broad red stripe on either side of it.

Henry pressed a speed-dial key. His phone was still on speaker, so I could hear everything. The number he was calling rang three times, then General Yao picked up.

In a tone of delight, he said, "Henry."

Henry said, "Am I interrupting anything?"

"I'm in a meeting, but I'm sure that the others will understand when I tell them who's calling."

He did so without bothering to cover the mouthpiece with his hand.

"Please turn on your television receiver," Henry said. "Channel two two eight seven."

We heard the set come on in Beijing.

Yao said, "It's nothing but snow."

Henry supplied an access code.

On the screen of our own television set, a hatch opened on the Spaceplane. Three space maidens floated from it in their vermilion suits and swam, as it seemed, to the satellite. It was a beautiful picture, but apparently Yao's companions didn't like what they saw on their own screen. Someone with a squeaky voice cursed in Cantonese. Somebody else shouted, and then began to cough violently.

Yao said, "Henry, what is the meaning of this?"

Henry said, "We're having a drill. The object you see on-screen is the primary communications satellite for China's space program."

On-screen, the cargo bay of the Spaceplane opened. A crane unfolded like origami from the cargo bay.

Henry said, "There are five other Chinese national defense satellites in orbit. Our ships can reach any or all of them easily and quickly. If necessary we can retrieve an entire satellite and return it to Earth or some other destination, or make repairs in orbits. This team, one of several, is specially trained to deal with just such problems. Should you ever need assistance, we'd be only too happy to do what we can to help out. We could even work on all six satellites at once."

In orbit, the space maidens waited, a few meters from the satellite. Each held a tool in her gloved hand, an effective prop, since all the world knew how good these women were with tools. We heard others in Yao's meeting talking to one another. It was a babble, everyone shouting at the same time. I caught a word here and there, but couldn't put their meaning together because they were using words I didn't know.

General Yao came back on the line. By now he had recovered his sangfroid, and he sounded almost like the original Yao, bland and false to the core.

"Very interesting, Henry," he said, and clicked off.

The Chinese troops departed the factory thirty minutes later. They were General Yao's men, Ng Fred reported over the telephone—from the same unit as the soldiers who always came with him. They were armed to the teeth, but they made no threatening gestures. Their conduct was exemplary. Their faces were expressionless. Their eyes looked straight ahead. They touched no one, asked no questions, made no demands, just spread out through the two factories, took up their posts, and waited.

"Did the officers explain why they were there?" Henry asked.

"They were mute," Ng Fred replied. "So were the men. Didn't speak a word the whole time."

"Why not?" I asked.

"Probably because they'd be the last to know why they were," Ng Fred said

6

THE TIME HAD COME TO move the crew of the mother ship into orbit, and Henry flew to their compound to bid them good-bye. From the air, their compound with its glittering windows and multitude of rooftops and trees and lawns and twinkling royal-blue swimming pools and green soccer fields and tennis courts and baseball diamonds might have been any suburban community outside any city in the developed world, except that in this case there was no city.

The commander of the mission met us on the tarmac. He was a Gary Cooper type—weather-burnt, slow-spoken, tall, gaunt, and handsome.

He and Henry clasped hands and spoke each other's names.

"Angus, meet my wife," Henry said. "My dear, Admiral Angus Henderson."

Henderson took my hand and squeezed it, relaxing his grip just before the bones snapped.

"An honor, ma'am."

The crew had assembled in the vast interior of a hangar. There were hundreds of them. They were a good-looking lot, all of them in tip-top physical condition—lean, quick moving, clear-eyed. They belonged to many nationalities. They radiated competence and chosenness. Whatever their gender or race, they were alike in manner and affect, as if they had all gone to the same school, which had fitted each of them out with the same manner, the same convictions. Give them a test and they would intuit the answers and ace it. Clearly they had lived up to their SAT scores or their countries' equivalents. They had lived in isolation and trained together in this compound for a year or more. Previously they had been astronauts, cosmonauts, pilots, military officers, physicists, chemists, scientists of many other disciplines, computer whizzes, engineers, academics, physicians, surgeons—name it. The genders were present in something like proportionate numbers. So were the races. Taken together, the crew looked like a scientifically selected sample of the best and brightest and most genetically favored of the earth's peoples. No doubt that was exactly what they were.

They were as orderly as a congregation of Episcopalians awaiting the first note of the organ. Smiles—white, bright, perfect smiles—flashed throughout the crowd. At the front of the hangar a Spaceplane stood on its tail like a religious symbol, its polymer skin gleaming in the artificial light. Despite the verdant look of the compound from an altitude of ten thousand feet, the parched scent of the desert filled the nostrils.

When Admiral Henderson mounted the rostrum, the entire group sprang to its feet. The explosive noise made by this unified movement of people was a single, simultaneous, profoundly military sound.

From the lectern, Angus Henderson gave a curt nod. The crew sat down.

"It is sometimes said in introducing an especially distinguished visitor that he needs no introduction," Henderson said. "That is seldom really true. Today, it is. Our visitor's name and his work are known to nearly everyone in the world. He is the man we work for. Ladies and gentlemen, Mr. Henry Peel."

Henry entered from stage left. His appearance was greeted by total silence. The hush was almost visible, as if a cartoon balloon had popped into existence above the audience in which a single incredulous thought, printed in bold caps, had popped simultaneously into several hundred minds: *"THIS* IS HENRY PEEL?*"*

This collective incredulity lasted, maybe, for a count of ten. Then the audience leapt to its feet and slapped hands together as if an applause sign had lighted up. Henry did not say *thank-you-thank-you* or make any other gesture. He just stood at the rostrum, smiling his fugitive smile and moving no other muscle as he waited for the outburst to run its course.

When it did, he adjusted the height of the microphone and said, "Hi, I'm Henry."

More applause, also appreciative laughter. The guy had a sense of humor! When quiet was restored, Henry began to speak in his usual unhurried way. He was perfectly at ease. Neither he nor anyone else had ever addressed a hangar full of people he was about to send into space for the rest of their lives, but he was so relaxed that you might have thought he was a member of Toastmasters International who did this sort of thing every day. He did not flatter the audience. They didn't need flattery. Being selected for this mission might be the ultimate meritocratic achievement, but they were accustomed to being selected and I suppose they took it for granted that they had been chosen to rescue the human race. Henry nevertheless managed to send them the message they wanted to hear: They deserved to be here. He was glad to meet them at last. He thanked them for the many invaluable contributions they had already made to the mission. The pilots among them had been flying the Spaceplanes and the mother ship itself, insofar as it needed to be controlled, by remote control for many months. About a hundred of them had visited the mother ship and the rest of the flotilla in orbit.

"As those of you who have gone aboard the mother ship know," Henry said, "the problem of weightlessness has remained the chief obstacle to the ultimate success of the mission. In fact, there was little point in launching the mission unless the crew could be capable, at the end of it, of walking off the ship onto the surface of the planet and doing the job they had returned to Earth to do. The physical and psychological consequences of the crew's adaptation to weightlessness over a journey that might last for several generations are obvious. Many doubted that such an adaptation was even possible. It was essential to find a solution before the mission was launched, even if it was only a partial answer to the problem that could be improved upon by the crew in the course of the flight. In regard to that problem, I have good news."

The audience's attention tightened like a collective muscle.

He said, "I can tell you that a system of artificial gravity is in the process of being installed in orbit within the mother ship and the Spaceplanes. It has undergone exhaustive testing in the laboratory and in space. It works."

This audience was far too cool to gasp or to applaud this astonishing news, but the feeling in the room changed. The lights dimmed. Monitors lit up. An image of the mother ship and its attendant Spaceplanes and other escorts appeared. The camera zoomed in until the flotilla filled the screen. An interior shot showing space maidens, dressed in coveralls, going about their tasks. One of them, an extremely pretty girl on a tall ladder, dropped a tool and it fell slowly to the floor twenty feet below, bounced some five feet straight up, fell, and bounced again, finally settling on the floor. In another shot about a dozen girls did gymnastics, leaping off the balance beam and floating back down to it while performing slow-motion somersaults in air. Another group of young women ran a race around the perimeter of the sphere in which the gym was located. They took tremendously long strides, covering meters with every step, and floating from one footfall to another. Mostly they wore their hair in tight pigtails, but one girl ran with her blue-black hair unbound. It floated around her head like a shadow in a painting.

The pictures stopped. The lights went on.

Henry said, "As you can see, the artificial gravity we have so far achieved is weaker than Earth gravity. To be precise, it is about twenty-four percent of Earth gravity, or roughly halfway between the gravity of the moon and the gravity of Mars. It is, however, adequate to maintain the health of human muscles and equilibrium, and we believe that its strength can be substantially increased during flight as the phenomenon is more fully understood."

"Increased by how much?" asked a man with a bass voice that would have made an umpire wince.

"Theoretically, to something close to Earth gravity," Henry answered politely. "I'm sure there are other questions. Go ahead."

He pointed to a woman in the second row.

"My question is simple," she said. "How did you do it?"

"Our friend Ng Fred, who can make reality out of any idea, and his workers fabricated the equipment in the underground plant you have all visited," Henry said. "The modules that power the system were lifted into orbit by booster rockets, then placed in proper position using remote control from Earth."

"Not that," said the blonde. "How does it work?"

"Diamagnetism," Henry said. "We created a magnetic field that resembles Earth's magnetic field."

"What about the metals in the ship?"

"The mother ship and the Spaceplanes, as you know, are made entirely of polymers. Where it was impossible to avoid the use of metal, aluminum and other nonmagnetic metals were employed."

He pointed at the man with the powerful voice.

"What about magnetism disrupting electrical systems?"

"That problem has been solved through superconductivity," Henry said. "That was less complicated than you might think, but a little too complicated to describe in a sentence or two, or even a paragraph."

"Give it a try, Henry," said the bellower.

"The equations and the blueprints are available in the archives of the mother ship," Henry said. "Any member of the crew can access them or anything else in the archives. No doubt Admiral Henderson will arrange fuller briefings so that you all get a better idea how this thing works. The idea of inducing artificial gravity in spacecraft through magnetism isn't new. It was tried on one of the Apollo flights in the twentieth century, with very minor but observable results. In a laboratory experiment in the same era, a frog was levitated, though not very far, by magnetism. Someone else, please. Microphones are available."

Many hands were raised. Henry called on half a dozen people. Mostly their questions were versions of those that had already been asked.

The last question was one that I would have liked to ask: "What effect will long-term exposure to the magnetism have on the human body?"

"Less than an MRI scan," Henry said. "Earth itself is a magnet, and this has done its species no harm over four thousand generations."

At least a hundred hands were still raised. Henry ignored them. They fell one by one. For another fifteen minutes, he spoke of other matters, as if the simulation of gravity was something that could not possibly bewilder anyone who had, until twenty minutes before, regarded such a thing as impossible.

TWELVE

1

IN THE DARK, HIS FAVORITE place for telling me things I did not wish to hear, Henry confided that he intended to remain on Earth when the mother ship sailed. I tried to change his mind—humanity needed him, he had a duty to be the good shepherd to the crew, did he not understand that if he died, his intelligence would die with him, depriving the future of whatever work remained for it to do? He wouldn't listen. As a last resort, I even asked him to consider the awful, to him, possibility that the crew of the mother ship might do to him what the Roman senate did to Augustus, and make him a god.

Henry refused to be wheedled. The fact was, he didn't believe it mattered much what happened to the organism that was himself. It was, after all, just one among billions.

But where did that leave me?

"You should make your own decision," Henry said.

"About what?"

"Going or staying."

"Would you prefer that I go?"

"No. But that doesn't mean you're obliged to stay."

"Oh, yes it does," I said.

Henry didn't argue. He never did. He squeezed me. He put his lips upon me. I wrapped him in my arms and breathed him in. I might not be able to see his face, but even in the perpetual darkness of one of the twenty-seven moons of Uranus I would have known him by scent and touch and taste and the unmistakable cadence of his breath.

The following morning, Henry called a meeting of the inner circle and asked everyone what his or her wishes were. Would they embark with the crew?

No one answered. No one wanted to speak first.

In the end, Ng Fred was the volunteer. "My wife doesn't wish to go," he said. "Gwen thinks it wouldn't be comfortable to be an outsider among people who have already chosen their friends and for the most part can't speak Mandarin. Furthermore, the *I Ching* has assured her that her children will be happy grandparents on this planet. I can't go without her and the children. Besides, it would be awkward for Angus Henderson. The ship doesn't need two captains."

Melissa, back in character, said, "How about you, Henry?"

I jumped between him and her question.

"I'm staying," I said.

Henry said, "We're staying together."

"It's good to know that," Melissa said. "Because I'm not going anywhere, either. For years I planned to save my son and daughter by sending them off as passengers on the mother ship. Now that the moment has arrived, they absolutely refuse to go. They fear boredom. They don't want to lose their friends or miss the new music. They're both sexually active now, they tell me. They don't want to leave that behind in exchange for a life in which everyone else is old, and as my daughter puts it, you can't even look out a window, and even if you could, what would be the use?"

The vote was unanimous. Garbo had wavered, Amerigo said, but in the end, she was like Ng Fred's wife and Melissa's kids. She didn't want to leave her friends behind and be condescended to by the crew because she didn't have a doctorate. She didn't want to wear polyester and eat pap and live in the void of space, and in the absence of art, for the rest of her life.

Not once during this whole process had I thought about the embryos. Now I did. What would those tiny organisms—their cells already possessed of all the data they would need to grow a brain, a heart, limbs, and the stuff that dreams are made on, if centuries from now they were implanted in a womb, any human womb—what would they remember? Not me, not Henry, not anyone like themselves, not the Earth as we had known it.

But then again, why shouldn't they remember, as we do, events that we cannot possibly have witnessed?

The next morning, Henry handed over command of the mother ship to Angus Henderson. The business was supremely Henryesque—unsentimental, brief, and matter-of-fact. Although the absence of ceremony must have jarred the instincts of a military man like Henderson, there were no salutes, no stirring music played by a brass band, no speeches. Henry handed the captain an envelope containing his instructions for the mission, shook his hand, and wished him Godspeed. Altogether, it was a gloomy moment, like the last day before a world war was going to begin and no one on either side had any idea who was going to win or who was going to come back.

Admiral Henderson took custody of the apparatus that had been summoned into existence by Henry's genius and dollars. If Henry's prophecy of cataclysm was going to be fulfilled—and judging by the expressions on their faces, no one present seriously doubted that it would be—money was about to become worthless, along with just about everything else that had value on Earth simply because the world pretended that it did. What use could there possibly be for currency aboard the mother ship—or for that matter, for whatever and whoever survived on Earth?

Within the hour, Henderson and an advance party of crew members were ferried into orbit aboard one of the Spaceplanes. Two more of these ships were parked on the tarmac. They had returned to Earth all but the one hundred space maidens who had decided to remain aboard—under one condition. Ng Fred, immune to the melancholy that bound the rest of us together, was amused by the message they sent him in this regard.

"They took a vote," he told us. "They will only fly if we send no men to join them."

Clementine, who up to this moment had been remarkably still, said, "What about the men you've been training for the mission?"

"They stay behind."

Clementine said, "You mean to say you've bowed to the ultimatum?"

"What's the alternative?" Ng Fred asked. "Angus Henderson won't launch without the women. The ship is their baby. They built it from scratch, on the ground and in orbit. They know it and care about it as nobody else does or possibly can. They're indispensable."

"How are the men taking this?"

"They're disappointed. Men have feelings, too."

"What about your feelings?"

"Frankly, a load has been lifted from my shoulders," Ng Fred said. "I've always been of two minds about adding the men. They're unpredictable, especially if they're Chinese, and they make women unpredictable."

Melissa said, "All I have to say is, good move, girls."

"The girls think so, too," Ng Fred said. "No more loudmouth thugs ordering them to do stupid things and beating them up in one way or another if they don't obey."

"Forgive my asking," Clementine said, "But doesn't this raise a question about replacing the space maidens through natural increase?"

"Yes, but it was easy to resolve."

"Of course—the embryos."

Amerigo answered. "The girls vetoed that," he said. "As a matter of principle, the embryos aren't sorted by race or ethnicity. You take what you get. The ladies are Han. They want Han babies, not funny-looking kids who are half something else."

"What an old-fashioned dilemma."

"Not really. The girls had thought it over. At their suggestion, the men have provided sperm samples. These have been labeled with DNA information and frozen. They will be loaded aboard the mother ship for future use."

Melissa said, "What a turncoat to your gender you are, Amerigo. You should be proud."

None of us, not even Henry, visited the mother ship. To me, and I think to most of the others, the ship, as soon as it was assembled in space, had become a concept, rather than an actuality. Even after it became visible as a glittering dot in the sky and an image on television screens, it remained beyond the reach of the mind—remote, untouchable, like everything else in the night sky. Yet it was something human beings had made while other human beings watched from five hundred miles below. It was as material, as earthly, and in its own way as familiar as a brick house on a suburban lot. Except that it wasn't.

2

AS SOON AS THE LAST member of the crew was safely aboard the mother ship, Henry and I went home. As the desert flowed beneath the wings of the airplane, I felt in my bones that I would never look upon its monotony again. The thought filled me with sorrow. This was a surprise for any number of reasons. Always before, when something came to an end, I had asked, "What next?" and awaited the answer, knowing that it would sooner or later come into being. Not this time. There was no next thing except chaos and darkness. I upbraided myself for yielding to despair, and then absolved myself by blaming Henry for it, unjust and unintelligent as this was. He, too, was silent and withdrawn, and as usual, I caught his mood like a cold. In all our time in Mongolia he had said nothing more about a honeymoon. That was all right with me. After months in the wilderness, I wanted to be in New York—no tropic islands, no deserts, no artificial gravity. I had found out through research that mountains are not so idyllically safe as I had thought. The Rio Grande Rift, where the planet's crust split apart thirty-five million years ago, ran through the Colorado Rockies. The Andes were nudged by the Nazca Plate just off the coast of South America, the Alps were being pulled asunder by tectonic forces, and the Caucasus, infested with pious bandits and kidnappers, was not a destination for sweet-hearts.

We returned to Manhattan. For our first anniversary, we went out to dinner, walking to the restaurant inside our ring of chaps. We clinked wineglasses. We smiled into each other's eyes. I touched Henry's wedding band and for once he got the signal and touched mine, too. He drank his customary dram of champagne. I did rather better by the Oregon pinot noir that came with the three or four mouthfuls of veal and the morel mushrooms and the dab of sauce and the herbal leaf that constituted the entrée. The politics of the veal, the cost of it, disturbed me. I could not help but think that there was something deeply wrong about paying so much money for food. I could have bought a hundred cans of Chef Boyardee ravioli for the price of the morsels of veal on each of our plates, and been more pleased with the taste. Alas, I had no place to hide the canned goods from Henry, who was as offended by the sight of a Chef Boyardee can as I was put off by the medallion of veal. Nevertheless, I ate it and said how good it was.

We moved at last to Henry's town house because it was at ground level instead of being the top floor of a skyscraper. At first I liked the change. It was wonderful to live with the art, to come to know it so well that you did not so much look at it as simply know it was there. But when Henry and I lived together, just the two of us, in the apartment, he was always present. At all times I could see him, hear him, smell him. Now he was swallowed by the house. I would rush through rooms, looking for him, listening for him. What if the end came all of a sudden, as it was bound to do? What if the roof collapsed between us, trapping Henry in one distant room, me in another, a mountain of debris or a wall of fire between us? When I wandered through the old-fashioned, labyrinthine house until I found him at last, I would smile like a starlet and say something cheery like, *Oh there you are!* Or *Hi there!* For an instant, his eyes would focus momentarily—*Ah, it's you!* He would vouchsafe a fleeting smile, knowing exactly what I was up to, then slip back into his own thoughts.

Henry was in this mode only in the daytime. We still catnapped the night away, waking often at more or less the same moments, and if Henry woke first I sometimes was wakened—I am not making this up—by a dream in which he called my name from a tremendous distance while I strained my eyes to find him and finally located him, a tiny figure stuck to a caramel-color landscape.

One night I said, "I want to go back to the apartment."

"Why?"

"Because it's home."

"The apartment is on the fortieth floor."

"So?"

"Forty floors is a long way to fall."

I knew. Imagine the Event as it might be. We are in bed. It is pitch-dark, so dark that you cannot make out colors or shapes—no moon, no stars, no glow of incandescent light above the city. The building shakes a little, then harder, then violently. Windows break, rain blows in, we hear a noise the like of which no human being has ever heard before. Then we are inside a thick cloud of dust, we choke, we gasp for breath, we are thrown across the room, we fall to the floor. This hurts, but not for long. The floor disappears. Gravity seems to strengthen. We are falling through a cumulus of dust. We cannot breathe, we cannot move, we cannot feel our bodies. In our terror we do not scream or call out the name of the one we love. For each of us, the other is already as good as dead. I think as I fall, of course I do, fool that I am. I try to remember how tall our building is, so that I can ask Henry how long it will take for us to fall to earth at thirty-two feet per second per second. My nose, my mouth, my eyes, my lungs are filled with dust. Will I suffocate before I hit the ground? Are such small mercies part of the plan, like the choir and the church bells in Henry's dream? Will a great white light suddenly shine, will my father appear, wearing his brown tweed jacket with the leather buttons, and beckon me into the light with a loving smile? If Henry dies first, even by a second, will he be there beside my dad?

How could anyone who knew anything about the history of extinction think such trusting thoughts?

3

THE SEASONS CHANGED. THE MOTHER ship and its escorts remained in orbit. The mother ship stopped transmitting video images to Earth. Admiral Henderson did not call home, nor did Henry call the ship. If you lived in a place—the Hsi-tau or rural New Mexico, say—where there was little artificial light, the naked eye perceived the mother ship in the night sky as a speck of tinfoil. Through a backyard telescope it was a blurry string of moonlets hanging inertly in near space. The public quickly lost interest in the flotilla and its mission. Most people had long since lost interest in what was to come. In their hearts, they did not believe in it. Natural catastrophes—meteors, flood or universal thirst, the death of species, fire or ice—that never came to pass were always being predicted.

Who had time to listen to yet another cry of wolf? Media coverage withered in the absence of information and audience interest. Even Henry did not know exactly what was going on aboard his own ships. He thought this was a good thing. The mother ship's mission had been designed to be completely independent. The ship and its crew were on their own, responsible for everything, without possibility of rescue—just like the United States of America had been. There was no Houston, no ground control, no spokesman the media could badger. Admiral Henderson's powers of command were absolute. He and he alone would decide when to cut the umbilical cord. Meanwhile, he was acclimating his crew to the lower gravity aboard ship, and to the reality that they were living in isolation from the rest of the species and would go on doing so for the remainder of their lives and, most likely, the lives of several generations of their descendants. The programmed flight was a round trip to Neptune, a voyage of 1.6 billion miles. Even at flank speed with Henry's revolutionary engines, that would take the psychological equivalent of forever. The mother ship would explore the solar system as it went along, seeking out likely spots for human colonization and opportunities for profit. The window for a flight to Mars and the outer planets opened every twenty-six months. This wouldn't happen for another eleven months. Henderson had been to Mars before. He was a Mars enthusiast. He had written a book and given lectures proposing that mankind should become a two-planet civilization. Almost certainly he would want to make another landing, and establish a base. Another possibility was a colony on Earth's own moon, assuming that the pilgrims could find enough hidden water to support life, or on one of Jupiter's moons, probably Europa, which had an oxygen atmosphere and a crust of frozen water. Europa's gravity was only about fifteen percent of Earth's, but within the spheres in which colonists would live, it could be increased artificially, as it had been on the mother ship and aboard the Spaceplanes. The fusion reactors could produce the heat and melt the ice necessary for human beings to live on a moon whose temperature at the poles was minus four hundred degrees Fahrenheit. The Spaceplanes would provide transport between the mother ship and the surface of the planets and moons of the solar system. The stars were out of reach of the technology now in Earth orbit. The nearest one, the red dwarf Proxima Centauri, was 4.2 light-years distant from our sun. Even at the speed attainable by the mother ship's brand-new ion thruster system, whatever that was, the journey to this star would take at least fifty thousand years. The otherworldliness of the mother ship's technology might be routine stuff to Henry and the folks aboard ship, but it was a mystery to me. If there were beings on Proxima Centauri's planets, the ship and its wonders might be Toys 'R' Us to them.

I didn't quiz Henry on his thoughts on this matter. The mission was accomplished. By day he was idle, as if between jobs. In the marches of the night he was interested in the combination of him and me, a far more agreeable subject than the number of protons and electrons in a particular ion. I wasn't such a fool as to trifle with what was by asking him questions whose answers would mean nothing to me.

In daylight, Henry's mind was completely elsewhere. Sometimes he smiled to himself. Sometimes he suddenly spoke a name or a thought. In other circumstances, or if he had been anyone but Henry, I might have sniffed his clothes for traces of somebody else's perfume or kept an eye out for strands of silky, dyed blonde hair. Instead, I left him in peace. We dined together, and although I almost never won, we played chess. We watched movies. I no longer drank wine except at meals. It's one thing to drink alone, another to be snookered while the person you love is stone-cold sober. For an hour first thing every day, we ran together in the park, usually just before daylight, right after we got out of bed. Whatever the time, the chaps were always with us—discreet, watchful, cunningly camouflaged. For the rest of the day, Henry folded his consciousness back into its chrysalis. He was waiting for the inevitable. The list of unanswered questions was not so very long: When would it happen, how would it happen? And what then? However, Henry's possibilities were peculiar to himself, so I had no idea what revelation he was waiting for. Part of him was absent, and I missed being in the presence of the entire man. Insane as it was, under the circumstances, to wish my life away, I hoped that the hours and days that lay between the question he was asking himself and the answer he was waiting for would pass with the speed of light.

If truth be told, I, too, was living a secret half life. Even when I was with Henry, even when I was writing, I thought of little else but my children. I don't mean just the embryos to which Henry and I had contributed the necessary ingredients—not *made*, mind you, in any human way in the many, many times we had simulated conception—but also the child Bear had deposited in me. He or she— surely "she," for I was now positive I had given birth to a female, because how could I have been condemned even by the most vengeful possible god to bring another Bear into the world? My daughter would now be almost as old as I had been when she was born. For most of her life I had forbidden myself to imagine her. I failed. She had been wandering for years in the outskirts of my consciousness—blue dress, supple little body, pretty little face, bouncing braid, cornflower eyes, sweet smile, quick mind, endearing giggle. She was another me, as my father, who loved me so helplessly, must have seen me when I was small. Was she looking for me? Is that why I kept catching these glimpses of her? Would she turn up one morning on the doorstep of this unfindable house and identify herself? Such prodigals showed up on doorsteps all the time, abandoned children who refuse to remain abandoned. Would she be so unmistakably herself, when she finally showed up, that no identification other than her mere materialization would be required? Would she love me in the flesh as she had loved me in my imagination, would she have sought me out in order to be with me at the end, to be cuddled and stroked and to whisper "Mommy"?

4

THE EARTHQUAKES STOPPED. ONLY THE most minor tremors were recorded by seismographs. This phenomenon was new to science. Clairvoyants and astrologers all over the world were given credit for having predicted it. The religious offered thanks for this answer to their prayers, and in some cases no doubt felt disappointed that sinners hadn't gotten what they deserved. Scientists mostly had not seen it coming, and they offered no unified explanation as to why it had occurred. Some thought that the core of the earth had already vented its excess energy in a series of small events such as the cluster of quakes that had devastated the Admiralty archipelago, and would now go quiet again. Others believed that this was the stillness before the darkness, and a hyperquake was imminent. Henry offered no opinion. The evidence of his worst fears was orbiting the earth, waiting to make sure the worst had happened before heading for Mars and Jupiter and Neptune.

The question was, how long would it last? I myself believed, with even less reason than a psychic or an astrologer, that the respite was temporary, that the planet had taken a geological moment to center its ch'i, and when it had done so, it would let loose the energy it had been storing. Would the result be an explosion of pop-corn—many, many small quakes happening all over the globe—or a single, focused surge that would open a seam in the planet as a dragon impatient to be born after millennia of gestation awakens and breaks out of its egg?

THIRTEEN

1

ON THE FOURTEENTH OF JUNE, Henry and I started running, as usual, at the break of day. He had the peculiar habit of taking his first step with his right foot instead of his left, so in the beginning of the run we were out of synch until I skipped a step. After this our shoes thudded on the pavement in counterpoint, Henry's thuds a fraction of a second quicker than my own and slightly more basso. I enjoyed the sound of it, *left-right, left-right, him-me, him-me.* The intensity of the light grew stronger as the iris of the day opened. Seldom had I ever been so happy. We were on the shady path that led from the Metropolitan Museum of Art to the running track around the Reservoir. The usual early-to-rise dog-walkers milled sleepily in our way. I wasn't wearing my contacts, so the people and the animals and the trees looked something like a Seurat tableau come to life. The people were all sorts, young and old, beautiful and not so beautiful—ectomorph, endomorph, even a mesomorph or two. The dogs were more various. Terriers and spaniels and collies were so out of fashion that they might as well have been extinct, and now nearly every dog owner held the leash of a creature beautiful and strange to behold. These exotic animals looked less like living, breathing canines born of bitches than fantastical living toys constructed by genetic artists through the manipulation of DNA.

Suddenly the dogs froze. Their noses pointed west, their ears pricked. Their coats bristled. They growled in unison. As if on cue, they barked in many different voices. Elsewhere in the park, other dogs barked, hundreds of them. Behind this choir, another, larger one sounded, muffled but coming from every point of the compass. Every dog in New York seemed to be barking. Every human being in the city knew what this meant. I shivered though I felt the rising sun on my back. Henry turned around and ran backward for a few steps. I would have done the same, but I was transfixed by the look on his face. He was *interested*, not afraid. He knew he was about to observe something no human eyes had ever seen before and might never see again, and (I knew Henry) he was correcting the picture of this moment that he had stored in his imagination by substituting the actuality. Or maybe, since he *was* Henry, no corrections were necessary. Even if I had not already guessed the truth, his expression would have told me everything I needed to know about the moment. The Event was happening at last.

It started to hail—small stones at first, then larger, jagged ones. They bounced off Henry's Yankees cap and struck my scalp and shoulders with such force that I thought I must be bleeding. Henry stopped running backward and opened his arms. I staggered into him at running speed, knocking us both to the pavement. I twisted an ankle and skinned a knee. The pain was intense, the kind of pain a child feels because it is new to her. A woman screamed and scooped up her dog, holding it tightly against her body as if it were a child. The dog, barking shrilly, struggled to break free. Other dogs and humans did the same, like members of an incredibly clumsy ballet company performing a work by an absurdist choreographer. Some of the dogs did get loose. Their owners chased them, calling their names.

Henry was squeezing the breath out of me. I twisted in his arms, and using only the one eye that could see the sun, half-saw it. Ever since the cluster quakes in the Pacific, it had been tinged with pink and tattooed with flecks of dark pigment, but now—maybe because of the way the scrim of hailstones refracted its light—it looked blue, and so did everything its light fell upon. The figures of the people and the dogs, the leaves on the trees, even the squat granite museum, which was the only building I could see, were the colors of gas flame.

Every nerve in my own body seemed to be centered in my skinned knee. These distractions made it possible for a moment to refuse to acknowledge what I knew was happening. With my good leg, I kneed Henry hard, may he forgive me, and he loosened his grip. I heard a rumbling sound and saw Henry's eyes, glowing with intelligence, as he recognized the sound. I, too, knew what it was. It grew louder. The ground shook. Dog walkers fell down, more or less in unison. The rumbling was very loud now. Henry turned me around so that we were facing each other, groin to groin, face against face. I felt him lock his hands on my back.

He whispered, "Ssshh, ssshh."

Was I screaming, too? I knew I was. How was such a thing possible? I felt deep shame.

A great dirty cloud of dust boiled over the western horizon. The ground beneath our feet shivered, then shrugged violently, like the hide of an animal tormented by flies. It trembled, froze, trembled again. Then, as it seemed, something broke beneath the surface. The ground jerked in the direction of the museum and Fifth Avenue. It moved maybe a foot or two, quite gently. We moved with it. So did the other human beings, some of whom were teetering for balance like tightrope walkers. Most of them fell down and were now sprawled on their backs, their arms crossed, their feet pointed in the direction in which the ground, which had detached itself from whatever had formerly fastened it down, was slipping and sliding. Up to this moment, everything had remained in place. But now the trees were bending. Already some were almost parallel to the ground. I heard a loud crackle as their trunks shattered, then a cacophony of explosions crescendoing into a single great explosion, and I realized—I don't know how—that the roots of trees were snapping in two beneath the soil. Severed trees fell down, smaller ones first, then the big ones.

Central Park, along with the rest of the city, was sliding fast now—accelerating—and Henry and I and everyone else along with it. There were no points of reference. Everything was moving, nothing was the same, the fallen trees traveled with us like jackstraws. Everything—trees, grass, buildings, creatures—was skidding, faster now, toward the East River. The rumbling was very loud now. Other noises intruded, every one of them composed of many separate noises that in the end coalesced into a single deafening roar. The sun was blotted out by the roiling cloud of dust. The city, the world, was sliding, just as Henry had told me it would all those years ago in this park. Not for a moment did I think that I was dreaming. This was real. I tried to free my arms so that I could throw them around Henry, but they were still bound to my sides by his arms. He was far, far stronger than I ever realized.

By now I couldn't see much because I was crushed against Henry, but I could see the museum. Though blurred by the dust, it looked the same as ever, solid and gray. Like everything else, it was about the same distance away as it had been before the ground began to move. Then it collapsed—in an instant, thousands of tons of stone just came apart and fell down.

Within myself I was calm, but who knows what noises I was making? Henry kept on whispering, "Ssshh, ssshh." I wanted to talk to him but I couldn't find my voice. Suddenly the ground jerked violently, propelling me at great speed. The movement tore me from Henry's arms. In front of us, a huge rock rose from the earth. It was sharp at one end, raked like the prow of a sinking ship, squeezing out of the ground as if two gigantic, invisible thumbs were extruding it. I was going to be flung against this rock. I had no idea how fast the ground was moving, and me with it, but it was moving much faster than before. The rock seemed to be stationary, earth furrowing around it, wet and yellowish. I tried to run. I couldn't even walk.

Henry picked me up, threw me over his shoulder, stood up, and began to run on a diagonal. Somehow I understood the geometry. It was impossible to run away from the rock, so he was trying to use the momentum of the earthslide to get off to one side of it. To do that, he would have to run slightly faster than the ground was moving. I didn't think this was possible, because the grass, the soil, and rocks of all sizes and shapes that were oozing to the surface all around us were moving far faster than any human being could run, let alone a man of forty-five with a hundred-pound woman slung over his shoulder. Henry lurched, he stumbled on a round stone and somehow kept his balance. He gasped—wheezed—for breath. He retched. I thought his heart might stop at any moment. He stumbled, then stumbled again. His cap fell off. I made a futile grab for it. He ran jerkily among the stones, which were rolling around like misshapen croquet balls and *click-clacking* against each other. As he tried to outrun all this, Henry's bony shoulder stabbed into my stomach. Panic, the like of which I had never felt before, detonated inside me. This had nothing to do with what was happening beneath Henry's feet. I had stopped using birth control a month earlier. I was late. I had meant to do a pregnancy test today, I had to fight myself to keep from fighting Henry—pummeling him, kicking him, screaming into his ear—to protect the child I might be carrying.

Henry was staggering almost to the point of falling to the ground, which seemed to be on the point of breaking apart. Cracks formed on its surface. These cracks, caused by the shifting of the incalculable weight of the entire crust of the planet, were going to widen. They were going to become the huge fissures every human brain could instantaneously picture as if they were a collective memory from the prehuman past, or in some incomprehensible way, a long-gestating memory of the future whose moment of revelation had finally come. The *Tarbosauruses* and *Oviraptors* Bear had dug up in China had been swallowed in their time by just such an earthy mouth, and in my mind's eye I saw Bear being covered up, too, like the specimens he had disinterred, and his own fossilized bones, all that was left of him, being dug up and exposed to air again millions of years from now.

We had seconds left to live. The child I was carrying would die before it lived. How could this nonsense about the damnation of Bear be my last thought?

Henry fell. I was thrown clear. I reached for him, clawing the ground as though groping for him in darkness. My body rolled as if tumbling down a steep slope. I couldn't get control of it. It rolled over stones, which dug into my flesh. My bones were going to break, I knew this, and the memory of another fracture admitted Bear back into my consciousness. He became the earthquake. Tiny as I was, huge as he was, I fought back. His strength was too much for me, as I had known it would be. He pulled me toward death.

Like him, I was one of the damned. What else could this mean? Henry was saved, I knew it. Old teachings came back to me. He was in the hands of another, more kindly captor. As in the past, I believed this while refusing to believe it. I was afraid to speak Henry's name, in case whatever was carrying him off to eternal bliss might hear me and change its mind. I could feel movement, not a falling sensation, not flight. I couldn't see. Why? Had I closed my eyes, had the sun been blotted out, was I going to be blind from now on, was I dead but not yet brain-dead? Any one of these possibilities was perfectly believable. I stopped asking questions. At last I had enough answers. I heard voices but could not make out words. I was rolling toward indecipherable sounds over a bed of stones. Pain was being inflicted on me. Would it never stop? I had never believed that such an end really lay in store for sinners. I had believed in oblivion. I let go of life, as the dying are advised to do as a signal of submission to the Almighty in the hope of light and silence and mercy. Something strong—stronger than Bear—grabbed me with many hands. It fixed me in place. I was wrapped in a storm of noise, all kinds of noise—explosions, screams, groans, crashes, sounds I could not name. If that was damnation, it was a brilliant cruelty, and how wise its designers had been to keep its true nature a secret from us.

ARK

Or most of us. Henry—I was sure of this—was, for the second
time, hearing a choir of counter-tenors singing songs new and beautiful to the human ear. He was hearing the church bells. The caveman was smiling back at him again. If the elect knew everything,
he must know what I was hearing, too, so even though he was the
lucky one, how could he be in a state of gladness, knowing that
neither of us could ever break through this impassable barrier of
unbearable noise, one to the other. Whether saved or damned, we
were marooned.

2

"IT'S ABSOLUTELY DREADFUL, OF COURSE it is," Clementine said, "but not so very much worse than what British and American bombing did to German and Japanese cities in the Second World War. Those half-starved, utterly defeated, guilt-ridden people—and to a certain extent, the British, too, by the bye—cleared away the rubble, stone by stone, and built up new cities, far better though perhaps less beautiful ones, in less than two generations. And so shall this generation and the next do the same."

Yet even Clementine, in whom the Event had reawakened the spirit of the Blitz, conceded that the damage done by the hyperquake was far greater than the devastation inflicted by any past war. Nevertheless, she regarded the outcome as a happy one. Before the batteries in our telephones went dead, we learned what happened from the mother ship, whose crew had observed the Event in its entirety, and measured it and photographed it and calculated its force. We now knew that most of the energy released by the core of the earth had been absorbed by the oceans, because it burst through the planet's crust along the Mid-Oceanic Ridge, a fifty-thousand-mile-long underwater mountain range with a rift along its spine that runs down the middle of the Atlantic Ocean from the Arctic to a point midway between the Cape of Good Hope and the coast of Antarctica, then turns east and passes south of Australia, putting out several branches along the way and bending gradually northward along the coasts of the two American continents. Colossal volumes of lava burst through the mid-ocean rift at temperatures of more than two thousand degrees Fahrenheit. Volcanoes and other mountains were formed beneath the sea all along this line, creating tsunamis that caused many deaths but did little damage to cities along the coasts that had already been transformed into heaps of stone and concrete and metal and glass by the slippage of the planet's crust. In fact the tsunamis served a useful purpose by washing many of the dead out to sea, thus lessening the severity of the epidemics caused by millions of rotting corpses. In Northern California, the detritus of coastal cities was deposited forty miles inland. Fragments of the Empire State Building—and, one supposes, the stones and crumpled masterpieces of the Metropolitan Museum of Art—were carried all the way across Long Island and deposited in the Atlantic, whose ash-gray, gritty waters washed the island's shores.

The fact that the Mid-Oceanic Ridge was located on the bed of the ocean meant that most of the damage was inflicted on the Americas and Europe, which were closest to it. An offshoot of the ridge that runs up what used to be the Red Sea devastated most of the Middle East, so neither of the great religions that had been attempting to obliterate each other when the planet convulsed could plausibly claim that the deity had chosen sides. They did so anyway, but since electronic communications and even paper mail no longer existed, they were forced to rely on ragged, wild-eyed pilgrims who wandered the scalped land dressed in robes and hoods, to spread news of the aftermath by word of mouth. The interior of Asia (though not the islands along its Pacific coast) escaped catastrophic damage. Ng Fred's factories were unscathed, the herdsmen of Mongolia felt only a slight tremor. The destruction of most of the United States and nearly all of the European Union meant that the wealth of those two manufactories of sin had evaporated, and along with them, international trade and the very idea of wealth and its relentless conscience, philanthropy. Asia, therefore, was in no condition to come to the rescue of the ruined half of the world even if its culture could have produced such an impulse. The destruction of the dollar and the euro demonstrated the inconvenience of bad luck in a world that now lacked an America ever poised to come to the rescue of those who hated it. In what used to be the United States, central government was in hibernation. It still existed, or so we sometimes heard, but the pillars and domes and cupolas of the alabaster city that had been Washington, D.C., were now strewn over the bottom of Chesapeake Bay like a deconstructed Atlantis. Naturally, those who fancied themselves the rulers of what was left of America, whoever they were, issued decrees. However, their commands and proclamations traveled from the capital, wherever that was, to the people at about the same rate of speed—that of a man on foot or mounted on a horse—that had applied during the administration of George Washington. The smart thing was to ignore them.

"Henry was spot-on about what was going to happen and how it would happen," said Clementine, "and I'm sure he'd be quite happy to know that he overestimated the effect. By the time the mother ship returns, the rescue of humanity will be quite unnecessary. Civilization will be up and running, and glorious human folly will rule the planet once again."

QED. One could admire or be revolted by Clementine's optimism, but there was no gainsaying that she had the right attitude. She was the only person in our little commune who ever mentioned Henry's name in my presence. The chaps and others who had attached themselves to us took great care not to upset the grieving widow. Clementine refused to look on me as a Victoria that had lost her Albert. In her tidy bureaucratic way, she regarded my husband as missing and presumed to be alive. That was the MI5 rule—always had been—when no corpse had been identified. Whatever his fate, Henry was still present in all our minds. It would be unthinkable to classify him as one of the dead, an affront to put him into the wrong drawer in the absence of proof that he was one of the uncounted millions that had perished in the cataclysm. Quite possibly he would turn up one day at the end of the lane, and a lookout with exceptional eyesight would recognize him and cry, "Henry is back!" He knew where we were because Clementine had established our commune on land that Henry designated for the purpose. For him, it would be no problem to calculate how far that property had moved and where it was now. It would be like him never to show up. In any case, Clementine was right: He deserved to be counted among the living as long as we didn't know for certain that he was dead. Clementine insisted on it for his child's sake. How else could the girl grow up with the necessary mental picture of the father she had never seen?

Clementine delivered my daughter with her own hands. As a young woman she had taken a night course in midwifery. Afterward, as a way of doing her bit, she had birthed many babies as a volunteer in a shelter for distressed young women. Even if it was she who said so as shouldn't, she remarked in a mock Cockney accent moments after the child's birth, no one knotted a neater umbilical cord than she, and indeed little Clementine—called Tiney because neither Clementine nor I could bear the thought of her being known as Clem—had a lovely belly button. The child spent more time on her namesake's lap than mine, and surely absorbed more sensible vibrations. In her gruff contralto Clementine sang her nursery songs. She also read to her—stories I wrote and Clementine illustrated. Because batteries had temporarily vanished from the world, photographs were a thing of the past, so she recorded Tiney's childhood by sketching her in charcoal or watercolors at least once a month. In these portraits, as in life, she looked just like the half-smiling, lama-like portrait of Henry that Clementine had painted and hung on the wall of Tiney's room. The child, after learning to talk in sentences, spoke in a voice in which fugitive Cantabrigian vowels skittered like trout.

It was Clementine who told me what the chaps had told her about my rescue and the disappearance of Henry when she debriefed them. I remembered nothing after the moment when he dropped me at the feet of the chaps because I had knocked my head against a rock. While I was out, according to the chaps, Henry had kept running with the skidding earth beneath his feet. It was, the chaps said, like watching a man as he ran down a steep hill. To me, as I listened to their description, it seemed like the Quasimodo from Henry's nightmare, now invisible, had wrapped his arms around him. Henry could not stop himself. It looked to the chaps like he was trying to regain his balance—trying to catch up with it, reaching for it as a kid will do when in danger of falling on his face.

They did not pursue him because they figured he would soon fall down and they could reach him more easily when the earthslide came to a halt. However, he did not fall, but just kept staggering on. By the time they realized they were losing him, they had already lost him, because another great slab of bedrock, glistening with moisture and smeared with mud, burst from the ground between them and Henry, hiding him from them. Afterward, they spent hours searching for him, turning over the bodies of the many dead and injured people who wore blue jeans, but he was nowhere to be found. They never saw him again.

All the chaps were trained battlefield medics in addition to the many other things that they were, so they knew exactly what was the matter with me—I had a concussion—and how to stabilize a person in my condition. After treating me, they carried my inert body, a dead weight, over mountains of rubble—on their backs, presumably, though they were too taciturn ever to describe this flight to me. The bridges and tunnels were gone, but this didn't matter because the Hudson and the East River had been dammed and filled in by dirt and debris, so they simply walked across, climbing over the obstacles they could not skirt. By some sort of chaps' magic, they knew exactly where they were going, even though their destination was no longer where it used to be. The outpost Clementine had set up was several hundred miles away. We walked—and after I came partly to my senses, sometimes ran—the whole way. At such moments, my head ached terribly as my bruised brain bounced against bone. The chaps foraged in the ruins of supermarkets and houses for food to eat and water to drink and pain medicine for me, which I refused to take because of the baby. For the moment, there was still plenty of everything. Sometimes they slaughtered and cooked chickens or livestock from the flocks and herds that roamed the countryside. The dead, human and other mammals, lay everywhere, covered with flies, crawling with maggots, oozing disease. Birds including escaped poultry and small animals including dogs and cats fed on them. Rats scampered in multitudes, a great gray moving carpet. I turned my face away from such sights and put my hands on my belly as if shielding the baby's eyes. Since waking up I had been absolutely certain that I was pregnant. At moments I was sure that Henry was speaking to me, reassuring me, through the child in my womb.

We also encountered living people. They stood beside the roads—or what used to be roads—staring at us dead-eyed as we jogged by, as though we had roused them from a collective sleep and they were not yet entirely aware that they were awake and walking. Sometimes the chaps sang cadence as they ran. Once in a while, gangs of younger survivors attacked us. The chaps, in their offhand way, neutralized them with expert brutality, hardly breaking stride as they made the kill. As a child on my grandparents' farm I had seen their three dogs attack a woodchuck and tear it apart in an instant. Watching the chaps at work was like watching that.

My concussion was a blessing of sorts. My memory of the last hour of Manhattan, my memory of Henry, my memory of practically everything, was blurred. My speech was slurred. Words eluded me. If asked a question I chased the answer around in the half-darkness of my mind like a name I couldn't quite recapture. I was tired to the bone, though my body did not seem to realize this and kept on functioning. Nothing to worry about, the chaps said, the feeling will go away. It never did—not really, not altogether. In my heart I didn't want it to. Nothing else was as it used to be. Why should my brain be different?

Our commune grew. People joined us, especially the educated

who wanted to be useful and young women who had no one to protect them from the gangs. If rape had made the women pregnant, as
was sometimes the case, our doctors and nurses delivered the babies
or performed abortions. Some of the women brought children with
them. More had lost or abandoned their families. Clementine, as
Henry's viceroy, interviewed each applicant. If they were suitable—
that is to say, intelligent, strong, free of disease and illusion, possessed
of a skill they could practice for the common good and teach to an
apprentice (Clementine loved farmers, carpenters, craftsmen of all
kinds, engineers, nurses, physicians and surgeons, dentists, soldiers),
they remained. If not, she sent them away. She was coldhearted about
this. It was her job to put together a team that would not merely survive, but thrive and breed itself up into a thinking and doing class.
Over time, this social Darwinism of hers resulted in a miniature raj,
with the lucky elite living on the green and pleasant island that was a
flawed replica of the perfect Blighty of their dreams. This paradise was
a replica, a symbol, a fancy, but a reality nonetheless. As before the
Event, everyone else existed outside the cantonments in dust, stench,
and desperation. In early days we saw these people when they fell
on our commune like Stone Age war parties, looking to steal women
and weapons and animals they could take home and eat. Some of
them named themselves after the fiercer Indian tribes—Comanche,
Apache, Mohawk, Cheyenne, Shawnee—and were said to practice a
religion whose eucharist was marijuana, just as they had done before
the end of civilization. Stoned or not, they were no match for the
chaps or for the new chaps the original chaps adopted and trained.
Our warriors punished them in battle and drove away such survivors
as they chose not to kill. After a while, the raids dwindled and finally
ceased altogether.

It wasn't a bad life—not much different, really, from the one led
by the whole of the human race until quite recently. The obsession
with time went away. The lust for possessions intensified because
there was so little to possess. Lust ruled the world, which was, on balance, a good thing in a world that needed to be repopulated. For the

first time since the Middle Ages, people lived entirely in natural light, and so close together and to the other animals, that the idea of privacy simply perished. The apocalypse was, in a way, a victory for the Greens to an extent that was almost comical. Pollution diminished to almost nothing. Colors that had not been seen outside of paintings since the Industrial Revolution reappeared. Quicker than anyone expected, the land healed. Flowers bloomed. New kinds of grasses grew. The trees came back. The ones that had fallen in the quake provided an inexhaustible supply of firewood and lumber. The hunter-gatherer stage quickly ended, though the tribes never disbanded, just huddled together as in the past, and continued to prey on one another. Commune by commune, agriculture was rediscovered. We raised food from the seeds Clementine had stockpiled, and from the seeds of those plants. Feral animals were captured and domesticated again. Inside the commune, we ate a healthy diet—grass-fed, free-range meat, vegetables and fruits fertilized with urine and manure. The demanding monotony of producing food and keeping nature at bay provided plenty of exercise for everyone.

Culture lived on. Like Marx's money, it seemed to have a life of its own and the ability to feed on its own body. Children were taught to read, write, figure, and conform. Books—long regarded as artifacts of a lesser civilization—were salvaged from ruined libraries and schools, musical instruments from schools and houses. When books, or memory, did not provide the necessary data, Clementine looked it up on Henry's sphere. Synthetic drugs disappeared. Quite soon the medicines collected from pharmacies were all gone. Except among small children and the very old, this didn't seem to alter the death rate very much. Others believed that the kids who survived would transmit their immunity to their own children and the species would end up being healthier and sounder genetically. Until the middle of the twentieth century, after all, mankind had demonstrated that it could increase quite handily in the absence of antibiotics. Meanwhile, there seemed to be fewer crazies than there used to be, and who knows but what the disappearance of pills had something to do with that.

For music, we sang, all together, usually at night, under the moon and stars that were gradually becoming brighter. Gradually the sun, too, stopped being the wrong color and went back to being the blinding star that human eyes were not designed to look upon. The planet was beautiful again in a way that most living people had never realized it was meant to be. The dust of the hyperquake dispersed quicker than had been thought possible, and the ash and smoke of new volcanoes were less of a problem than Henry had thought they might be, partly because most of them were bubbling away underwater, attracting fishes to their warmth, instead of releasing dust and ash into the atmosphere. Tiney and her playmates took the only world they knew entirely for granted. Thanks to Clementine's storytelling, the planet she lived upon was, to her, a Neverland in which children flew over the housetops in their nightgowns, holding hands with happy fairies that rang like bells, and a flying boy played the flute in his calmer moments, and nothing that was naughty or nice ever came to an end.

Because I was Henry's wife, I lived as a vestal. No male dared to look at me with lust. To my great surprise, chastity suited me. All my sexual memories had to do with Henry. Other lovers, even the ones who had been more expert than Henry, even Adam, dissolved. Henry was the love of my life. I fantasized about finding his grave and lying down beside him one last time. Only my love for Tiney kept me from wandering off in search of his unfindable sepulcher. Gazing at our daughter as she played—golden hair, golden skin, golden hints of her father's mind—I understood at last the meaning of the word *seed* as it applies to the begetting of children. From Tiney or her descendants, another Henry would sooner or later be born. I was sure of this. It was a banal thought, but what difference did that make? As time went by, I had fewer and fewer visitations from the past. My memories faded, my dreams about what used to be ceased. Though I remembered them, I never wondered whatever happened to Melissa or Adam or my abandoned child. Even Bear sank irrevocably into the mists.

Henry would never appear at the gate. I was sure of that. It was too unlike him. It was possible that somebody else would come, and though the visitor looked nothing like Henry, would insist that he was Henry. If that happened, would I play along like the wife in that medieval tale of impersonation? Would I sleep with the imposter, would I talk to him in the dark, would I make this absurdity into an idyll?

I didn't think so, but how could I know? Maybe impulse—my oldest friend, *mon semblance*—was not so withered after all.

If Henry *was* alive, the best thing he could have wished for, the most desired thing, was that he might at last pass through the world unnoticed. We did nothing that might cause him to be remembered. The last thing Henry had said to Clementine, she told me (*why hadn't he said this to* me?), was that the commune should not be named for him, that there should be no monument, no biography, no gossip calling itself history. In accordance with his wishes, our commune did not bear his name. No child born there was ever named Henry. The formula worked. Quicker than even Henry might have hoped or thought possible, he was forgotten outside the tiny circle that had known what he looked like, sounded like, or how sometimes he loosened his grip on his singularity for a fleeting moment and smiled a whole, delightful smile instead of the furtive semi-smile that was nearly always on his lips.

I remembered everything. How Henry was, how he looked, how he had found all those grails and carried them out of the labyrinth and into the light. In the deepest recesses of my self, I thought, even while scoffing at the possibility, that he might sooner or later turn up. One morning just before I woke, he would call. Even if he came back as an old, old man, as ancient as I myself would be by that time, I would know him, as no one else could, for the Henry he was inside his disguise of raddled flesh and twisted bone. I would know what worlds spun behind his rheumy eyes.

Even if he looked me in the eye and smiled that unfinished smile and swore that he was Henry.

ISBN: 978-1-4532-5820-0

The Mysterious Press

MysteriousPress.com

Published in 2011 by
Open Road Integrated Media
180 Varick Street
New York, NY 10014
www.openroadmedia.com

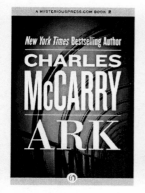 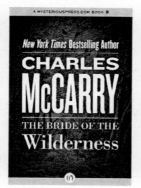 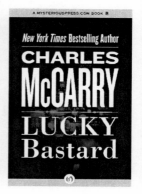

Videos, Archival Documents, and New Releases

Sign up for the Open Road Media newsletter and get news delivered straight to your inbox.

FOLLOW US:
@openroadmedia and
Facebook.com/OpenRoadMedia

CPSIA information can be obtained at www.ICGtesting.com
Printed in the USA
BVOW030548100412

287126BV00001B/3/P